# EMBERS OF THE OLD WORLD

## THE HORSEMEN CHRONICLES
### Book One

Published by Mission Point Press
2554 Chandler Lake Rd.
Traverse City, MI 49686
(231) 421-9513
www.MissionPointPress.com

ISBN: 978-1-943995-25-7
LOC: 2017902348

Printed in the United States of America.

# THE HORSEMEN

## EMBERS OF THE OLD WORLD

### by ERIC WOOD

MISSION POINT PRESS

*To my family, who have always believed in me.*

# PART I
## The Mission

WHEN THE FIRST OUTBREAKS of the virus occurred, there was some disagreement in regards to its name. Within six months, the newswires were filled with stories of diseases like Rocky Mountain Hemorrhagic Flu, Hong Kong Sleepwalking Sickness, and Kali's Wrath. Approximately one year after the disease first appeared, and it was understood exactly how it worked, one name had gained prominence worldwide: The Horsemen Virus. To this day scholars disagree on the origin of the name; the majority believe it refers to the four distinct strains of dangerous Infected produced by the pathogen, each corresponding to one of the mythic 'four horsemen' of the bible. Others believe it refers simply to the fact that the disease brought with it the same thing as the biblical horsemen: the Apocalypse.

*The Origins, Structures, and Effects of the Horseman Virus; Official Colonial Records.*

# 1

SAM STARED UP at Deacon's blood-red eyes and tried to ignore the Ravager's oversized pistol. Not the easiest thing to do, when its barrel was hovering an inch from your face. Close enough Sam could smell the thing: burnt gunpowder and dirty cleaning oil. Close enough he could taste its metal.

He set his jaw in defiance as Deacon clicked back the hammer. Despite his pounding heart, Sam's breath remained steady. The end would come any second. But now, after everything that had happened, after everything he had done and everything he had gone through, here at the end he was no longer scared. Just disappointed.

"I'd ask if you had any last words," Deacon said in his too-friendly voice, "but I stopped asking that question a long time ago. The answers are always less interesting than you'd expect."

It wasn't supposed to happen this way, after all. Sam was supposed to be the one holding the weapon; Deacon the one on his knees at the end of the barrel. Sam had never had much in this diseased and broken world, but the past week had taken all of it. And now he wouldn't even have his revenge.

He tilted his head to the side and spat on the ground, keeping his eyes fixed on Deacon. He said nothing.

"Okay then," Deacon said, "I guess that's that. Goodbye, Sam. I can't say it hasn't been interesting. But I win."

A tiny stream of rocks trickled down the cliff face ahead of him, and Sam closed his eyes. He felt the pistol press against his forehead, and he took in what was likely his final breath.

✝

*One week earlier*

The gunshot rang out across the long-abandoned city, echoing off moss-covered walls and rusted-out cars. The boar lurched forward, just a single step, before keeling over and collapsing. Sam exhaled and lowered the rifle. He worked the lever, discharging the spent casing. *Two hundred and twenty-five yards, right through the heart,* he thought. *Vincente couldn't have done it cleaner.*

Of course, now they would have to figure out how to get the dead beast back to the Colony. This neighborhood was as far into the remnants of old Rapid City as Sam had ever been, and it was over ten miles back to the first set of walls. He did a quick calculation in his head, based on his bike's fuel level and their approximate combined weight, and decided they should be fine dragging the thing back if they scavenged a few extra gallons of gas.

"What the hell was that?" Vincente demanded, emerging from the broken storefront to Sam's right. The long-ago broken glass crunched under his heavy work boots. "Are you trying to attract every Plague-Head within a five-mile radius?"

Sam rolled his eyes. "We cleared the area hours ago, V.

What, do you think those things are laying a trap for us or something? Infected don't think, they just do. Isn't that what you always tell me?"

"Just be glad it's still daylight, or we'd have worse things to worry about than Plague-Heads."

Vincente Ramos and Sam Brennan didn't look much alike. Vincente was short, and had dark skin, darker eyes, and long, brown-black hair, tied up in a utilitarian bun. He also had a thick, dark beard and an ever-present smile. Sam, on the other hand, was tall and wiry, with blond hair shaved short, pale eyes and a more or less permanent scowl. His face was clean shaven, mostly because he was tired of Vincente mocking the thin, patchy hair that grew on his chin and jaw when he didn't.

"We could have missed one," Vincente said. He peered down the debris-strewn street at the dead boar and nodded. "Nice shot, though."

Vincente was twenty-seven and looked older; Sam was seventeen and looked younger. Vincente had come to the Black Hills Colony just after Sam's mother had died, and in the years since, Sam had come to think of him as something between a brother and a father. Neither one of them had anyone else.

"How picked over was that place?" Sam asked. According to its sun-faded sign, the shop had once been a pharmacy.

"There were a few bottles left," Vincente said. "Ones that rolled under the shelves and into the corners. I don't recognize the labels; we'll see what the higher-ups think when we get back to the Colony."

The Old World chemical printers could synthesize medicine, but only from recipes they already had. The printers needed inputs, and unfortunately the Colony's population of two hundred people didn't include any chemists. That art had been lost twenty years ago, when the Horsemen Virus stampeded mercilessly across the world.

So if you needed inputs, you scavenged. For years now, people like Vincente and Sam had ventured out from behind the safety of the Colony walls and into the Wilds, digging out the last useful bits from the embers of the Old World. It was dangerous work — the world at large belonged to the four strains of the Infected — but Sam loved it. Sure, every time he went out into the Wilds he wasn't sure he would come back, but at least he knew he would see something new. It definitely beat working the crops or toiling away in the machine shops, where he was in constant danger of dying from boredom. Still, he dreamed of the day when he could travel further out than Rapid City.

There was a clattering sound behind them. Sam and Vincente swung around as one unit, raising their rifles. Sam tried not to exhale too hard when he saw it was only an empty aluminum can sliding across the street, urged on by the wind. Sam lowered his rifle and tried to *will* his heart to slow down. He didn't want Vincente to see how much the noise had startled him.

"I guess I'm getting jumpy in my old age," Vincente said, rifle still poised. "I could have sworn that was something bigger than a soda—"

Glass shattered above them, and bodies rained down onto their heads.

&#8224;

The first thing Vincente would have done when he entered the pharmacy was to clear both floors, so Sam was more than a bit surprised to find himself pinned underneath a hissing, writhing Infected. But here he was.

He pushed the Infected off himself and rolled back onto his feet, cutting his forearm on the broken glass in the process. The Infected moved nearly as quickly as he did, in its mindless, feral way, and Sam found himself crouching face to face with a cloudy-eyed, green-skinned horror.

"Plague-Heads!" Sam shouted the warning despite the fact that Vincente was only a few feet away. It was a reflex that the sergeants had drilled into him with countless days of practice before the Elder's council had given him permission to join Vincente on scavenging runs.

Sam pulled down his mask and tore the shield off his back, moving without thinking. He popped open the clear plexiglass shield just in time to catch the spray of red-and-black infective vomit the Plague-Head spewed at him. He stepped forward and bashed the Plague-Head with the shield, reaching down for his baton to collapse the Infected's skull. His hand came up empty; the baton must have come loose. *Of Course.* It was probably rolling around on the ground with his lost rifle.

The Plague-Head grabbed the top of his shield with broken-nailed fingers. Sam had to clutch the shield with both hands to keep the ghoul from ripping it away. The thing was surprisingly strong for having been locked away in the pharmacy's upstairs, away from the nourishing rays of the sun. Someone must have corralled it up there quite recently...

Sam heard the distinctive crack of a gunshot, and the wall above him exploded. Brick and plaster rained down on him and the Plague-Head both. He put his shoulder into the shield, and shouting, he shoved the Infected forward and into the broken storefront, letting the shield go with it as both tumbled back into the gloom.

A second shot boomed, this one much closer, practically

on top of him. His ears began to ring just as he realized the shot had been Vincente's, who was currently aiming at something just behind Sam's head.

Sam located his fallen rifle and picked it up. He swung it over to the Plague-Head he had just fended off, found its head, and pulled the trigger, putting the creature down for good. However, his sense of victory was short-lived: bullets kicked up a spray of gravel from the ground just to Sam's left, forcing him to take refuge inside the broken shopfront.

"War party?" he asked Vincente as he hunkered low, the adrenaline in his veins keeping the worst of the fear battened down.

Vincente nodded once. "War party," he said.

☩

The Horsemen Virus produced four distinct varieties of Infected. The Plague-Heads — Greenies, or Pesties, or Carriers, depending on who you were speaking to — were mostly feral creatures, whose only purpose in life was to pass the Horsemen Virus on to new hosts. They were vicious, and often surprisingly quick, but they weren't much for smarts.

The Ravagers were a different story.

More shots peppered the walls around them as Sam and Vincente ducked into a narrow alleyway.

"At least the grunts still can't shoot," Vincente said, smiling a smile that didn't reach his plainly-anxious eyes.

"But what are they doing this close to the Colony?" Sam asked him, putting words to the obvious question. "I didn't think there were any Ravagers within a hundred miles of here."

"Well, those gunshots tell a different story."

Hoots, animal laughter and gravel-voiced taunts echoed after them as the war party of Ravagers gave chase. Less common than the Plague-Heads, Ravagers were often far more dangerous, as they retained enough of their previous human intelligence to communicate and plan and hunt. And this hunting party had found its prey.

Sam followed Vincente out the other side of the alley, across the next road, and into a partially collapsed chain restaurant. They ducked behind an overturned host stand and peered back the direction they had come.

"Did you get a look at them?" Vincente asked. "Any kind of count?"

"I was a little busy with that Greenie," Sam said, trying to sound more composed than he felt. "Truth be told, I didn't really *see* any of them."

"There were at least four. I got one of them. That leaves three. Could be more."

Even if the war party hadn't seen them come into the restaurant, they would find them eventually. Ravagers had a dog's sense of smell, matched with a badger's tenacity and fury. Once their bloodlust was up — and as Sam understood it, their bloodlust was almost always up — the war party wouldn't quit until they had killed their quarry. As brutally as possible.

"We can take them when they come around the corner," Sam said. "With both of us shooting, there's no way they'll be able to cross the street and the parking—"

The sound of a back door being thrown open silenced him.

"Come out, come out, wherever you are," a deranged-sounding voice said, emerging from somewhere in the restaurant's dark interior. Every fiber of Sam's body wanted to bolt out the front door as fast as he could, but Vincente put a hand on his shoulder and steadied him.

"Keep your rifle sighted back the way we came," Vincente whispered urgently. "The other two will come as soon as they think this one has our attention. When they do, you need to put them down."

"But what about the one inside?" Sam asked.

Vincente snapped open his baton and pulled a long-bladed knife from his belt. "I'll take care of it," he said, maneuvering towards the back of the building.

✝

There weren't two more of the Ravagers waiting across the street. There were four.

Three men and one woman, each looking like something between a caveman and an outlaw biker from the television archives. They began to cross the street in a slow, spread-out jog that made Sam think of a loping pack of coyotes. He would have to take down all four before they reached the restaurant, or he was as good as dead. Fighting a Plague-Head was frightening, but not terribly difficult as long as you were prepared. Ravagers, however, were not mindless infecting or eating machines. They were brutal, unrelenting fighters that enjoyed both inflicting and receiving pain. Sam wouldn't be able to stand against one of them, much less four.

Behind him, Sam heard a series of heavy crashes and insane, bestial yells. He wanted to go and help Vincente, who undoubtedly was locked in the fight of his life, but if he left this spot they would both die. Instead, he centered the leftmost Ravager in his rifle sights, exhaled, and pulled the trigger.

The shot tore through the Ravager's chest, taking him off his feet. Upon seeing their compatriot go down, the other three Ravagers sped up, laughing and zigzagging back and forth as they crossed the street and entered the weed-choked parking lot.

Sam worked the rifle's lever, ejecting the cartridge and replacing it with a fresh round. He repositioned the rifle, leading his second target, and squeezed the trigger. The Ravager twisted to the side as the shot ripped through his neck and shoulder. He toppled to the ground a moment later. *Two down,* Sam told himself. *Halfway there.* He reloaded, trying to keep his focus. The two remaining Ravagers had made it halfway across the lot by the time he aimed again.

He fired too quickly and missed his third shot. They were almost here. He reloaded and fired again, and this time caught the third Ravager square between her eyes. One left. There were more crashes behind Sam as he grabbed the rifle lever and pushed the cartridge free. He had a vision of the Ravager coming up behind him, coated in Vincente's blood, and clubbing him on the back of his head as he sighted the final approaching Infected. But no: he was actually going to do it. Kill four real-life charging Ravagers. He smiled crazily as he took aim, imagining the story he would tell. He pulled the trigger.

The rifle clicked, and Sam's smile died. The rifle was empty; he had lost count of his shots. There was no time to reload, and his baton was gone. He would have to fight the Ravager — who was armed with a revolver and what looked to be a meat cleaver — with the empty gun, and pray for a miracle. The Ravager screamed a disconcertingly joyous war cry as he leaped across the restaurant's broken doorway, and Sam lost his nerve. He dropped the rifle and cowered away, waiting for the death blow to fall.

It never came. Sam open his eyes to see the Ravager standing in place, a confused look in his blood-red eyes and the handle of Vincente's knife sticking out of his forehead. The Ravager fell to his knees, and then onto his face.

Vincente walked out of the kitchen doorway, from where he'd thrown the heavy knife. Sam scrambled to pick his rifle back up, all the while trying to wrap his mind around the fact that he was, in fact, still alive.

Sam worried that Vincente was going to yell at him for not standing his ground, but instead the older man just patted him on the shoulder. "Nice shooting, kid," he said. "You just saved us both. Now let's get back to the bikes before more of them show up."

In response, Sam doubled over and threw up.

# 2

THEY RETURNED TO THE COLONY more or less empty-handed.

The outer walls of the Black Hills Survivors Colony were made of simple corrugated metal, long since turned red and blue with rust, and stood at the edge of a hilly, pine and spruce forest. A sniper wearing an Old World gas mask — today it would be John, if Sam remembered the watch schedule correctly — pulled open the gate ahead of them. Vincente and Sam rode their dirt bikes through without slowing down.

At first glance, the wide stretch of land between the outer and inner walls didn't look much different than that of the Wilds. Looks could be deceiving, however. Motion sensors and laser trip wires studded the trees and the bushes and the rocks, each carefully hidden from the untrained eye. Sam had long ago memorized the positions of each and every one. Up until a few months ago, intra-wall patrol was as close as he could get to the outside world, and he had worked diligently to earn his way up to his current position on the Scavenge-and-Scout detail. He still recognized each sensor-carrying tree by sight, even at 40 mph and even with his nerves worn raw from the day's fight.

It wasn't long before the inner walls came into view. Even obscured among the trees, the bone-white twenty-foot ramparts — steel, ceramic, and bulletproof plastics, state-of-the-art Old World engineering — were hard to miss. The blue laser-sights of the two automated machine guns picked them up a couple of hundred yards out, and Sam had to raise a hand just to keep the weapons' azure lights out of his eyes.

The two dirt bikes churned twin trails of mud and rock as they skidded to a stop at the inner wall gates. Unlike those at the outer walls, these doors wouldn't open automatically, no matter how clear or familiar their faces were to the camera operators inside. Sam and Vincente raised open hands at their sides and looked up at the camera's blinking light, waiting for the security operator to match their faces against the ones on file. It didn't matter that they were the only ones that had gone out that day, nor that they had gone through this very process dozens of times in the past months. Protocol was protocol, as Sam had repeatedly been told, and following it wasn't optional. It was what kept the Colony safe and its inhabitants uninfected. It was what kept them alive.

After a few moments of waiting, whoever was at the security monitors must have finally been satisfied that they were not, in fact, Plague-Heads or Ravagers, because the gate hissed and slid slowly open. The pair revved their engines and moved their bikes forward into the wall's antechamber. They waited while the door behind them slid shut and they were sprayed down with disinfecting mist. Sam heeled down his kickstand and got off his bike, walked over to the clearance kiosk, and took two test strips. He returned to the bikes and handed one to Vincente. Each of them swabbed the inside of their cheeks, and then, careful to keep the still-green strips visible to the cameras the entire time, Sam returned them to the kiosk.

There was another short wait before the wall's inner door hissed open and they reentered the Black Hills Survivors Colony.

╪

The Colony was a mix of Old World high technology and new world functionality. Multi-floor laboratory and fabrication facilities existed side by side with single-story machine shops and barns and barracks. High-tech, shiny white buildings were scattered among newer, hand-built structures of scavenged metal, hand-chopped wood, and fabricated plastics.

No sooner had Sam and Vincente entered the Colony's interior than were they were forced to wait as a school teacher led a line of small children across the dirt and stone road ahead of them, like a mother duck trailing a string of ducklings. One of the children raised a hand in the air and twisted his wrist, and in response, Sam revved his engine, to the delight of the children and the scolding stare of the teacher. To their left, a group of elderly Colonists hung laundry up to dry; to their right, a handful of Sam's old classmates worked to harvest a square of high, bushy corn stalks.

Sam was home, and already he was getting anxious to go back out.

The last remnants of the day's earlier terror were still there in his belly, but now that he was back and safe, those remnants were joined by something else. It was a feeling that had been growing for years now, steadily claiming greater portions of his head and of his heart. It was a feeling like a limp weight slung over his shoulders, a feeling like an itch at the corners of his thoughts. Each morning he woke here in this Colony it seemed a little less like his home.

He had lived for his entire seventeen years on this square mile of earth, surrounded by the same mountains and the same trees and the same people. The high, white walls all around him should have made him feel safe — he had certainly been told that enough times by the Elders, after all — but instead those walls felt like the ever-tightening bars of a cage. He knew from his books just how big the world really was, and a cold pit of dread formed in his stomach any time he thought of just how little of it he'd seen.

Sam pushed those feelings out of his mind and tried to focus on his next, most urgent, task. Now that he was back, he was suddenly starving. He needed to get himself some food. No matter how else he felt about the Colony, it had no shortage of hot meals. *See, I'm already focusing on the positive*, he told himself, smiling as he stepped off his bike and followed Vincente to the motor pool. There, they handed off their bikes to the mechanics, along with their padded armor and weapons.

Malik, the head quartermaster and mechanic, looked over Sam's metal and plexiglass helmet with a look on his face that was equal parts disappointment and disgust. "Is this plague-spew?" he asked, turning the thing over in his hands, his arms stretched out away from his body as far as they would go.

"It's disinfected," Sam said with a shrug as he emptied his rifle and handed it over to Karen, the other quartermaster. "It was an eventful run."

"Not a productive one, though, by the looks of your packs," Karen said. "Elder Jed wants to see you, Vincente.

"For your sake, I hope it's not about how light you are on scavenge."

Vincente nodded, flashing his trademark rogue's smile at her. Sam rolled his eyes; he could practically see Karen melting under its spell. Vincente had an effortless charm with women, one of the many skills Sam had tried to pick up from him, with exceedingly limited success.

"Wait for me in the barracks," Vincente said to Sam. "When the old man's done with me, we'll head down to the mess and catch some grub."

"Now we're talking," Sam said, rubbing his hands together. As he did so, he caught sight of the dried, black-and-red Plague-Head vomit that still caked his coveralls and his body armor. His lips curled, and his hunger vanished. Well, it almost vanished. "I think I'm going to need a shower."

Vincente laughed. Sam was about to point out that Vincente didn't look any better, but then he remembered that what covered his friend's chin and chest was Ravager blood. Sam's thoughts flashed back to that charging Ravager, to how close he had come to death. To how he had frozen up — lost his nerve.

His own smiled vanished. He vowed to himself he would never let something like that happen again. He knew he wouldn't live forever, especially not in this world; but on the day he did finally meet his end, he would go down swinging.

"The Elder actually wants to see both of you," Karen interjected. Vincente and Sam both looked at her in surprise. "I know, right?" she added.

The Elders talked to Vincente, and Vincente relayed the orders to Sam. That was how it always worked. *Until today, apparently.* Sam didn't know whether to be excited or afraid. In either case, it looked like his shower would have to wait. He was going in front of one of the Council Elders.

✝

The Colony Headquarters had always reminded Sam of a hospital, or maybe an alien space ship. The hallways were a spotless white, lit from above and below with antiseptically bright glow panels and cleaned by a small army of tiny, whirring robots. Attendants and secretaries passed them in similarly white coveralls, their footstep echoing off the walls of the otherwise silent corridors. Sam had always felt grubby and unkempt on the few occasions that he had been allowed inside these futuristic walls, but never more so than he did today. The last attendant they had passed had actually pressed himself against the wall as he walked by, keeping as far away from Sam as was physically possible.

When he had been younger, it had been assumed that Sam would eventually be spending most of his time in these immaculate halls. From his first aptitude tests, when he was barely five years old, Sam had ranked at the top of his class in math, abstract reasoning, and spatial analysis. All the qualities valued in Colony leaders; traits the Elders were known to prize above all else. Even today, long after he'd decided on the course of his life, Sam wondered what things would be like if he'd simply stayed on the path that had been laid out for him. He'd probably be not too different from one of those white-clad attendees rushing by, looking down their nose at him. Likely he would be on track for his own office, even a junior administrative position. It would be a life that others in his class would kill for, and certainly a great deal safer and more respectable than scrounging around in the trash heap of the outside world. But to Sam it sounded like a prison sentence. Being cooped up in this shiny, hi-tech box, away from the real world...he shivered.

Vincente brought the two of them to a stop in front of Elder Jed's door. "You nervous?" he asked.

Sam shook his head. Nervous, after all, wasn't quite the right word. Uncomfortable was more accurate. Sam didn't know the Elders any more than the majority of other Colonists did. Mostly they existed to him as a handful of voices that read announcements over the Colony's loudspeakers. Occasionally he would see them, a group of well-dressed old people, scurrying from headquarters to the fabricating labs or vice versa. They were, for the most part, a mystery, and that was how he preferred to keep them. As far as Sam was concerned, they could keep to their fluorescent, indoor world, and he would keep to his.

"Not nervous," Sam said.

"I'm not sure if that's a good thing or a bad," Vincente said, looking him over. "Just try not to talk back to him. Or correct him. Or insult him. In fact, just try and keep as quiet as you can. Silent would be best."

"I have great people skills," Sam answered, smiling and shaking his head as Vincente knocked on the Elder's door.

+

Elder Jed's office didn't look anything like what Sam had imagined. Rather than the bright, minimalist whites of the building's outer hallways and plazas, this room was all warm woods and rich leathers. It was as if they stepped into another world when they crossed its threshold — an older, now-deceased world. The room reminded Sam of a hunting lodge, or a rich man's cabin, back from when either of those things still existed. The office had a brick fireplace, for god's sake; Sam doubted that was part of the building's original plans.

"Thank you, gentlemen, for seeing me on such short notice," the Council Elder said, standing up from his dark walnut desk and gesturing toward two empty chairs. "I know you have recently returned from a salvage run, and you must certainly be tired."

Vincente thanked the Elder for his concern. Sam, following his friend's instruction, simply nodded. Elder Jed didn't look a day over thirty, with a close-cropped brown beard and wrinkle-free, nut-brown eyes. Sam knew he could be far older — the rumor was the Elders had access to Old World anti-aging treatments, or at least had used them at one time. All Sam was sure of was that Jed had been one of the original Colony leaders at the time of the Horsemen Virus's outbreak, just over twenty years ago. So unless a particularly mature tween was running the Colony on I-Day, Elder Jed was older than he appeared.

"I know you were both probably looking forward to some well-deserved rest," the Elder continued, "but unfortunately that won't be possible. We need you to go back out tomorrow morning."

"Elder, if I may?" Vincente said. "We just survived an ambush by a Ravager war party. Not only are me and Sam in no shape for another run, but our security forces need to be briefed on these new developments. If a tribe of Ravagers has migrated into our area, we need to prepare for a possible attack."

"The Ravagers will be dealt with, Mr. Ramos, I can assure you of that," Elder Jed said. "In point of fact, the Ravager problem is precisely why we need you and your protégé to go back out on such short notice."

"It's going to take more than a pair of scouts to beat back a whole Ravager tribe," Sam said. "Even Vincente and I aren't that bad-ass."

Vincente winced, and Sam felt his cheeks warm. He had momentarily forgotten his friend's only command — not to speak — and not only that, he had cursed in front of the Elder. *Screw it,* Sam thought, after a moment's pause. *This old guy wants us to go right back out, into the teeth of the Ravagers.* He was lucky Sam didn't throw something at him.

"What my colleague *means,* Elder," Vincente began. Elder Jed smiled and raised a hand to quiet him.

"It's fine, Scout Ramos," the Elder said, chuckling. "The young man isn't wrong. Assaulting a band of Ravagers with a single scout patrol would be ill-advised. Regardless of how 'bad-ass' those scouts may be.

"The task I have for you is far more within your skill set," the Elder continued. "And I wouldn't ask you to go back out so soon if we had any better options. Unfortunately, we do not. The very survival of this Colony may well depend upon this mission's success. Are you and young Mr. Brennan up for it?"

Vincente sighed. "It would help if I knew what 'it' was," he said. "But yes, I can handle another mission, if that's what we need. Sam, though, needs his rest. He's too young and too green to go back out so soon."

"I'm fine to go back out right now," Sam protested. "If you're going, V, so am I." *Too young?* Sam thought. *I'll show Vincente who's too young.* The older scout knew far more than Sam at this point, but physically, Sam was at least as capable. *And I've always been the better shot.*

"I'm afraid I have to agree with the young man," Elder Jed said. "I have been looking over your metrics. Your mission success rates have risen dramatically since Mr. Brennan has begun to accompany you. Due to this mission's importance, we need the best, and that means both of you."

Vincente looked like he was going to argue further, but the Elder again raised his hand. "I'm afraid I'm going to have to insist, Vincente."

Vincente sighed as he rubbed his beard and considered the Elder's request. Sam knew, however, that the decision had already been made. The Colony needed them to go back out, and go back out they would.

"Tell me the mission," Vincente said.

## 3

AT LEAST SAM GOT TO SLEEP one night in his own bunk.

After Elder Jed had secured their agreement to undertake this mysterious and vital mission, Sam had been dismissed so Vincente could be briefed further in private. Apparently Sam was good enough to hold the Colony's survival in his hands, but not trustworthy enough to know the assignment details. He was too tired and too hungry to be properly disgruntled, however, so instead of arguing, he left the Elder's building and headed to the barracks, where he ate two normal-sized dinners before collapsing into his bunk and promptly falling asleep.

Vincente shook Sam awake just before dawn the next morning. Sam shambled out of his bunk and over to outfitting, where he and Vincent put on their traveling clothes, grabbed their packs, and made final preparations to head back out into the Wilds.

This assignment was to be Sam's first long distance ranging — the Rangers like Vincente called them LDR's — as well his first overnight mission. He told himself it was just the next logical step in his career path: he'd started on inner wall guard duty, graduated to intra-wall patrol, and then to short scavenging runs. An LDR was nothing more than the next level up. He kept telling himself that, because each time he thought particularly hard about camping out there in the Wilds, among the hordes of Plague-Heads, the packs of Howlers, and the marauding war-parties of Ravagers, he had the overwhelming urge to sprint back to his bunk and pull the covers up over his head.

Despite his worries, it was exciting that the Elders had chosen him, of all people, for this vital mission. *Well, they actually chose Vincente,* Sam reminded himself. Vincente, Lead Ranger, who had more experience with long distance scouting and recon than anyone else within the Colony. *But they chose me to accompany Vincente. That counted for something, right?*

Exciting was how he was going to choose to think about this LDR. He was *not* going to think about how many scouts and rangers had gone out on an overnight, and were simply never heard from again.

"You packed the extra MRE's?" Vincente asked, as they cut through the early morning fog toward the armory and the motor pool.

"One week's supply for two. I counted it twice," Sam replied. Overhead, the sun had just begun to light up the peaks of the northern mountains. They glowed orange against the indigo sky, like floating islands of fire.

"Extra socks?"

"In both packs," Sam said. He listened to the sporadic chirps of the morning's first songbirds. He breathed in the smell of the dew on the air, and the fresh-cut grass all around him. He wondered how different morning would be, out there in the Wilds.

"Fire supplies?"

"Yes."

"Cookpot?"

"Uh-huh."

"Walkies?"

Sam scoffed and rolled his eyes. "We went through the supplies last night, V. You woke me up to load them, and you looked them over yourself. I put everything you inspected in the bags, so you can stop asking me about every little thing."

Vincente turned around to face Sam, his ever-present smile nowhere to be seen. He put a hand on the younger man's shoulder. "Out there, Sam, every detail matters. Those supplies could very well be the difference between if we live or die out there. You understand that, right?"

Sam sighed. "Yes, I understand," he said.

"So," Vincente said as he resumed walking. "Batteries?"

"Yes," Sam said, following dutifully after.

✝

When they got to the armory, they went through the checklist again, this time for their weapons and armor. Rifles? Check. Pistols? Check. Knives? Check, Check, and Check.

"Is it all like Rapid City out there?" Sam asked. "Just more abandoned buildings, more trash?"

Vincente, busy strapping on his shin and wrist guards, shrugged. "Yes and no," he said. "Most of the old cities and towns look the same, sure, but the further you get away from the Colony, the more the new world crops up."

"More Infected?"

"Yeah, but not just that. There's more Infected, sure, but also more animals. Horses and cows and pigs — a lot of the Old World farm animals gone semi- or all-the-way feral. There's also stranger ones, like herds of buffalo and prides of lions. One of the old rangers swore to me he saw a family of gorillas, living in the woods south of here. Escaped from the zoos, I guess. And then there are the people."

"Uninfected people?" Sam asked. "You mean the other Colonies?"

Vincente shook his head. He strapped the expandable plexiglass riot shield to his back, the collapsible baton to his thigh, and the folding longbow to the back of his belt. "I mean the ones that live outside the Colonies: traders, scavengers, nomads, and independent tribes. There are more out there than you think. Not near the Colonies, of course, but once you get a little ways away, you'll begin to see them more and more."

Sam knew people — Uninfected — lived out in the Wilds, but he had always assumed they were madmen, highwaymen, and hermits, little better than Infected. He had heard stories about the nomad societies following the new great herds, as well as the so-called 'Free Cities' of the Rockies; all children had. But he knew they were just that: stories. It surprised him to hear that there really was a whole world of Uninfected — of *people* — out there. However, what surprised him even more was how casually Vincente had brought it up.

"You never talked about them before," Sam said. Of course, no one spoke of the greater Wilds, beyond occasional whispers and rumors and ghost stories. Since he was old enough to know what they did, Sam had always suspected that the scouts and the rangers knew more about the Wilds than they let on. But he couldn't believe that Vincente would lie to him, not for all these years, without a good reason. Either the real truth of the outside was too terrible to speak of, or someone high up — and the only people who could be that high up were the Elders —

demanded the truth be suppressed. Sam didn't know which possibility disturbed him more.

"You never asked," Vincente said, focusing on his work. Sam wondered if what he was really saying was 'you didn't need to know.' Vincente grabbed his plexiglass facemask and nodded towards the motor pool and the bikes. "Let's get moving; I want to be past the outer gates before sun up. We've got a whole lot of road ahead of us."

Sam grabbed the last of his gear and followed after Vincente, who was already walking. "The Jackson Colony?" Sam said. "Old Wyoming? That is where we're heading, right? Are you ever going to get around to telling me what our actual mission is?"

A single groggy-looking mechanic stood next to their bikes, which were freshly cleaned, fueled, and ready to go. He tossed the first set of keys to Vincente, who snatched them expertly out of the air. "Maybe once we're clear of the walls," Vincente said.

Sam rolled his eyes as he took the second pair of keys. There was plenty Vincente wasn't telling him about the mission, of course, but what was really starting to rattle around in Sam's mind was what Vincente had just said about the Uninfected in the Wilds. He had said that it was only when you got *away* from the Colonies that you started to see the Uninfected. Sam looked out the door of the garage at the green grass, the swept streets and the carefully tended crops of his peacefully sleeping Colony, and one question refused to stop shouting back at him.

*What was it about the Colonies that kept the Uninfected away?*

They passed the outskirts of old Rapid City soon after they left the outer Colony walls. It felt strange to Sam, not slowing down and turning his bike toward the mass of stout, crumbling buildings. Instead, he and Vincente kept on the gas and continued to burn pavement, heading out toward the unknown west.

Vincente had told him things would look different, further out from the Colony. But after a few hours of hard driving, Sam just wasn't seeing it. What he was seeing, all around him, over and over again, was more of the same. Rusty signs; cracked and pock-marked roads; slowly crumbling buildings. Shrubs and grasses that had once been carefully cultivated and pruned now gone bushy and wild, reclaiming the yards and gardens of their former tenders, long dead and unburied.

There were fewer trees, however. So that was different. And fewer hills, and rocks, and mountains. More flat. Though Sam knew that would change. The mountains around Jackson — the Tetons — would make the crags around their home Colony look like mole hills. But Sam was disappointed by the emptiness. He'd yet to see any of the herds of buffalo or wild horses Vincente had promised, nor any —

There, out in the distance, just before the horizon. Vincente saw it a second after Sam, and they slowed their bikes to a stop. It was massed around a patch of ranch homes and a single drunkenly-leaning grain silo, and from this distance it looked like nothing so much as a pulsating, writhing clump of green-and-gray mold.

It was a full swarm of Plague-Heads. It took Sam a moment to realize, as he stared out at that horrible mass, that his mouth was hanging open.

The term 'zombie' had been frowned upon for as long

as Sam could remember. Plague-Heads didn't eat people, after all, brains or otherwise. For sustenance, their mottled green flesh absorbed sunlight; at night, they would wolf down clumps of dirt for the minerals. That didn't mean they weren't dangerous; far from it. Everything that had made them human was long gone, replaced by one single-minded, animalistic purpose: to spread the Horsemen Virus. They were driven to attack the Uninfected, and would do all they could, in their violent, mindless fashion, to make sure they spread the infection onward. Most famously they did this through projectile vomiting, but equally as often through biting, clawing, and tearing at the flesh of their target. Plague-Heads, the standard-bearers of Pestilence itself, were in fact the only way the Horsemen Virus still spread, and they did their job extremely well. This was all basic stuff, taught to every Colony child in first year biology class.

Still, seeing them massed like that — mindless things that were once thinking, feeling people, now something both more and less than human — it was hard not to think of the old stories of the living dead.

"Looks like we're going to need a different route," Vincente said, taking out his old, marked-up map.

Sam watched the Plague-Heads mill back and forth among the ancient cadaver of the Old World farming village, trying to ignore the beads of cold sweat that had formed on his brow.

"A different route would be good," he whispered.

✝

"Well, this is new," Vincente said. He lowered his binoculars just as Sam raised his own.

A few miles ahead, Sam could see what appeared to be some kind of settlement. A wall of rusty metal and water-stained plywood ran in a ring around an intersection of the Old World roadways, enclosing buildings that were once a drugstore, a gas station, and a Taco Bell. The settlement's tall, swinging gate was propped open, and though Sam couldn't make out any people, the structures inside looked to be intact and in good repair.

"It looks new-built," Sam said. "I take it this place was put up sometime after you were last here?" Sam was still getting used to the idea of Uninfected civilization out here in the Wilds, but Vincente was well used to it by now. So why did Sam's friend look so concerned?

"It's new," Vincente confirmed. "But that's not what's bothering me. Look at the gate."

"It's open," Sam said, feeling a small surge of encouragement in his scouting abilities. "It was one of the first things I noticed. I thought that was a little odd, but then again, I don't see any Plague-Heads, and there's plenty of open ground to spot them coming. And I know Howler packs don't hunt till night. So…maybe they didn't see the need to keep it closed?"

"No," Vincente said, slowly scanning the horizon with his binoculars. "Any settlers reckless enough to leave their gates hanging open wouldn't have gotten this far into construction. So we've got a red-flag there. But there's still something else that's got my neck hair up. What is it?"

Vincente was fond of these sorts of tests. He would find something he thought Sam needed to notice, refusing to move forward till Sam had picked it out. Sam considered it little more than a glorified guessing game, albeit one that might one day save his life. All the same, standing here all day didn't sound like his idea of a good time...luckily, he was pretty sure what V wanted him to notice.

"The sign," Sam said.

"The sign?" Vincente asked, his voice soaked with poorly-feigned cluelessness.

"The sign," Sam repeated. He pointed at the giant metal sign just ahead of them, built from what looked like a quarter of an Old World billboard, which had been torn down, painted with its new, crudely-drawn message, and then propped back up on a single metal pole. "It says 'Trading Post Ahead. Plenty of Supplies. All welcome.' It may as well read 'Please Come and Rob Us.'"

"There are three more signs out there," Vincente said. "One on each road heading toward the walls. That settlement is a trap."

Sam nodded. It made sense now. The people out here were likely not the kind of folk you would want to invite in for dinner. They were robbers and worse. Nice, harmless people wouldn't choose to live outside the safety of the Colonies, but highwaymen would. And if you were a highwayman, why spend the time and energy hunting down travelers to rob when you could just direct them straight to you?

"You're sure?" Sam said. "We're going to need supplies eventually."

"It doesn't make sense," Vincente said, ignoring Sam's question. "No one would put that much effort into a trap that no one could possibly fall for."

"Maybe it was built by someone else, and then some bad guys came and took it over. Then they turned it into the trap."

"I guess it's possible," Vincente said. "It's less worrisome than the alternative."

"What's the alternative?" Sam asked.

"The alternative is that Ravagers set this trap. It would mean they are learning to think ahead, to plan, rather than being fixated on whatever is right in front of their faces and how to kill it."

Sam shivered and said nothing.

Slowly, they turned their bikes around and drove away from the intersection settlement. Vincente rechecked their map and found them a new route, one that gave the place an extra wide berth. Neither Sam nor Vincente was anxious to see who — or what — had set the trap.

A single eye tracked the two riders through a rifle scope as they approached the outpost. The outpost that a particularly cunning band of Ravagers had turned into their trap. The riders stopped some distance away and considered the trap; finally, thinking better of it, they turned and drove away.

*Smart,* the eye's owner thought. *Or smarter, at least, than the Ravagers who had baited the trap.* The figure decided to follow and see where the riders were heading.

There was no hurry, after all. The meat would keep.

# 4

THEY STOPPED JUST BEFORE SUNDOWN and made camp. Vincente selected a mostly-intact suburban neighborhood, found the least decrepit-looking house, and the pair set out their sleeping bags in the upstairs master bedroom. The house was empty, but in surprisingly good shape.

After sweeping a few years worth of accumulated dust, dirt, debris, and animal leavings from the room, Sam sat down and started their portable stove, trying to imagine what it must have been like to grow up in an ordinary old house like this. What it must have been like to grow up safe in a pre-Horsemen world. He couldn't do it. He may as well have tried to imagine growing up on Mars.

Later, as Sam finished the last of his MRE, Vincente stood at the bedroom's wide, long-ago broken window and scanned the horizon with his binoculars. His rifle leaned against the wall next to him, ready in case any Ravagers or Uninfected highwaymen had picked up their trail.

"It's been over an hour, V," Sam said. "If you haven't seen anyone by now, I think it's safe to say we haven't been followed."

"You're probably right," Vincente replied, "but it never hurts to be sure. In any case, these past few minutes I've mostly been watching those smoke trails on the southern horizon."

*Smoke?* This was a new development. Sam stood up and joined Vincente at the windowsill. His friend was right: there were three distinct columns of greasy black smoke rising against the orange and red of the sunset sky. Sam grabbed Vincente's rifle and peered through its scope as he tried, unsuccessfully, to identify the burning's source. Whatever was on fire, it was far away.

"Should we be worried?" Sam asked. He and Vincente had come from the east, and in the morning, their path would continue more or less southwest. They wouldn't be heading directly toward the smoke trails, but they were close enough to tomorrow's route to bother him. Based on Vincente's expression, they bothered him as well.

Vincente lowered his binoculars and shook his head. "They're worth keeping an eye on," he said. "But it's too early yet to start borrowing worries."

A howl sounded somewhere in the distance. The call was too short and too guttural to be a coyote. *Not a coyote at all,* Sam thought. He recognized the sound from the Colony recordings.

"Howlers," he said, an icy pit of fear coalescing in his gut. A second, lower-pitched howl answered the first. The first had come from the east; this one was from the west. Sam swung the rifle barrel in the howl's direction, his heartbeat ticking steadily upward.

Vincente gently took the rifle from Sam and propped it back up against the wall. "The Howlers are nothing to worry about, either," Vincente said. "That's why we sleep inside."

Sam shook his head. The Howler calls were unsettling, but they weren't the thing that was bothering him. "Ravagers," he said. "Howlers. Plague-Heads. Uninfected highwaymen, even." He turned away from the window and stalked back toward the fire, rubbing his hands together. "The watch captains and the Elders spend so much time teaching us about them, and only them. They teach us how to recognize them, how to avoid them, how to kill them." He turned again and paced back toward the window. He knew he must look like a lunatic, but he couldn't stop himself. He felt compelled to keep moving. "And sure, they scare me alright; I won't pretend that they don't. But it wasn't a Howler that made me an orphan, V. And it's not a war party of Ravagers, or a herd of Plague-Heads, that worry me now that the sun's gone down."

"Ah. You're talking about the fourth kind of Infected," Vincente said, staring out the window. He ignored Sam's pacing, either out of sympathy or irritation. "You're talking about the Reapers." He chuckled softly to himself. "Well, kid, I can tell you right now, you don't need to worry about Reapers."

"You're not going to try and tell me Reapers aren't real, are you V?" Sam said.

"No, they are very real," Vincente said. "Rare — extremely rare — but they're real. But that's not why you don't need to worry about them."

"Well, what is the reason?"

Vincente walked over to the stove and sat down, finally starting on his own dinner. "Because if a Reaper wants to kill you, Sam, there isn't a whole hell of a lot you'll be able to do to stop it. Now, quit scaring yourself with ghost stories, sit down, and help me finish my soup. You'll need your energy tomorrow."

✝

The figure in black listened to the Howlers bark their animal calls back and forth through the waxing darkness. The figure wasn't worried; the beasts might hunt at night, but she *owned* the night. The occasional glints of light, coming from the upper window of that Old World mansion, worried her more. The riders were cautious, and they had optics, the quality of which the figure was still unsure. She had been careful to conceal her path, but the riders were obviously experienced scouts, and there was no guarantee that they hadn't already spotted their tail.

The figure paused at the edge of the tree line at the hill's crest, looking down into the gently sloping valley below. She surveyed the landscape, trying to imagine what path the riders would take in the morning. Why did she care, the figure wondered? Why was she even bothering to follow them at all?

She couldn't answer that. Answers came to her less and less these days. In any case, the smart move would be to hit them tonight after full dark. Kill the riders and take their supplies. Take the food. Turn back east.

*But no,* she thought, *not yet.* She would wait.

Another Howler called, closer this time. No more than a hundred yards away. The figure set down her bag of bones and drew her knife.

*I'll give them one more day. Tonight, I hunt.*

✝

Sam and Vincente each sat atop a sleeping bag and slurped soup. Outside, the sky had turned an inky black, and a thin crescent moon had risen. Between the two of them, a small lantern glowed dimly.

"Tell me again about what was it like, before you came to the Colony?" Sam asked. In the past, most questions like these Sam posed to Vincente were only answered with deflections and terse silence. Back home, talking about the past, especially about the life one led before entering the Colony, was considered extremely impolite, not to mention unlucky. It was worst with the older people, the ones that remembered what it was like before the Horsemen Virus. More than once Sam had walked in on an old-timer watching entertainments made before the Plague, weeping silently. Sights like that tended to discourage conversation on the topic.

Even with Vincente, who Sam could talk to about almost anything, the topic of their past lives had rarely came up. Early on, when Sam was little, the subjects were too fresh and painful, and then after a while their mutual silence just sort of settled into a habit. With Vincente, Sam talked about scouting, or shooting, or other, easier topics. With the rest of the Colonists, Sam kept it even more superficial. The head doctors would probably tell him it had to do with losing his parents early on; that he had put up walls in his own head, as high and as impenetrable as those that guarded the Colony itself.

Hell, Sam and Vincente didn't even talk about Shayla, the widow who had fostered the pair of them for a few years before cancer had taken her. Their past lives were behind them, buried, and until today Sam had been perfectly happy to let those memories lie.

But now that they were out here, overnight in the Wilds, outside the safety of the Colony walls, it felt important to Sam that he asked. Things were changing for him, and with this mission he was no longer a child. He was a real scout now, and an adult, and he was going to act like it. Part of that meant working to take down his walls. If he couldn't do that with Vincente, who could he do it with?

"I don't remember a lot," Vincente said, staring down into his soup. "There was a lot of running, and a lot of hiding. Hiding from war parties of Ravagers during the day and from packs of Howlers at night. Hiding from the Uninfected, the highwaymen. Our group changed a lot: people joined, and people left. A lot of people died."

Vincente set down his tin bowl and stared off into space. "I don't remember a lot of those people's names. I feel bad about that from time to time."

Sam nodded silently. Looking at Vincente's face, he regretted asking about it. Vincente's parents had died when he was eight, Sam knew that, and he had come to the Colony three years later. He had lived through the early days of the Infection, and those were bad times. Sam had assumed Vincente had gotten past whatever traumas he'd experienced during those three years in the Wilds. But, based on his friend's expression, he hadn't.

"I still see those faces, sometimes, in my mind," Vincente continued. "It's funny, I don't remember a single one of their names, but I remember every one of their faces. They come back to me at the strangest times, and always when I'm back out in the Wilds. I saw the face of the group's oldest man, the one with the bad hip who was slowing us down, the first time I caught a mask full of Plague-Head spit. That guy got ripped apart by…I think it was four Plague-Heads when he opened the doors to a winter clothing store without looking inside first. The things just came flooding out, and he got swept up by them. I saw the face of the woman who used to sing to the group every night the first time one of my scouting partners got killed. They were both taken by Howlers after they left camp to go to the bathroom."

Sam didn't know how to answer that, so he just nodded silently. He hadn't realized until now how much of a toll the Wilds had taken on Vincente. Generally, Sam only saw the lighter side of his friend; the quiet wit and teasing jokes and easy smiles. He understood now that Vincente had hidden this part from him, for his own protection. There was no need to burden a child with memories like these, no reason until now. Sam had always resented growing up behind the Colony's narrow walls — for as long as he could remember, he had wanted to escape and see the wider world. Well, here it was.

"I remember every one of their faces, and I remember every one of their deaths. I carry them with me, every single day. If you can do one thing for me, Sam, it's this: If you see me die, don't carry it with you. Set that burden down and move on with your life. If I can only teach you one thing about living out here in the Wilds, it's that. Because sadness, and regret, those things won't just kill you outright, no. Instead, they'll steal a little bit of your life every day, until you lose the will to live without even noticing."

Sam listened to Vincente intently, pale faced. It wasn't till now, his first night in the Wilds, out among the fires and the Ravagers and the never-ending calls of the Howlers, that he understood just how lucky he had been. But it also made him wonder. Given how dangerous the Wilds were, why would someone choose to live out here?

Vincente shook his head ruefully and looked away. Sam could tell he didn't want to speak further on this matter, so he changed the topic.

"Why do the Uninfected out here keep away from the Colonies?" Sam asked. "Why do they live outside the walls at all?"

Vincente thought about the question for a while before answering.

"The world is a complicated place, Sam," he finally said. "And people are strange. And more than that, a lot of them lie. The powerful lie most of all."

"That's not really an answer," Sam said.

Vincente stood up and returned to the window. "Now is as good a time as any to learn that you can't trust everything the Elders tell you," he said. "Just keep your eyes open while we're out here. If you still have questions by the time this mission is done, I'll do my best to answer them. Now, kill that lantern and try to get some shuteye. You've got the second watch, and I don't want to worry about you nodding off while I try and sleep."

"So what are we really doing out here?" Sam asked.

"We're going to figure out why we lost contact with Jackson."

"And?" *There was more.* Sam was sure of it.

Vincente shook his head and sighed, still staring out into the night. "And we're looking for something," Vincente said. "Something very important, Sam, and you're just going to have to trust me on that." After a few more moments, he added, barely above a whisper, "Something very dangerous."

"Sam," Vincente hissed, shaking him awake. "Get up. We've got company."

Sam was wide awake and on his feet instantaneously. He

and Vincente returned to the window, where they looked down through the night vision of their rifle scopes at the group of people just entering the gated subdivision.

More accurately, it was a group of people and mules. Specifically: four people and two mules. The animals were weighed down with packs, and the people wore ancient-looking gas masks, which in the green and black of the night vision gave them a vaguely sinister, alien-like appearance.

"Highwaymen?" Sam asked, his voice a whisper.

Vincente shook his head. "I don't think so," he said. "They look like traders, or maybe a supply caravan. Highwaymen don't bring pack animals with them. And they wouldn't be crazy enough to travel at night and risk the Howlers."

"And a caravan would?" Sam asked. "Could they be dressed up to look like traders? Part of another trap?"

"I doubt it. Those four are the only ones I've seen for miles. Plus, how would they even know someone was here? If this is a trap, it's a damned elaborate one."

"Elaborate like a fake settlement with roadside ads?"

"Well, there's elaborate, and then there's convoluted," Vincente said. He set down his rifle and went over to their packs. He grabbed a pair of walkies and tossed one to Sam. "I'm going to go down and talk to them."

"What?" Sam hissed. "Are you crazy? What if they decided to rob you, or worse?"

Vincente smiled. "I've got a good feeling about them," he said. "Besides, you'll be up here covering me."

"I can only fire one gun at a time, V. They have four guns. If shooting starts, we're going to lose."

"Well, I guess we'll have to make sure the shooting doesn't start then," Vincente said. He drew his pistol and checked the load before returning it to his leg holster. "We need more gas, Sam, and after what we saw at the last settlement, there's no guarantee the ones on my map will still be around. We need to trade while we have the chance."

Sam sighed. "I'll get the laser sights," he said.

After dashing around the house making preparations, Sam returned to the bedroom windowsill overlooking the subdivision. He set the walkie down to his right, picked up his rifle, unfolded the collapsible bipod, made sure a round was chambered and adjusted his scope, trying to ignore the uneasy churning feeling in his stomach. Outside, the trade caravan had crossed most of the subdivision and was now just under a block away.

"I'll head out when they are two driveways away," Vincente said over the walkie. "They'll probably be a little jumpy, but you stay cool. Don't shoot unless they do first."

Sam listened to his heart pound for what seemed like an eternity before the caravan reached the designated driveway and Vincente stepped out into the road, hands empty and open and out to his sides.

"Ho, travelers," Vincente said. He had left the channel open so Sam could hear what he heard. His greeting sounded silly to Sam's ear, but he wasn't the one with experience in the Wilds, or experience dealing with its denizens.

There was a flurry of shouts and motion as the four outlanders reacted to Vincente's sudden appearance with a combination of surprise, fear, and quickly-brandished weapons.

"Who the hell are you?" one of them shouted.

"Put down your weapon!" another yelled, despite the fact that Vincente's hands were clearly empty.

"Freeze!" a third bellowed. "Or I'll put one between your eyes." Sam admired this one's confidence, though he was less a fan of the threat. He centered his crosshairs on Mr. Confident.

"I mean you no harm, gentlemen and/or ladies," Vincente called out. "I am no highwayman, and certainly no Infected. I merely wish to exchange news, and perhaps some goods, with fellow travelers of the open road."

Vincente's smile was wide enough that Sam could see it even from this distance. His voice was friendly and inviting and completely without fear, despite the four guns pointed at him. Sam had doubted the older ranger's plan, but it looked like it might actually work—

"No, I don't think so," one of the masked travelers said. "How about you unstrap that blaster from your hip and kick it over to us, and then you lie yourself down on the ground, eh? I'm afraid we're going to have to take whatever it is you got."

Sam quickly shifted and centered each of the four travelers in his sights, holding the crosshairs briefly on one after the other in turn. *I told Vincente this was a bad idea.* And Sam would explain that to him again, in detail, once this was over. Assuming they actually lived through it, of course.

"I don't think that's how you want to play this," Vincente said to the travelers, his voice as calm and friendly as ever. "I'm just looking to trade. There's no reason this needs to go poorly for you."

"Poorly? For us?" one of the travelers said with a laugh. "You've got four guns pointed right at you, boy."

The other travelers began to laugh as well.

"I could say the same thing about you," Vincente said.

That was Sam's cue. He squeezed the button on the side

of his rifle grip. Four red dots appeared: one on the chest of each of the four caravan travelers. The laughter stopped instantly.

Sam had spent the last few moments before Vincente left the house setting up the remote laser sights. They were each slaved to his rifle scope, and he had quickly targeted each one on a different traveler when things started to go south. The lasers weren't attached to any weapons, but there was no way for the hostile gunmen to know that. Sam had come up with this trick himself, a few months back, and had engineered the remotes himself. The other scouts had loved it, and it had become a part of the standard kit soon after. Sam grinned. *It was nice to finally see the trick's effectiveness first-hand*, he thought.

Slowly, each of the gunmen lowered their weapons to the ground, and then raised their hands.

"I knew it was just a matter of time before we all saw sense," Vincente said. "Now, I believe we were talking trade. What do you have in the way of gasoline?"

# 5

VINCENTE DIDN'T LIKE THE LOOK of the Jackson Underground Colony.

He had told Sam upon their arrival that he didn't like the look of it. After nearly an hour of staring down at it, the two of them lying on their stomachs and freezing their asses off at the top of the ridgeline, he didn't like the look of it a single bit more.

Sam was starting to wonder if V liked the look of *anything* out here in the Wilds.

After securing a quite favorable deal from the supply caravan — a team of imaginary snipers does wonders for your negotiating position — Vincente and Sam had spent the next day driving across the open, crumbling highways of old Wyoming. Their day of travel had been, for the most part, uneventful. Sam had seen a small herd of wild horses, which had been pretty cool, and the smoldering remains of two settlements destroyed by Ravagers, which had been far less cool. Eventually, the high plains turned to the foothills of the Tetons, and after that to the forested mountains themselves. From there, Vincente had directed them to the hidden trail that had led them through the woodlands and up to the entrance to the Jackson Underground Colony.

"The door is open," Vincente said. "The door shouldn't be open."

The Jackson Underground Colony was built into a small cleft in the base of a mountain. As its name suggested, the entire Colony was underground. From outside, the only evidence that it was there at all was a truck-sized metal door set in the stone, painted to match the rock around it. Even knowing it was there, Vincente had to point it out to Sam before he could locate it.

The door was at least four feet thick, all solid steel. It made the walls of Sam's home Colony look like balsa wood. By Sam's estimation, whoever was inside would have been protected from anything short of a nuclear bomb. As long as they didn't mind living underground, in the dark, twenty-four hours a day...

"What is this place, really?" Sam asked.

"It's our destination," Vincente said.

"No kidding. But you can't keep telling me this is a Colony. I mean, who would choose to live there? Literally under a rock."

"Like I said, we're here to retrieve something important. What does it matter where we're getting it from?" Vincente countered. "Don't get distracted, Sam. Focus on the what, and not the why."

*Yeah, why let a little thing like the truth distract you?* Sam thought. But he let it go. There was probably very real danger beyond that open door. He could get answers from Vincente later.

"Okay, then. That open door," Sam said. "Do you think it's another trap?"

"If it is, I don't understand the bait," Vincente said. "I mean, look at it. Would you really want to go through that door without knowing what was on the other side?"

Sam would not. The only thing beyond the heavy steel door was stark, looming darkness. It reminded Sam of a cave or a mineshaft. *Or a gateway to the underworld*, he thought. It was far from an inviting passageway.

"So what do we do?" Sam asked.

They had lain on that hilltop for what felt like days, watching and waiting. They had prowled the area, looking for any dangers or clues or signs of recent activity. There had been none, besides that damned door. There were zero signs of movement; zero signs that anyone was even in the area. The place looked like it had been abandoned. Vincente had tried to hail the Colony's inhabitants over the radio, every five minutes, like clockwork. Every attempt had been met with silence. It was like the Colony had never existed.

"I suppose we have to go in, eventually," Vincente said.

Sam peered into the grim darkness of the Colony's entrance, and sighed. "Yeah," he said. "I guess we do."

Their mission was to investigate why the Colony had gone silent. Obviously, the answers lay within the mountain. And something else was in there, too: something they needed. Sam knew there was more to the mission, information that Vincente insisted on keeping from him. But they had a job to do, and they would get it done. And more than that, Sam trusted Vincente. If Vincente was going in there, Sam would be right behind.

They made their way slowly down the hill and toward the door, scanning the area with their rifles all the way. As before, the place was lonely and silent, seemingly abandoned. If something was waiting for them, it was waiting deep within the mountain.

At the doorway, they paused and put on their night vision goggles. Inside, the rifles would be too unwieldy, so they left them behind, drawing out their hip-mounted pistols instead.

"Ready?" Vincente asked, staring ahead into the black.

"Ready," Sam answered. He pulled his goggles down over his eyes and flipped them on, and the world turned to shades of green.

☦

The figure in black watched as the riders approached the gate of metal and prepared to enter the mountain. She could smell the stink of Ravager all around, and no place was it stronger than at the opening of the tunnel. It was more than just general Ravager stench, too: yes, she recognized this particular smell. This particular Ravager.

The figure in black would wager anything that the Ravager leader known as Deacon was inside. Deacon, the madman from whom the figure in black had so recently escaped.

And she wondered: were the two riders aware of what awaited them within the mountain?

She removed the black scarf that enclosed her head. Immediately, the sun began to itch at her skin, even filtered as it was through the canopy of pine above.

This was madness.

She should leave. Stick to her plan; turn around and head back east. She owed no assistance to these riders, any more than she owed revenge to Deacon. Survival was all that was important. It was the first lesson she had been taught. The most important lesson, the one above all others.

And yet she found her feet were already moving. She found herself walking silently down the hills and toward the great door of the mountain. She found herself following the riders, down into the darkness within.

☩

Vincente entered the tunnel first; Sam followed.

The night vision helped Sam see where he was going, but it didn't do much to make him feel comfortable. If anything, the distorted green of the goggles made the underground Colony feel even more oppressive and claustrophobic.

The entranceway was a square concrete tunnel that slanted downward steeply enough that Sam had to lean backward to keep his balance; the temperature was noticeably colder than outside, and the air was musty and stale. And it was quiet. Not silent — there was a sort of humming wind that might have been a ventilation system — but it was eerily dead compared to the world above. There were no birds or animals down here, at least not that Sam could hear. No insects, either; not a single cricket-chirp or buzzing fly. The only sounds of life were the soft crunch of their boots and the softer, racing rhythms of their breath.

It took a surprisingly long time for the ground to level out, and Sam wondered just how deep they had gone. With no small amount of unease, he reflected on how much earth and rock currently sat above his head, ultimately deciding it was far more than he was comfortable imagining. Unsuccessfully, he tried to put it out of his mind.

The main part of the Colony looked like something between a natural cavern and an underground highway. The wide corridors extended in front of them as far as the night vision could see. Every few feet on the ceiling was an unlit electric lamp, and on either wall were regularly spaced square metal doors. The doors were smaller than the one at the Colony's entrance, but otherwise they were identical, and every one of them Sam tried was locked. Vincente didn't bother trying a single one. He knew where they were going, and apparently it lay straight ahead. They continued to walk.

It wasn't long before they saw the first signs of conflict. It was smeared just outside the first open door they came across: blood. A splash of matte black in Sam's night vision, stark against the bright neon green of the stone walls. Vincente raised a silent fist, and both of them stopped.

Vincente motioned to Sam, telling him to wait at the doorway while he checked the room beyond. Sam peered in after him — the room looked like some sort of laboratory — and made out the shape of a body on the floor as Vincente knelt down to inspect it.

Sam had seen dead bodies before — you couldn't be a scavenger without coming across any number of the Old World's dead — but most of those corpses had been little more than bones. This body was fresh; for all Sam knew it could have been alive last week, yesterday, an hour ago.

He felt a wave of nausea and bent over to wait until it passed. His heart started pounding, and he began to get dizzy. Feeling worse, he lifted the goggles off his eyes. This was a mistake.

Without the goggles, Sam found himself surrounded by complete and utter darkness. Darkness so thick it felt like it was crushing him. He slammed the goggles back down with a gasp, and the bright green light stung his eyes.

*We shouldn't be here*, he thought. *This place is a tomb.* He felt his throat closing up; it was getting harder and harder to breathe.

*I need to get out of here*, Sam thought. He wanted to run,

but his legs wouldn't move. Bright white spots began to form in front of his eyes, and he knew he was moments away from passing out.

Vincente put a hand on Sam's shoulder, returning him to the present. Sam took a deep, cleansing breath, and found the world was back as it should be. His dizziness faded quickly, though he still felt a bit queasy and disoriented.

"It's okay, Sam," Vincente said. "Just breathe."

He did just that for a few seconds. Gradually, the last bits of the nausea and dizziness melted away. "I'm sorry," Sam said, feeling suddenly embarrassed. *What just happened to me?*

"It's just a spot of panic," Vincente whispered. "It will pass."

"It's gone," Sam said. "I'm fine. So, what happened to that guy?"

"It looks like he died from a blow to the head, though it's hard to tell in this light exactly what was used. I could tell it wasn't recent."

"This place is dead, V," Sam said. "We're only going to find more dead bodies the further in we go. We've done our job, so let's just get whatever it is we need and get the hell out of here."

"It shouldn't be too much further," Vincente said, a waver in his voice betraying his own unease. "It's in the senior Elders' offices. Past the main lab, straight ahead."

*Okay, good,* Sam thought. *Straight ahead, grab this mystery object and then get back to the daylight.* He should have been relieved, but instead he felt an ever-mounting frustration. Since he was down here, risking his life, he deserved — Hell, *needed* — to know what it was they were after.

"Vincente, just tell me what we really came here for," Sam said. "I can tell you're not surprised by the state of this place, which means the whole 're-establish contact' part of our mission was always bullshit. We came here to get something. Something secret. I deserve to know what it is."

"It's not important," Vincente began. *That information is need-to-know*, Sam knew is what he meant.

Vincente started forward, then stopped and turned back toward Sam. He sighed and shook his head. "Okay, fine," he said, after a few moments of consideration. "I guess there's no reason to keep it a secret any longer. This place, the Jackson Underground Colony, is a research station. Genetics, medical, and agricultural science; work going back to pre-infection days. They have codes here, for a cure to a very specific disease, and we need it. That's it."

"A cure?" Sam said. "To what? The Horsemen Virus?"

That couldn't be possible. Colonies all over the continent had tried and failed for years; the virus had proven to be impervious to all attempts at a cure.

Vincente shook his head. "Not the Horsemen Virus. Or, not exactly. It's a cure for something new, a mutation of the original Horsemen Virus. A new strain, one that attacks crops." Vincente paused, and when he spoke again, his voice was grave. "It's the only known cure for a disease that is, at this very moment, killing each and every wheat plant in the Black Hills Colony."

"What are you talking about?" Sam said. "I would know if our crops were failing. Everyone would."

"That's why Elder Jed didn't tell you the details of our mission," Vincente said. "He couldn't risk a panic. But they can't keep it a secret forever. When it comes right down to it, we have to find this cure or our Colony is going to starve."

At that moment, they saw a faint light flickering ahead of them down the tunnel. They heard the voices a moment later.

Sam and Vincente were not alone inside the mountain.

# 6

THESE TUNNELS SMELLED OF DEATH. Death and things worse than death. The figure in black might have considered the darkness her home, but this darkness was something else entirely. She wanted to be away from here, gone, as soon as she could. Nevertheless, she continued down, down deeper into the mountain.

She heard the two riders, who were still far ahead. She heard them whispering to one another, their voices too soft from this distance for even her ears to make out. She heard something else, too. Something further away, down inside the heart of the mountain. She tilted her head, and she listened.

Laughter. And crying. Yes, it would be good to be gone from here.

But still, she continued to move forward, silently cutting through the velvet blackness of these dank tombs. She continued, down into the mountain.

†

Vincente jogged silently toward the source of the light and the voices, with Sam right behind. While Sam could admit it *was* possible the voices belonged to the Colony's original inhabitants, after all that he'd seen he didn't think it likely. Why was the door open? Why hadn't they answered any of Vincente's hails? Or any from Black Hills Colony, for that matter? And then there was the matter of the dead body. *No,* Sam thought, *in all likelihood, those voices belong to whoever is responsible for this Colony's destruction.*

*Well, at least we still have the element of surprise.*

The voices were coming from a room at the end of the road-like stone corridor. Unlike the side doors he and Vincente had passed, this portal appeared to be machine-driven, and large enough to drive a small vehicle through. Another difference from the side doors: this one seemed to have been blown off its hinges by explosives.

Vincente came to a stop with his back against the wall on one side of the door, with Sam directly behind him. Sam leaned around to glance into the room. From the flickering, uneven light inside, it seemed to be lit by fire, rather than electric lights. The room was large — far larger than the side rooms — and seemed to be at least two stories tall. Sam and Vincente were on the top level, up against the room's weirdly underlit ceiling. Wherever the firelight was coming from, it was low enough that Sam couldn't see its source. This had to be the main lab.

An anguished moan rose up from the room's unseen depths. A chorus of cruel laughter followed immediately after. Vincente pushed Sam back from the door and signaled for him to be quiet with a finger to the lips. Then he motioned forward, and the two of them, pistols out, crept silently into the room, keeping to the shadows.

The light of the fire began overloading Sam's night vision, so he pushed the goggles up and off his eyes. Disorientingly, the world went from green and white to orange, red, and black. It took his eyes a moment to adjust to the low light, but once he did he was able to get a better idea of the room's layout. The laboratory was roughly the size of the basketball court back home, and it was three levels high. He and Vincente were now crouching on a grated metal catwalk, which circled the room and connected the levels with a wide, descending ramp. Doors were on every level, one per wall, and on the room's ground floor were computer consoles, lab stations, and what looked like the splintered remains of half a wooden conference table.

The other half of the table had been hacked apart and turned into an enormous, roaring bonfire at the center of the room. Just in front of the fire, with their backs to it, were three bloody and bruised middle-aged men. Each of them sat, tied down with electrical wire, in three wheeled-bottomed office chairs. They weren't alone.

The room was filled with Ravagers.

&#8224;

Above, an air duct whirred softly, sucking up the smoke and the smell from the fire below. Where the power driving it was coming from, Sam had no idea. What he did know was that the fan noise would be invaluable in concealing their movements from the Ravagers below. If they even needed it; it looked like the creatures were already plenty distracted.

"What are they doing down there?" Sam whispered to Vincente.

"Nothing I want to see," Vincente whispered back. "That door across from us, on the second floor, that's the Elder's record room. That's where the drive we need is located."

At that moment, one of the larger Ravagers pointed a

sawed-off shotgun in the air and fired. The shot boomed in the enclosed space, and Sam heard a handful of pellets ping off the grating just below him. For a brief, terrifying moment he thought they had been spotted, but looking back down, he saw the Ravager was focused intently on the prisoners he already had.

"Alright boys, enough pussyfooting around," the Ravager said. "The first one of you that gives me the boss man's codes, he gets to live. The other two?" He shrugged and pointed the shotgun at the prisoners, and then pointed to the crackling fire.

"Shit," Vincente whispered. "I had hoped we could wait them out, wait till they lost interest and left this place. Now it looks like we aren't going to have the luxury. Shit. They must be after the drive...how did they even know it was here?" He sighed and shook his head. "Alright, new plan. Wait here, Sam."

He began to move toward the ramp down to the second floor. Sam reached out and grabbed his arm.

"What the hell are you doing?" Sam hissed. "How are you even going to get into that room?"

"I have the codes," Vincente said. "There's eleven Ravagers down there. That's way too many to fight. Even assuming that's all of them, which I don't." Vincente rested a hand on Sam's shoulder and leaned in close. "Now, listen very carefully, kid. If anything happens, you run. Understand? You don't try and help me, you don't fire your weapon, you don't even let them know you're here. You run, and you don't stop till you reach the Black Hills."

"V..." Sam began.

"We don't have time," Vincente whispered. He smiled. "Relax, Sam. What's the worst that could happen?"

Sam sighed, but he let him go. It was Vincente's call, but

to Sam, the plan sounded insane. Actually, everything about this seemed insane. He briefly wondered if he was dreaming, but unless he'd taken an unremembered blow to the head, he didn't think himself capable of dreaming up something this surreal. *Why did V have the codes to a foreign Colony's secure records room?* Sam wondered. *How did a war party of Ravagers get inside this Colony, and how did they know about the secure storage? How did they even know what secure storage was?* Admittedly, Sam hadn't actually *seen* a Ravager in person till just a few days ago, but everything he had been taught about them described them as little more than misshapen cavemen — barely-human killing machines. The one below, the one speaking to those prisoners, didn't seem like a mindless brute; instead, he sounded like an all-too-human psychopath.

And he seemed to know exactly what he was looking for.

"How do we know you'll let us live, even if we tell you what you want to know?" one of the prisoners said, speaking with a trembling voice marred by a slight lisp, owing to his severely split lip. "We need some kind of assurance you'll keep your word."

The Ravager paced back and forth, nodding slowly to himself. "Assurance, huh?" the Ravager said. "Some kind of assurance."

Vincente silently crossed the catwalk ramp above as this large Ravager, who seemed to be the leader of the band, considered his prisoner's request. Vincente reached the second floor, on the opposite side of the room, just as the Ravager suddenly turned and viciously kicked the prisoner squarely in the chest. The man grunted as the force of the kick knocked him back and over; chair and prisoner both fell straight into the heart of the bonfire.

Sam winced, looking away as the man screamed and burned. Mercifully, it was over quickly. The man's screams faded, overtaken by the cackling and hooting of the assembled Ravagers.

"You want an assurance?" the Ravager leader roared. "Here is my assurance. One more of you is going in that fire. Which of you mooks that is, well, that's up to you."

Sam couldn't get a clear look at the Ravager's face from his position above, but he could get a general idea of him. The Ravager was tall, and like every other of his kind, he was covered in thick slabs of muscle. His dark, oily hair was cut short, and he was missing a jagged chunk of it, owing to a thick, nasty-looking scar which looped up and over the crown of his head from the base of his skull, ending over his right eyebrow. He wore a bear hide as a cloak, with the dead animal's head worn back and seemingly staring up at Sam. He had thick, metal shoulder pads, and besides his fingerless leather gloves, his arms were bare.

If his appearance was unsettling, his voice was even more so. It was gravelly and low and disturbingly cheery — almost melodic. And if Sam had any doubts that this man — this *Ravager* — was capable of extreme violence, those doubts had burned up with the last screaming prisoner.

Just above the Ravager's head, on the second-floor railing, Vincente crouched in front of the door, having successfully crossed the ramped bridge undetected. Unfortunately, he was having less success getting the door open. Vincente was still hidden, despite the fire's light; his small movements as he worked at the door were shrouded among the dancing shadows. But only barely. If any of the Ravagers happened to look up, Vincente was sure to be noticed. *Come on,* Sam thought, trying to *will* the door unlocked. *Come on. Just open, dammit.*

One of the prisoners began to cry. The other's head drooped, and he stared at the floor.

The Ravager leader tapped at the floor with the tip of his shotgun. "Well?" he asked. "Don't go and speak all at once." He grabbed a broken piece of conference table and tossed it into the fire, the wood sailing between the two prisoner's heads. "Time's running out, friends."

Just above, Sam caught a flicker of movement. Finally, Vincente's door had unlocked. Sam watched as his friend eased it open and disappeared into the Elder's office. Sam exhaled slowly. *Almost there,* he thought. *Just hold out a little longer, guys.*

Sam knew the prisoners were going to die. Later, when they were free of this, he knew he would feel sad for them. But right now, he couldn't spare the worry. He just couldn't. He told himself there was nothing he could do for them — he *knew* there was nothing he could do, not against eleven Ravagers — and that helped ease his conscience. Kind of.

"Deacon," one of the other Ravagers said, walking up to the scar-headed leader. This one was a young woman with the left half of her bright red hair shaved down to the scalp. "The last of the outriders just radioed in. They say they found a dead Howler. Back of the neck opened up, not more than a quarter mile from here. Fresh."

The lead Ravager — Deacon was apparently his name — rubbed his hands together and laughed. "It sounds like we've got ourselves a Reaper in the neighborhood," he said. "This day just keeps getting better and better."

Vincente reappeared at the office door. He looked across the room at Sam and nodded, gesturing toward him with a small, white computer drive. He had found the data.

Deacon leaned back and lifted a foot, twirling theatrically on his heel to face his prisoners. He pumped his shotgun and the sound echoed off the chamber walls. "It looks like your time is up, gentlemen," he said. "Because as of this moment, I've got a Reaper to hunt. Now you two just know I'd like to stand here and continue playing grab-ass with you all day, but that's just no longer in the cards. So, tell me those codes now, or I start cutting pieces off you."

The crying prisoner began to wail. The other prisoner, the one who until then had been staring at the floor, looked up at Deacon, defiance and resolve burning in his eyes.

"Roger doesn't know the codes," the prisoner said, apparently referring to his weeping compatriot. "And I'll never tell you, do what you will. You'll never even get inside that office."

Deacon began to laugh, quietly at first, under his breath, the sound building till it seemed to fill the room. After a moment, the rest of the Ravagers joined him.

"Look what I did to the front doors of this lab," Deacon said. "Blew 'em right in. Like they were nothing. You think that itty bitty little door will stop me?"

Deacon pointed up at the office door. His gaze, and that of every other Ravager, followed his hand.

Directly to Vincente.

Sam's heart dropped.

"Well, hello there," Deacon said.

# 7

A LOT OF THINGS HAPPENED all at once. The Ravagers raised their weapons. Vincente began to run. Then the room exploded into chaos.

Sam wasn't sure if Vincente fired first, or if one of the Ravagers did, but once the first gun went off everyone began to shoot. The room was filled with flashes and smoke and booming, deafening explosions. Sam's sight danced between the bridge — watching Vincente's mad dash — and the floor below, filled with shooting, frothing Ravagers. Sam's finger twitched, but he couldn't bring himself to pull the trigger. There were too many of them; what could he do? Besides, Vincente had told him — ordered him — to hold his fire. It was all happening so fast.

Some of the Ravagers only had clubs or crude spears, but the majority had scavenged guns, and at that distance, it was hard to miss. Vincente got further than he should have, but bullets quickly began tearing through him. One cut through his leg, another through his shoulder, and a third right under his left arm. He fell first to one knee, and then to his stomach. He tried to crawl the rest of the way. Sam began to move out of the darkness to help him, but Vincente raised a hand, urging him back. Sam shouldn't have listened. He should have crossed the rail, risking that field of death, and pulled his friend to safety. But something in Vincente's eyes stopped him. On the floor below, the Ravagers ceased fire.

Vincente was injured, but he wasn't dead. That was thanks to the grated metal of the bridge-ramp, which had blocked most of the bullets. Unfortunately, those same bullets had torn huge chunks of the bridge away, and the mangled structure was quivering in mid-air, barely staying aloft. It swayed drunkenly to one side, and then to the other, the metal screeching as it twisted further and further against the supports that anchored it in place. A terrible series of pings sounded just in front of Sam as the bridge began to tear free from the rest of the catwalk. To Sam it all seemed to happen in slow motion: one by one each individual link of grate began to first bend, and then finally to break.

Below them, the Ravagers taunted and laughed like demons.

Vincente, bloody and broken, lying in the middle of the bridge, raised his head and looked up at Sam.

"Go, Sam," he said, his voice barely more than a whisper, his lips speckled with blood. He struggled to pull something out from under his chest; a heartbeat later he had the white computer drive in his hand. He held it up to Sam, and made to throw it the rest of the way across the bridge.

He never finished the throw.

The bridge let out one final metallic scream and broke free. The span of twisted metal swung down and away from Sam, and Vincente fell.

✝

Gunshots ahead. Despite herself, the figure in black smiled. *Finally, something interesting,* she thought.

The shots were coming from the same direction as the faint source of light ahead of her. She broke into a jog and headed toward the light and the violence, moving effortlessly despite the near-black of the tunnels. She could see fine in this light, better than the riders could in daylight. Better than the Ravagers could in any light. One might think this was the reason she felt no fear as she moved, sprinting now, through the underground dark, towards violence and combat and no doubt a number of deaths. But that wasn't the reason.

She felt no fear simply because she no longer knew how.

✝

Sam crouched in the shadows, just behind the torn off edge of a bridge that was no longer there. He tried to force himself to think clearly. The effort was not going well.

He couldn't breathe. He didn't know what to do. Vincente was still alive — he had to be. Sam couldn't imagine the alternative.

But how could he go about saving him? *You can't,* a voice inside Sam said. *He's already dead. Even discounting the gunshots, he couldn't have survived that fall. And what did I do to help him? Nothing.*

At that thought, Sam's paralyzed fear turned to rage. He found the leader — Deacon — and centered him down the barrel of his pistol. If Sam shot, he would give away his position, would give away his very presence. He couldn't kill them all, and he couldn't outrun them. If he fired, it would be as good as killing himself. But at that moment, and thinking about Vincente down there, dead or dying, Sam simply didn't care.

Sam followed Deacon with his pistol's sights as the giant Ravager paced back and forth, considering the fallen wreckage. Both of the scientists had been mercifully smashed to death under the metal, along with at least two Ravagers. Sam could see one of the muscle-bound Infected lying pinned on his back, his wide blood-red eyes staring up at nothing. Sam's finger trembled against the trigger, but still he didn't fire.

Deacon noticed the dead Ravagers a moment later. He walked up to the nearer of the two and prodded its head with the muzzle of his shotgun. Satisfied the Ravager was dead, Deacon reared back his head and he laughed.

"Damn! Did you all see that? Smashed right down, the whole damned thing. Crushed both our egg-heads here straight dead. Man, I've never seen anything quite like it." He turned around wildly, looking for someone. "Roach, dig out our mysterious gentleman caller and see if he's still shuffling along this mortal coil. Maybe he'll be able to answer my questions. Because these boys definitely ain't." Deacon looked to the splattered remains of the scientists, sighed and shook his head. "Was gonna slow-roast 'em over the fire, too. What a waste."

"Found him, chief!" a female voice called. Sam located her — it was the same Ravager who had spoken before.

Lying at her feet, face down and unmoving, was Vincente. Sam sucked in a single, sharp breath. At least Vincente hadn't been caught under any of the falling wreckage. *There was still a chance.* Sam gripped his pistol a little tighter, and he waited.

Roach bent over and put a hand on Vincente's neck. Sam held his breath, listening to his heart pound.

"Nope," Roach said, matter-of-factly. She removed her hand from Vincente and stood up straight. "He's dead."

✝

Silence now, or as close to it as the rabble ahead was capable of keeping. The figure in black held her breath, slowed her heartbeat and tilted her head. She listened.

There were between eight and ten living people in the large room just ahead of her. At least one of them was severely wounded, likely dying. One was on her level, the rest below. Fifteen to twenty feet down, she believed. And there were...four others in the surrounding tunnels. Two groups of two, patrols, most likely. Each pair was creeping slowly around from opposite directions through the side tunnels, moments away from flanking the remaining undamaged rider. Four, all of them Ravagers, and by the sounds of their movements, all of them large.

The figure folded her thumbs around the back of her index fingers and squeezed, cracking her knuckles. She then repeated the process with each remaining pair of fingers. The sound of the pops echoed softly off the stone and steel walls in the pitch black of the tunnels.

*Four Ravagers,* she thought.

*That shouldn't be a problem.*

✝

*He's dead.*

Sam's vision flashed red. He swung his pistol back to Deacon, feeling the blood boiling in his veins as his trembling finger curled back around the weapon's trigger.

"Well, shit," Deacon said. "What a worthless sack of...

didn't even have the courtesy to let me torture him first. All of my fun, spoiled. You know—"

Sam fired. Deacon's head jerked to the side, and he spun away from Sam. *I may have just signed my own death warrant*, Sam thought, *but at least I took that bastard with me.*

Instead of falling to the ground, like he should have, Deacon instead straightened back up. His face turned toward Sam — now with a fresh red line marring one of the cheekbones — and he smiled.

"See, boys and girls, I told you he wasn't alone." Deacon pointed a thick, dirty finger up at Sam. "Bring that one to me."

Sam did what he should have done before. He turned and he ran.

# 8

SAM RAN AWAY from the laboratory, into the black of the tunnels. Bullets chased after him, the booms of Ravager guns echoing off the stone walls, the shots pinging off the bridge's twisted metal railing.

Even just a few feet away from the light of the Ravager's bonfire, the darkness of the tunnels fell over Sam like an icy wave of black. It got so dark, so fast, that it was like someone had flipped a light switch inside his head. His breath was suddenly loud in his ears; his limbs practically vibrated with adrenaline.

Sam had been scared before, more times than he cared to count. Hell, just a moment ago when he'd seen Vincente fall, followed by that scar-faced Ravager — Deacon — pointing up at him with his awful, carnival smile, he'd thought that was easily the most scared he would ever feel. But there was something different about the terror that flowed from a darkness so total and absolute. Something hardwired into the deepest reaches of his DNA. It was a prey's fear.

Suddenly, Sam remembered the night-vision goggles perched on his forehead. *Stupid*, he thought at himself. *This is how you get yourself killed. You give in to the fear, and you forget to think.*

He pulled the goggles down, bright green details mercifully replacing the wall of black. He saw the tunnels, winding away in front of him, eventually leading back to daylight and escape. He saw the rows of sealed metal doors, the gently swaying dead lights overhead, the side tunnels carved out of the stone to either side.

One of the side tunnels just ahead of him was lighting up in his rapidly in his night-vision. *This can't be good.*

The torch swung out from the tunnel, followed by the burly Ravager carrying it. He saw Sam, snarled and aimed the torch in a savage sideways blow. Sam ducked as the fire overloaded his goggles, turning his vision a bright white.

He wasn't quite quick enough.

He dodged the torch, but the Ravager's arm caught him high on the forehead. It glanced off him — Sam was slick with nervous sweat — but Sam's goggles caught on his attacker's wrist, and they were torn off his eyes and ripped from his head. The torch slammed against the wall just above him, its burning end smashing free and scattering on the ground around Sam's feet.

Instinctively, Sam stomped on the glowing embers, plunging both he and the Ravager back into darkness.

He dove to the floor, if for no other reason than to get away from the flailing, roaring Ravager. Sam focused on his breathing, ignoring the pounding of his heart and the high waves of terror beating at the dams on the edge of his mind. *Focus or die,* he told himself, over and over. *Keep your focus, Sam, and maybe you'll survive.*

The good news, if there was any, was that the Ravager didn't seem to be able to see in the dark any better than Sam. He could hear the whirs of its bat swinging back and forth above him, cracking harshly with the stone walls. He scooted rapidly away from the sound, remembering that he still carried a weapon of his own.

He listened, focusing his hearing past the sounds of the bat, honing in on the Ravager's heavy, wheezing breath. Sam raised his pistol — his arms and the weapon both invisible in the black - and pointed as best he could toward the Ravager. He fired.

Sam caught a frozen flash of vision as the weapon discharged. A tall, gangly Ravager, his lips pulled back from dirty broken teeth. The jagged, pointy edges of a club-like torch, ash-stained and broken. Floating balls of black blood, suspended in the air, above a fresh gunshot wound at the top of the Ravager's right shoulder.

Sam fired two more times, and the Ravager went down for good, giving Sam a moment of respite in the darkness. But he was still not alone. He heard the sounds of more Ravagers approaching, grunts and laughs and yelps of pain, along with thwacks and dull thuds which might have been the monsters running into each other, or possibly fighting with one another. *Focus, Sam.* In the dark distance, he saw the gradually brightening light of approaching torches. He needed to find his goggles: without those, he would never find his way out. It was only a matter of time before more Ravagers made their way up here; once that happened, he was done. He had to be gone from here. Now.

Sam extended his arms out in the dark and patted at the cold stone floor, praying the goggles hadn't been irreparably broken in their fall. He inched forward on his knees, tapping to his right, to his left, crawling first one way, then turning and crawling back the other. Behind him, he heard a sharp metallic tapping coming closer and closer: *Tap, Tap, Tap,* as if the noise was birthed from the darkness itself. He would have thought that by now his eyes would have adjusted to the dark — that he would be able to at least see *something. Tap, Tap, Tap.* But the darkness was unyielding, absolute. *And where the hell were those damned goggles?*

Finally, his fingers found something other than empty ground. It was the goggles. *Tap, Tap, Tap.* Sam gripped them with trembling hands and pushed them to his eyes, wanting to get an idea of what was around him before even taking the precious seconds to strap the goggles back into place.

He immediately saw that the source of the tapping was an aluminum baseball bat, wielded by a second Ravager. This was a short one, short and fat, with a bare belly hanging out from a shirt that looked like it was made for a small child. Luckily for Sam, this one had been too stupid to bring along a torch. Sam doubted that luck would last.

The Ravager held a sharpened rod of rebar, point down, and was stabbing at the stone ground in front of itself like a spear fishermen wading through a stream. He was practically on top of Sam — his next stab landed between Sam's splayed legs. Sam fumbled with his pistol; the next stab would be through his gut. The Ravager must have heard the noise, because his wide, wild eyes seemed to meet Sam's own in the dark. He grinned, raising his spear for a killing blow. Sam got the pistol up and fired just in time, emptying the rest of the clip into the Ravager.

The rebar rod fell harmlessly to the ground beside Sam. A half a heartbeat later, the Ravager's dead body fell somewhat less harmlessly on top of him. Sam heard the sound of cracking glass as the weight of the fresh corpse pinned him to the cold floor.

Sam was again in darkness, this time with the goggles still firmly attached to his face. He forced his hands between himself and the dead Ravager, pushing the still-twitching body aside with a grunt. Ahead, gunshots lit up the dark in bursts; strobed images, forms of figures, seemed to be fighting amongst themselves. He took in a steadying breath, checking over the goggles lenses with his fingers.

Sam's heart fell as he felt out the jagged edges of broken glass. The lenses had been shattered.

What he'd feared before had now happened. The goggles

were busted. They were dead, and if he couldn't think up a new plan he knew he'd be following quickly after.

More shots ahead. Dark, then light, then dark. Shapes and noises seemed to be all that existed down here. He struggled to his feet. More shots, closer now. He saw a frozen image of a small Ravager kicking a taller one in the face. Another image of a Ravager running his way. A third, of the same Ravager colliding in mid-air with one of its own kind. They both fell to the ground in a tangle, the smaller one atop the larger. A weapon went off accidentally, pointed Sam's way; he heard — almost felt — the bullet snap by his ear.

And then one of the creatures was on him. Standing nearly nose to nose, close enough that he could hear their breath. Close enough he could smell them — sweat and dirt and blood, but less of the animal stink he had come to recognize as a Ravager hallmark.

A hand gripped his shoulder. Sam pointed his pistol at where he expected the Ravager's face to be. His arm was shoved hard to the side, and his shot went wide, his wrist caught in the vise-like grip of a surprisingly small hand. He tried to wrench the pistol back toward the Ravager, but his opponent had the leverage, or the strength, or likely both, and he was unable to move the weapon at all.

"Stop it, fool," the Ravager said, her voice surprisingly composed and sane-sounding. "We've got to go, now, if we want to get out of here in one piece."

Sam was at a loss. Whatever new trick this Ravager was pulling, it was a good one. He wanted to believe her; maybe she was even telling the truth. He was desperate. He relaxed his gun arm.

"Fine, we do it your way," he said. She loosened the grip on his wrist, and he felt her turning away from him.

He was desperate, but he wasn't stupid. He jerked the pistol back toward the source of her voice and he fired.

Sam heard the shot ricochet off a wall somewhere in front of him. He didn't have to worry if he had missed: he knew he'd missed, because he was suddenly hurtling through the air, upside down.

The Ravager had re-grabbed his wrist as soon as his finger tightened on the trigger. She pulled him around and flipped him over her hip, tossing him about like he weighed nothing.

Sam flopped hard onto the cold stone of the tunnel floor, biting his lip in the process. So, *this is the end,* he thought as the taste of blood flooded his mouth. *Killed by a little girl, down here in the dark.*

The Ravager sighed. "Fine, hard way it is," she said. Sam felt, for the briefest of moments, terrible pain as she cracked a fist against the base of his skull. And then he didn't feel anything at all, for a good long while.

# PART 2

## The Girl

'PLAGUE-HEAD' ORIGINATED as a slang term even before the Infected were recognized as something no longer human. It referred to the fact that those who survived the initial days after exposure to the pathogen began to exhibit the overwhelming compulsion to violate their quarantines and ensure the virus was passed on to new hosts. This desire first expresses itself subtly, but quickly the Infected becomes irrevocably single-minded and violent. Later notes, after the Fall, recorded the curious fact that despite their mindlessness, these 'Plague-Heads' seemed remarkably well-adapted to the post-societal world. This news struck a blow against those hoping for a quick return to pre-Horsemen society.

*The Origins, Structures, and Effects of the Horseman Virus; Official Colonial Records.*

## 9

WHEN SAM AWOKE, he was outside. He was sitting in the dirt with his back to a tree, his legs extended out in front of him. He was cold. His limbs were sore and his mouth was dry, and he'd just had the absolute worst nightmare.

His head pounded. He put a hand to the back of his neck and winced in pain; it felt like he'd been worked over with a potato masher. He closed his eyes, remembering again the terrible darkness of those tunnels. He sighed, holding onto — for just a few seconds longer — the comforting lie that it had indeed been nothing but a bad dream. That Vincente wasn't dead. *That I'm not all alone out here. That I'm not now completely alone in the world.*

Sam exhaled and opened his eyes. He wasn't sure where he was or how he had gotten there, and his thoughts were still fuzzy. Nothing was going to be gained by sitting around feeling sorry for himself, so he blinked away the pain in his head and began to take in his surroundings.

It was night. No, it was late twilight: a thin line of orange cut across the black at the western horizon. Overhead, through the scattered pines, he could see stars. Crickets chirped; cicadas buzzed. In front of him, maybe fifteen feet away, there was a small fire, tended to by a small person.

It was a young woman. She had auburn hair, tied in a thick knot at the base of her skull. Her skin, even in the flickering crimson light of the fire, was a striking, almost painfully bright alabaster white. She wore all black: loose-fitting cargo pants and a light black coat over a black tank top. A long, heavily-notched machete leaned against a tree beside her. The blade seemed to glow blood red in the light of the campfire.

The girl worked at the fire — barely more than a pile of glowing embers — with a thin, sharp stick. The smell of cooked meat reached Sam's nose; he watched as she stabbed at the center of the flames and pulled a charred and ash-caked hunk of animal from the coals. Sam's mouth watered; among the many things he was feeling right now was hunger. *How long have I been out?*

He closed his eyes, and the full weight of what had happened finally fell upon him. The mission. The underground Colony. The Ravagers.

Vincente.

The images flashed through Sam's mind: his friend, hit by multiple bullets, lying on the catwalk ramp. The ramp breaking. Collapsing and falling. Deacon, that horrible monster of a Ravager, laughing at the carnage. The other Ravager, barely more than a girl, kicking at V's limp body.

'*He's dead,*' the Ravager had said.

✝

A wave of nausea washed over Sam. Vincente was really gone. It didn't seem possible. Even after all the deaths he had witnessed or heard about, all the other scouts and the travelers and the refugees... Even the deaths of his own parents, which had happened so long ago. The memories felt like they belonged to someone else. He truly didn't believe Vincente could actually die.

As far back as Sam could remember, Vincente was the one who had all the answers. He was the one that got things done, the one that showed Sam how things *should* be done. He was so capable and so unflappable, it didn't seem possible that he could lose. That he could fail.

That he could die.

But he had died, down there in the underground, at the hands of the Ravager Deacon. Vincente was the closest thing that Sam had to a family, and he had given his life trying to save the rest of their home Colony. *So,* Sam decided, *I may not have anyone left in this world, but I still have a purpose.* He would complete the mission Vincente had been given. He would bring back the cure to this mysterious crop disease, saving the Black Hills Survivors Colony. *And if I have the chance to kill this Deacon in the process? That would be a nice bonus.*

But first, he had to get away from this mystery girl. She may have pulled him out of that dank hole Jackson called a Colony, but in Sam's experience, even back in civilized society, people didn't do things like that for free. *And out here, in the Wilds?* He doubted he would like the price.

Her back was to him. She was hunched over near the fire, sawing at the hunk of meat with a hunting knife. Sam slowly got to his feet, as quietly as he could, bracing himself for a moment against a heavy wave of dizziness and a fresh bout of nausea. Confident she wasn't going to turn, he backed slowly away from the fire and his kidnapper. He took care to watch his step, to avoid dry twigs or anything else that would give away his movement. He stepped back over the edge of the firelight, into the dark of the freshly falling night. Still, she didn't turn, didn't show the slightest sign she even realized he had woken up. Once he was confident he was out of sight, Sam turned to run.

He got two steps before something grabbed his ankle and pulled him from his feet. His chin hit the leaf-covered ground, and he saw stars. His left leg was numb; it felt like it had been ripped from his hip. He rolled onto his back, grunting in pain, looking down to see what had caught him.

It was a tiny rope, tied tight around his ankle. It was thin and nearly invisible, but it held quite firm. Sam bent forward and tugged at the binding; the rope led back toward the fire. He worked at the cord, looking for a knot to untie. There was none. He heard the soft crunch of footsteps approaching. He reached for his knife. It was gone. *I don't know why that surprises me.* His belt and all his pockets were also empty. All his supplies had been taken.

Sam scrambled to his feet as the girl reached him. She stood a few feet away, turned to a silhouette of black by the fire at her back. Her hands were on her hips. She remained silent.

Sam made his hands into fists. *This time, you're not sneaking up on me in the dark*, he thought. He didn't like the idea of hitting a girl, but then, she *had* taken him prisoner. And she had hit him first. *Desperate times, and all that.* He took a step toward her and swung, counting on the element of surprise.

His left foot jerked forward. A moment later, the ground slammed into his back. Sam felt his spine rattle. He gasped as the fall knocked the wind from his lungs. It was that damn rope. She had obviously been holding it, had tugged it the instant he moved to hit her. He cursed his foolishness: with the fire at her back, he must have been lit up as if by a spotlight.

But he had to keep moving. That was the key: never stop moving. He spun around, grabbing the rope with his left hand. He would be ready if she tried that trick again. He located the girl — she didn't appear to have moved — and dove at her knees. She took a single step to the side, faster than Sam would have thought possible, and he was again face down in the dirt. He popped up to his feet and turned to where he expected her to be, but the space was now empty. He whirled around to see her standing a few feet away. One hand was on her hip, the other held—

"Dammit," Sam said, a moment before she pulled the rope and jerked him onto his back for a third time. This time, he stayed down. He was tired, his whole body now hurt, and this clearly wasn't getting him anywhere.

"Are you finished?" the girl asked. She sounded annoyed, and perhaps a bit bored. What she *didn't* sound like, despite so thoroughly wiping the floor with Sam only moments earlier, was even a little bit tired or winded.

Sam caught his breath and eased himself, slowly, to a sitting position, facing this devil of a girl.

He lifted one exhausted arm in conciliation. "I'm done," he said. "No more fighting. You proved your point."

"Good," she said. "Then dinner is ready."

Sam sat in the dirt and leaves, his back now up against a different tree. At least he was warmer than when he woke up, as he was closer to the fire. A hunk of charred meat — pronghorn, the girl had said — lay uneaten on his lap. He smelled the burning pine, he listened to the fire crackle, and he watched the girl who was both his savior and his captor.

Closer to the fire now, he was able to get a better look at her. She looked to be about his age — somewhere between 15 and 20, if he had to guess — and up close, sitting and gnawing at a leg of pronghorn, she looked far less imposing than she had when she had been embarrassing him in the dark. From here, she looked like she could have been one of his classmates from the Colony, rather than someone capable of carrying him through miles of underground tunnel and forest. Or someone capable of so thoroughly and effortlessly kicking his ass, for that matter. His eyes lingered on the small patches of freckles on her cheekbones. Sam didn't know why those stuck out to him, but they did.

She looked up at him from her dinner. "Eat," she said, her mouth full of meat. Her fingers glistened with grease in the low blaze of the fire; the light made her eyes appear black, depthless. "The meat is good. I used salt *and* pepper."

"Why are you keeping me here?" Sam asked. He was trying to make a point by ignoring the food, but it *did* smell good. In fact, the scent was making it harder and harder to remember exactly what point he was even trying to make.

"I'm keeping you alive," she said. "Same reason I brought you out of that hole." She picked a bit of gristle out of her teeth and tossed it into the fire. "I know where you want to go, by the way. It's foolish, and it won't work. I'm doing you a favor."

"You don't know anything about me," Sam said. "You had no right to take me, no right to keep me here. You have no right—"

"Right?" she said, laughing. "No *right*? You're in the Wilds, you spoiled Colony boy. The only rights you have out here are the ones you take and the ones you can defend. And *maybe* the rights someone else is kind enough to grant you. Right now, you have the right to sit there and eat the meal I so kindly provided for you. Tomorrow, you will have the right to wake up still breathing. Those rights you can have for free."

Sam's first instinct was to argue further, but he fought back the urge. He was in a precarious and undoubtedly dangerous situation. He needed to approach it with intelligence; with guile and with care.

The first thing he needed was more information. To get that information, he would need to play nice. He worked at a small piece of his meat. Below the char, it was still hot enough to burn at his fingertips. He wondered how the girl managed to tear into her portion with such gusto.

"My name is Sam," he said. "What's yours?"

"Sam," she repeated, nodding. "I'm surprised you would tell me your real name, Sam. A good rule of thumb is not to give your captor any more information than you absolutely need to. That's a piece of free advice."

"So now you're my captor?" Sam said. "I thought you were trying to help me." He did his best to keep his tone light, to hide his annoyance and his fear. He thought he did a fair job of it. He chewed and swallowed his pronghorn. She wasn't wrong about the meat: it was surprisingly tasty.

Her eyes, seeming both amused and annoyed in equal measure, settled on him briefly before returning to her meal. She shrugged. "It can be two things, can't it?"

Sam looked back across the fire at her, trying to gather any information he could from her facial expressions. Either she was good at hiding what she was thinking, or he was just bad at reading her. *Probably both*, Sam thought. Whatever else she was, she was still a girl.

There was still something that was bothering him, something he couldn't quite put his finger on. Finally, it came to him.

"How did you know my name was Sam?" he asked. "I mean, that Sam was my real name?" There were a number of reasons that came to mind, and none of them were good.

She looked up at him again, and slowly shook her head. "Refer back to free piece of advice number one. If I hadn't known for sure Sam was your real name — if I was *lying*, as people are known to do — well, I certainly know now. I'm starting to wonder how you survived out here this long, Sam."

*Dammit, I should have thought of that,* Sam thought, grimacing. There was something about this girl that infuriated him. *Well, two things, if you include the whole holding-me-captive issue.* "I guess I should thank my lucky stars that I've stumbled across helpful folk like you," he said, with some bitterness.

"Yes, you should," the girl answered sternly. "I suppose the other rider was your boss? Vincente, I believe his name was. He did seem to be the brains of your little operation."

Sam's anger flared, then died. Rather than shooting back with a biting retort, he just stared down at the ground.

Her mention of Vincente should have made him angry, but instead it made him sad. And frightened and frustrated, and a thousand other negative emotions Sam didn't want to think about particularly hard. He couldn't stop wondering how things had gone off the rails so quickly. He wanted to shout at her, to insult her, to say something that might make her feel bad, though that seemed impossible. But none of this made any sense to him; he had no idea what he was supposed to do. So he said nothing.

This silence seemed to have an effect on the girl that his anger and his words had not, because for the briefest of moments she stopped looking so infuriatingly self-satisfied.

"I'm sorry," she said. "I know he was probably your friend. Sometimes I talk before I think." She lowered her food and stared into the dying fire. "I don't do a lot of talking, as a normal matter of course."

"It's fine," Sam said. For a moment, he actually felt bad for this strange, arrogant young woman. He didn't mind the feeling: it pushed his own worries a little bit away from the center of his attention. "So, how did you know our names?"

"I followed you, of course," she said. She seemed to remember again about the meat in her hands, and took a large bite out of it. "If you're curious, I picked up your trail just before that disguised Ravager outpost, the one you so smartly avoided. I've learned a great deal about the both of you since then. You know, for scouts, you talk surprisingly loud."

"Why?" Sam asked.

"I don't know. Poor hearing, maybe?"

Sam sighed, shaking his head. "No, why were you following us?"

"For the same reason I saved you from certain death, Sam," she said. "I need something from you."

Sam rolled his eyes. "Of course you do," he said. "You need something from me. That's why you sneaked after me; why you knocked me out — my head is still throbbing, by the way. It's why you dragged me up to this god-forsaken heap of rocks, and why you tied me to a tree with some sort of -" he lifted and dropped the cord tied to his foot, "- some sort of magic rope."

He stopped and stared at her till she looked up from her meat and met his eyes with that inscrutable, angry look that seemed to be her default expression. "You know," he continued, "some people just ask for what they want. That is some free advice for you. Might save you some trouble in the future." He shook his head. "You can't even be bothered to tell me your name, and you want my help?"

The girl tossed the remains of her meal to the side and stood, any semblance of good nature now drained from her expression. She stared at Sam like she was trying to bore holes through him with her gaze. "We have an early morning tomorrow," she said. "Don't try and run again — I'll know." She turned and began to walk away from the fire, grabbing her machete as she went. She walked toward the pile of supplies, her own and the ones she had taken off Sam. She stopped after a few steps and turned back toward him.

"My name is Abigail," she said. "Get some sleep, Sam."

# 10

"GET UP."

Abigail kicked him in the leg, and Sam opened one eye. He had slept as poorly as he had expected to on the damp, leaf-strewn ground, and judging by the deep indigo of the sky, it was barely dawn yet.

"Screw off," he grunted, turning away from her. As little desire as he had to continue lying here with nothing but a flat stone for his pillow, he had even less for jumping up eagerly every time Abigail barked a command.

A heavy pack hit his side, surprising the last bits of sleep out of him. He sat up with a start and noticed it was the supplies that she had taken off him yesterday. *Or most of them, at least.* He was acutely aware that Abigail had kept his rifle, as well as his pistol. The former was slung over her shoulder, the latter strapped to her waist. Sam felt naked without them. Judging by the self-satisfied smirk she shot him, that might have been the idea.

Now that he was awake and sitting up, she tossed him his knife, still secure in its black leather sheath. He immediately moved to cut the rope from his ankle, and found it had already been removed.

Sam got to his feet. He now had a good idea of Abigail's level of trust in him: she might still consider him a threat if he had a gun, but not a knife. He considered proving her wrong, but dismissed the idea almost immediately. Whatever else she had done, Abigail hadn't harmed him, and Sam wasn't so hardened that he would knife her in the back. If he even could — after yesterday's encounter, Sam doubted that attacking his tiny jailor would go very well for him, element of surprise or no.

*Still, she trusts me enough to give me the knife,* Sam thought. *That's a start.*

"What's the plan for today, boss?" he asked, flashing what he hoped was a thoroughly trustworthy smile.

Abigail turned toward him and looked him over, her lips pursed, her expression a mix of disturbed confusion and narrow-eyed suspicion.

"East," she said. She pulled a black cotton hat over her ears and wrapped her mouth and nose with even blacker cloth. She looked ridiculous; like nothing so much as a ninja from one of the old movies he'd watched back at the Colony.

"I don't know what is going on behind that look of yours, Sam," Abigail said, the dark cloth muffling her voice but not her uneasy contempt, "but I don't like it. Don't make me regret removing your rope."

"I wouldn't think of it."

"Good. Don't think of anything else, either. Just follow."

She turned away from him and began walking without another word.

Despite himself, Sam laughed. And then he followed.

☨

"Well, it's getting harder and harder to pretend this isn't a pattern," Abigail said. Sam was glad she was finally talking sense.

He and Abigail had spent the entire morning walking due east, mile after mile toward the steadily rising sun and whatever unknown destination Abigail had in mind. In that time, they had been forced to change their route twice to avoid Ravager patrols. The one ahead of them now was the third.

"For what it's worth," Sam said, "I didn't see a single Ravager the last time I came through here. Something is definitely going on."

"I know something is going on," Abigail hissed. "That's what I just said. Now shut up and let me think."

They lay side by side in a copse of trees at the top of a gently sloping hill. Ahead of them was a stretch of Old World road, cracked and broken; at the end of that road loomed the dilapidated remains of a small Old World town. Within the town was, to the best of their knowledge, a war-party of six Ravagers. Four of them patrolled along the town's narrow borders, while two more sat up in the water tower at the town's center. One of these tower-occupying Ravagers was scanning the horizon with an Old World astronomy telescope, and the other with a high-powered, thoroughly modern sniper rifle. Endless, flat plains surrounded the long-dead town in every direction; there was no easy way for Abigail and Sam to pass undetected.

"I have an idea," Sam said.

Abigail's sigh was muffled by her ninja-wrap. "If you're going to suggest, yet again, that we turn around and head back west, you can keep it to yourself," she said.

"I figured you would say that. But if we can't go forward,

and you won't let us go back, then we've only got one option left."

"And what option is that, genius?" Abigail asked.

"Isn't it obvious?" Sam said. "We're going to have to kill every single Ravager down there."

✝

Sam hadn't meant for her to take his plan seriously. He was trying to get the stupid, stubborn girl leading him to finally see reason. To see that they couldn't just keep trudging forward; to see that they had to go back. He was trying to get her to understand that he was right.

Unfortunately for him, Abigail took his plan quite seriously indeed. Which was why Sam found himself back with his rifle, and about to take the most difficult shot he had ever attempted.

"I want to go on record saying this is a bad idea," he said. He concentrated on staying relaxed. On keeping his breathing steady, and his heart rate low. He stared through his scope, watching the Ravager in the tower and trying to keep himself from imagining the Ravager staring back at him through the scope of his own rifle. He tried to keep his crosshairs from jumping around.

"This was your idea," Abigail said. She lay beside him, watching the target through her binoculars. Sam tried not to notice her shoulder brushing against his. "Wind is coming in from the north, northwest, about five miles per hour," she said. "And there is no record. For the record."

"You do know that the second I pull this trigger, the rest of them will know we're out here."

"I'm counting on it," Abigail said. "Put him down."

Sam raised the crosshairs a bit to account for bullet drop,

then moved them to the left to compensate for the wind. He took a deep breath, and then he let it out. *Here we go,* he thought.

He pulled the trigger.

The rifle fired. The shot rang out as Sam worked the lever, kicking out the spent round and loading in the next. The bullet was on its way, moving faster than the sound of the shot; the Ravager hadn't yet reacted. Sam waited with his breath held, counting his heartbeats. One, Two, Three.

A splash of red appeared on the white of the water tank as the Ravager flew backward. It all happened silently from Sam's point of view.

"Target down," Abigail said. She laughed. "That got them moving."

Sam ignored her and located the water tower's second Ravager. He found him trying to rip the sniper rifle from the body of his dead compatriot. Sam aimed for center mass, and fired again. Three heartbeats later, the shot reached the tower.

It missed.

The round bounced harmlessly off the water tower just above the Ravager's head. The Ravager looked up at the strike, and then directly at Sam.

"Shit," Abigail said. "We're made. Damned Ravager is smarter than he looks. You need to put him down."

Sam had already loaded a third bullet. He watched as the Ravager's rifle swung in his direction. Its muzzle flashed. Sam gritted his teeth and fired. He knew as soon as the round was gone that he had missed. He reloaded, trying not to think about the bullet coming his way.

"Put him down, Sam."

"That's the plan," he replied through clenched teeth. "Please be quiet."

The Ravager's shot hit just in front of them, skipping over their heads. It probably hadn't been as close as it seemed, but it was still pretty damned close. Sam focused on remaining calm and making his next shot count. Abigail remained silent, and for that Sam was grateful. He needed all the concentration he could muster.

Unlike Sam's weapon, the Ravager's rifle was semi-automatic. That meant there was a large number of bullets heading Sam's way, very rapidly. He couldn't get up — the cover of the trees and bushes was his only advantage. His only chance was to put a bullet through the Ravager as quickly as he could.

Another couple rounds landed around them. Sam ignored them as best he could. He aimed, he fired, and he reloaded. Another bullet hit just to Sam's right; sand rained down on him. He missed again. He fired again.

This bullet hit. The Ravager spun and toppled over the water tower's railing, plummeting to the ground. Sam sighed in relief. His heart was beating so hard he was afraid it was going to crack his ribs. He rested his forehead on the ground.

Abigail patted him on the back. "Good job, Sam," she said. "I mostly never doubted you for a second. Now, give me back that rifle. We've still got four more of them to deal with."

✝

Ravagers did not give much thought to tactics. Even when under attack from an unknown assailant, they didn't coordinate with one another, didn't think to work together. Their overwatch had just been taken out, yet they didn't even bother figuring out from which direction the shots had come.

The closest one took cover behind a half-collapsed house, looking in the wrong direction. Abigail and Sam had crossed most of the open ground between their cover and the town before the Ravager finally looked in their direction. The Infected popped his head out from cover and took aim at Sam.

Abigail shot him in the head with Sam's pistol, making a clean kill from fifty yards out.

The second Ravager ran in a straight line toward the sound of the shot. Abigail took position behind the corner of a derelict pizza parlor and waited, with Sam right behind her. When the Ravager passed, she stepped forward and neatly buried her bowie knife between its shoulder blades.

"Two apiece," Abigail said, laughing. Ravager blood covered the exposed skin around her eyes. Sam didn't know what to say to that. He wasn't sure which bothered/fascinated him more: her complete lack of fear of the Ravagers, or the apparent glee she took in killing them.

Abigail tilted her head, listening for the approach of the remaining two Ravagers. Satisfied she had located them, she grabbed Sam's shirt and pulled him across the street. They came to a stop against the corner of another crumbling building. Sam heard the Ravagers approaching, and this time, he followed Abigail as she dashed into their path. He raised his knife, ready to finish off the Infected if Abigail had trouble with them.

Except this time, it wasn't Ravagers. It was a group of three snarling Plague-Heads: their grasping hands clenched into claws, their chins dripping with infectious vomit. Sam yelled out a warning, and Abigail pushed him back — a moment before the lead Plague-Head puked a spray of viscous black-red liquid. Sam watched as Abigail turned her head, trying to get out of the way of the spew; Sam's heel caught in a crack in the pavement, and he fell backward.

The back of Sam's head bounced off the sidewalk. Explosions of light bloomed in his vision. For a moment, it felt like he was asleep — everything went silent. The darkness lasted only a moment before he was back awake and moving. He stumbled to his feet, the world spinning around him, and located Abigail. By the time he made it to her side she was putting a bullet into the last standing Plague-Head.

He could smell the infectious vomit on her, but couldn't tell where it had hit. The black fabric hid the poison's exact location. *If any had gotten in her eyes or her mouth,* Sam thought, *or an open wound…* If it had, then she was already infected. Which meant she was as good as dead.

He took an uncertain step back from her. Infection moved fast; everyone knew that. The transformation, if it was going to happen, would begin at any moment.

One minute passed, and then another. Abigail scanned the alleys and street for any more Infected, seemingly oblivious to the danger she was currently in. *Had been in,* Sam thought. Enough time had passed. She was not infected.

Abigail peeled off her face wrap and pulled off her hat. Her auburn hair had come free from its tie, and it fell down to her shoulders. Still, Sam didn't see any vomit on her face. He breathed a sigh of relief. And then he wondered *why he was so concerned. Why should I care what happens to her?* Sam wondered. *Why do I care about her at all?*

"There's still two more Ravagers out there," Abigail said, her voice utterly free of both concern and fear. If she had at any point worried about infection, Sam hadn't seen it.

It didn't matter. *We still have a job to do.*

"Which way?" Sam asked her.

Instead of answering, her eyes went wide. *Finally, some semblance of emotion,* Sam thought. But he didn't understand.

An explosion sounded, just behind him, and something kicked him in the right shoulder, hard. Sam took an unsteady step forward. His arm was suddenly numb. He watched as Abigail raised her pistol toward him and fired a single shot. He raised his remaining good arm to try and stop her, but it was too late. *At least she missed,* he thought. Still, why did he feel so funny?

His legs gave out, and he fell to his knees. Abigail rushed forward and caught him just as the street tried to jump up and smack him in the face. He looked up at her, and was surprised to see actual worry in her eyes. It made him smile. He didn't know why. He did know he wanted to lie down, and she was kind enough to lower him to the pavement. He lay on his belly, wincing as she lifted his shirt. Vaguely, he realized for the first time that the right side of his back hurt. It hurt a lot.

*Shit,* he thought. *I've just been shot, haven't I?*

Abigail lifted his head and turned it back toward her. She rolled her eyes at him, and he knew he was going to be okay.

"It's just birdshot, you big baby," she said. "You'll be fine." She was smiling. She didn't look bad when she smiled, Sam thought. But as nice as that was, it didn't change the fact that he had been *shot in the back.* Birdshot or otherwise.

"You wait here, Sam," Abigail said, testing the edge of her knife with a thumb. "I'll be right back. I've got a Ravager to interrogate."

About ten minutes later, a vehicle rumbled to a stop beside him. It was an old extended cab pickup; it had lost both of its doors, and gained about eleven distinct layers of crudely drawn graffiti. Abigail was behind the wheel.

She got out of the idling truck and helped Sam into its passenger seat, careful not to touch his wounded back.

"Our last Ravager friend was kind enough to lend us his truck," Abigail said. She reached across Sam and buckled his seatbelt. "We had a little chat, before he died. It looks like our Deacon problem is worse than I had feared."

She jogged back around the front of the truck and hopped into the driver's seat. She turned to Sam and smiled. "The good news for you, Sammy, is that you get your wish. We're heading back west. It's the only chance we still have of staying alive."

## II

THE RAVAGER WHO CALLED HERSELF ROACH took in the sights, and laughed. She sat on the sheep-men's tractor and chewed on the leg of one of their goats. She watched as the sheep-men they had left alive — the 'Uninfected' as they called themselves, like they were somehow better than her — were herded into one of their own plastic-glass cages. Cages just like the ones in which the sheep-men had been holding the Spewers.

Roach had been trying to figure out what the sheep-men were doing with the Spewers, those dumb, stumbling dead things. The only use she knew of for a Spewer was to scare the sheep-men. She doubted these 'Uninfected' wanted them for that purpose, but then, she didn't much understand anything they did. They weren't like her, like a Ravager. She tried to ask one of the sheep-men why they kept the Spewers, but he had just cried and screamed. Maybe she should ask the Spewers, ha. She took another bite of her goat and smiled at the thought.

All around her, the sheep-men's Colony burned. Roach laughed. Fire always made her laugh.

Music blasted from DeeJ's speakers. Next to them, his generator belched thick puffs of black smoke. Drunken laughter and the sounds of smashing and breaking and cracking bounced off the sheep-men's pretty, white walls. *Not so pretty now,* she thought.

Her people had climbed the walls late last night, and the place was theirs by morning. Roach had smashed in two sheep-men's heads herself, and blasted a third with her scattergun.

It had been a good night.

Her sack of loot sat beside her, underneath her scattergun and her head-cracker. Some of it was new — stuff she had taken last night — and some of it, not much, was old. Her special things, things she kept. Things that were hers alone. She had long ago learned to keep her stuff close, and her special things closest of all. Not because the others would laugh at her — they might, until she cracked their heads — but because…well, she didn't really know why. Because she liked them. Almost as much as she liked smashing.

Still, some of the others thought that, just because she wasn't the biggest, she'd back down if they stepped on her. She loved that they were that dumb: it led to all sorts of violent fun.

Just today Broke-Jaw and Bowser had tried to take her winnings, and she'd gotten to teach them both a lesson in respect. She looked down at the bloody and torn ridges of her hands, and she laughed.

Deacon hadn't punished her for breaking Bowser's leg, but then he also hadn't punished the two idiots for trying to take her loot. That was fine by Roach. Hands off: that was Deacon. That was why he was Chief. That was why Roach and the rest of their band loved him.

That and his smarts. Deacon was the smartest person Roach had ever known.

In the past months, Deacon had led them in taking three

of the sheep-men's Colonies. Colonies others of the People said couldn't be taken. The sheep-men were too smart, they said. They were too well-armed, and they were too careful. Even the King, with all his numbers and his vehicles down south, didn't attack Colonies, Deacon said. According to Deacon, that was what was holding the People back. If Deacon were King, things would be different; Roach just knew it. And she couldn't wait.

Still, Roach wondered about Chief Deacon's obsession with the Reapers. Roach had never seen one — she didn't know anyone who had — but she had seen what they left behind. If anything in this world scared her, it was the Reapers. Though she would never admit that, of course.

She turned away from the cages and looked over to where Deacon was meeting with the sheep-men bounty hunters. Roach's lip curled at the sight of them; she cleared her throat and spat. Bounty Hunters. They may be wild sheep, but they were still sheep. She didn't know why Deacon kept contact with these parasites. Lately, he had taken to having some travel with the army. Even welcomed them into their base. No one else could have gotten away with a decision like that but Deacon. The chief was different — he was free from the normal rules, and they all knew it.

Allowing was one thing, but actually stomaching the sheep-men? Roach couldn't do it, herself. She didn't know why Deacon bothered dealing with these weak and worthless things. She only knew Deacon had his reasons, and she didn't question Deacon.

"The way I see it," Deacon began, strutting one way and then slowly back the other in front of the wild sheep. He held his fire ax casually draped across his shoulders, one hand on the head, the other braced on the handle. "The way I see it, you four are the best bounty hunters in these high plains. You're assuredly the bravest of your kind, coming here to meet with me." He walked over to the plastic-glass cage holding the surviving Colonists. "Or maybe just the stupidest," he said.

He flipped the ax off his shoulders and swung at the cage. It hit with a thump, and the Colonists jumped back; a few screamed. Deacon roared with laughter, slapping his knee and shaking his head back and forth while lolling his tongue at them. Roach kept her eyes on the bounty hunters: the short one on the left narrowed his eyes in contempt and leaned away from the chief almost imperceptibly. Like he was somehow above this whole affair. *I don't like the look of that one*, Roach thought. He stood there smug, rolling a little cigarillo in one hand, his pale skin almost pink in the low sun. The other three stood there like statues, thinking whatever thoughts sheep thought.

"The work I've got to offer you won't be easy," Deacon said, "but it just might be fun." He turned and stalked back toward the bounty hunters, dragging the head of the fire ax on the pavement behind him. It trailed a tiny stream of yellow sparks. "The truth is, I'd do the job myself, but my calendar is all filled up." He shrugged and tilted his head to the side. "We've all got a boss, after all."

"What is the job?" one of the bounty hunters asked. This one wore high leather boots and a cowboy hat. Roach didn't like his eyes: they were beady and too close together. She wanted to smash him. Deacon turned to look at him, smiling and wide-eyed, tilting his head the opposite direction. The chief swayed slightly like he always did when he looked someone over, moving back and forth like a snake.

"Eager, are we?" he said. He leaned to his left, then swung himself around on one heel to look at Roach. "Are you hearing all this, Roach?" he called out to her.

"Yeah chief," she said, staring at the bounty hunter and smiling.

Deacon spun back around, hefting the ax head. "An eager beaver," he said. In one smooth, quick motion he swung the ax and brought the bladed edge to rest a millimeter from the eager bounty hunter's throat. "Well, I guess I'll just have to tell you then. Hmmm?"

They stared at each other in silence for a few tense moments. Then Deacon pulled back the ax and spat to the side. "One of you four is going to bring me back a Reaper."

Deacon let that hang there between them for a minute. While she waited, Roach tried to guess which of the four had the best chance of actually living through this job. For sure not the impatient cowboy. Maybe the one next to him: the one with the shiny metal goggles that reflected everything, the left side of his stupid sheep face entirely covered by gruesome-looking burn scars. This one was her personal favorite.

Or maybe the old guy, the one with the snowy beard and the bow and arrow. He had survived to be an old sheep-man, which meant he was either good or lucky.

Or would it be the short haughty one, all in black? The one who had flinched away from Deacon when he'd scared the sheep-men in their cage. For sure not him. No, Roach reckoned that none of these bounty hunters would live through an encounter with a Reaper.

But Deacon said they could do it, so Roach believed it. She just didn't see how. At the end of the day, they were still just sheep-men. And the only things sheep-men were good at were hiding and dying.

"The Reaper is a female," Deacon said. "Dark reddish hair. That's all the description I got for you. But you know how Reapers are. She's traveling with a boy, a teenager. The boy is dressed like..." He turned his head towards Roach. "How would you say the boy is dressed, Roach?" he called out.

"Like the guy that won't wake up," she said. The Colony scout they had caught earlier beneath the mountain still hadn't revived, though he clung to life with an impressive tenacity. Deacon had insisted on bringing him with them, for reasons Roach still didn't understand. Probably something to do with the shiny white drive they had taken off of him. The same drive Deacon now kept in his pocket.

"Well, they can't see that guy, now can they?" Deacon called back.

Roach shrugged and continued to gnaw on her goat leg.

"It's so hard to find good help," Deacon told the bounty hunters flippantly. "Well, I guess he dressed like a fancy Colony scout. I hope that helps."

"Pay?" the one with the bandana asked.

Deacon smiled. "That's what I like to hear. Right to business. Double standard rates: gold or grain, you take your pick. But I want that Reaper alive. We have...a history. I intend on making it suffer, personally."

"And the boy?" the same bounty hunter asked.

"Oh, him I most certainly need alive. Me and him are going to have a little talk, since his friend insists on not waking up. So I guess I'm going to make both of them suffer."

Deacon laughed, and the bounty hunters continued to look uncomfortable. Finally, one of them spoke.

"Can I borrow some of your Plague-Heads?" the one in the goggles asked, his voice a wet rasp. "It's for the job."

"That's a strange request, and I don't understand it," Deacon said, "but I like it, and I'm dying to see what you've got in mind. How about three?" Deacon walked up to the bounty hunter and poked him in the chest. "You get infected, though, well…if you still have a working brain in that head, I'm going to say I told you so."

The bounty hunter nodded silently.

"Bringing a Reaper in alive is a tall order," the old one said. "What if it dies in the process? Is there a partial payment?"

"The partial payment," Deacon answered immediately, "is that I put you on a spit, cook you, and then I eat you. How is that for partial payment? Anyone dies on this job, gentlemen, it had better be you."

The cowboy, the one that had asked about the job, shook his head. "Killing a Reaper is hard enough. Bringing one in alive is insane. Keep your gold and your grain, Ravager. I'm out."

Deacon opened his hands and shrugged. "Fair enough," he said. "You can't blame a guy for asking, can you?"

The bounty hunter turned to walk away, and Deacon swung the ax. Roach was always amazed at how fast Deacon could move; one moment the ax-head was resting on the ground, the next it was buried in the top of the bounty hunter's skull, pinning his cowboy hat down into his brains. The sheep-man fell to his knees, and then down to the ground.

Roach whooped and tossed the remains of her goat leg away as she hopped off the tractor. She stared daggers at the rest of the bounty hunters, silently daring them to try and make a move against her chief. Sadly, none of the surviving three were that stupid.

Deacon put his foot on the dead sheep-man's back and wrenched free his ax. "Any more questions, boys?" he asked the remaining bounty hunters. There were none.

"Well then," he said. "Get hunting."

# 12

ABIGAIL WORKED AT THE BACK of his shoulder with a pair of needle-nose pliers, and Sam tried not to scream. The bottle of vodka they had found in the store below helped with both of their tasks.

They sat on the roof of an Old World Wal-Mart. Climbing a service ladder hadn't exactly been easy for Sam, but they needed somewhere with a good vantage point, and this was the tallest building they could find.

"You know, this would have been a lot worse if you had been shot with a real bullet," Abigail said. Sam winced as her heated metal pliers again stuck into his back. A moment later, Abigail pulled free yet another shotgun pellet and dropped it, clinking, into a ceramic 'Free Hugs' mug. "If this had been buckshot, the whole side of your body would be ribbons. You should consider yourself lucky."

"I'll be sure to count my many blessings, just as soon as all the metal is out of me," Sam grumbled. "You tell me how lucky you feel, the next time you get shot."

"The trick," Abigail said, again sticking Sam with the pliers, "is not to get shot. You should try it next time."

"You are just full of advice, aren't you?" Sam said. He took another small slug of Vodka. This time, he didn't choke when the fiery liquid hit his tongue. "You know, I'm not the only one that got lucky today. I watched that Plague-Head puke all over you."

"You and me must have different definitions of luck. That Plaguie ruined my favorite shirt."

Abigail was currently wearing a pink and white t-shirt featuring Minnie Mouse and the words 'Happy Birthday Jenny!' on its front, scavenged from the store below. It was about five sizes too large.

"If you had turned your head, even a half second later..." Sam began, imagining himself in that situation. "Do you ever worry about getting infected? Ever wonder which one you'll turn into? You know, God forbid it ever happens."

Abigail thought about his questions while she took a break from torturing him, reheating the pliers with her lighter. "There's nothing you can do except just try and be careful, right?" she said at last. "So it's useless to sit around and worry about it. That's my view."

"So you never think about it? Like, at all?" Sam asked. "Not even living like you do, out here in the Wilds?" He stared off into the distance, where the setting sun had turned the mountains into a jagged line of black. It looked like the horizon of another, much older, world. "I think if I had been that close to a puking Plague-Head, and with no shield and no mask, I would...I don't know what I would do. But you? You didn't even let it slow you down. You took down the Plaguies, and the Ravagers, not even caring if the Horsemen Virus was already running through your veins."

"Like I said, there's no point wasting time with worrying," Abigail said.

Sam took another sip from of vodka. "I think if I had to pick, I'd go with Howler." The pliers seemed to be hurting less, and he found himself wanting to talk. *God, I'm get-*

*ting drunk, aren't I?* He needed to keep it together. Abigail already thought of him as some innocent, sheltered Colony kid; she didn't need to know he had never tasted a drop of alcohol till tonight. "Howlers aren't pretty, sure, but they seem like they have a little more mind left than the Plague-Heads, and they're not as destructive and...I don't know, not as evil as the Ravagers. They aren't as violent."

"Oh, they're plenty violent," Abigail said. "But I see what you mean. They only kill what they need to eat. The Ravagers kill everything, just for the sheer fun of it." She paused, working at a particularly stubborn pellet. "You wouldn't want to be a Reaper?"

"A Reaper?" Sam said with a laugh. "Are you kidding me? No. Reapers are supposed to be just like Ravagers, but worse. A Ravager smashes and pillages and kills, but a Reaper is death itself. I mean, it might be cool to have their...whatever, their super-powers — though even those are probably a myth — but just...no. They're the worst of all of them. They're more slaves to their desire to kill than Plague-Heads are to spreading the virus, and more violent than Ravagers, and they have a hunger more insatiable than a Howler's. Have you ever seen a picture of one? They're supposed to have scaly wings under their arms and fangs that hang down below their chin; pointy ears and gray skin."

Abigail scoffed. "Did you see that in one of your Colony movies?" she asked.

"Well, those might be a little exaggerated, but I bet there is some truth to them. The other Infected don't exactly look like you and I, do they?" Sam said. He shook his head, the motion stinging his back, though not as much as it would have without the liquor. "Reapers drink blood, for God's sake. No, screw being a Reaper."

Abigail was silent for a few seconds, and Sam could practically hear her rolling her eyes behind his back. "Have you ever even met anyone who's seen a Reaper? Like, in the flesh? A lot of people say they might not even be real," she said.

"That Ravager, Deacon, sure seems to think they are," Sam said. "It sounded like he wanted to catch one almost as much as he wanted to catch me." His chest felt tight for a moment, and then he hiccupped, shaking his whole body and sending a fresh wave of pain coursing through his shoulder. "Why does he want to catch me so badly, anyways?"

After Sam had been shot, Abigail had tracked down and incapacitated the last of the Ravager patrol. She had learned from him — how, Sam wasn't going to ask — that Deacon had issued standing orders to his Ravagers for Sam to be captured and brought back to him. Sam was sure his interest had to do with the drive Vincente had recovered: *What else could it possibly be?*

"The Ravager didn't know," Abigail said. "It probably took all his brainpower to remember to keep his little band where Deacon told him."

"Then how come Deacon is smart enough to set patrols at all? I thought Ravagers were all big dumb idiots."

"I've…dealt with this Deacon before; he's different. He's smarter than he should be. Smarter than any Ravager I have ever seen. I can't help but thinking there might be some connection between Deacon's intelligence and whatever it was you were looking for underneath that mountain. Why else would he have been there, after all? The whole thing is… troubling."

She had finished removing the birdshot, and had moved on to stitching the wounds closed. "You're not wrong about that," Sam said. He took another sip of vodka. His back barely hurt at all now, and his thoughts were beginning to become a bit slippery. His concerns about Deacon and the drive suddenly felt very far away. "How long have you been out here?" he asked.

"Out where?"

"You know, out here." Sam waved his good arm, gesturing toward the black mountains and the purple-blue skies. "Outside a Colony. Out in the Wilds."

"I've been 'out here' my whole life," Abigail said. "Most people don't live in Colonies, you know."

"You mean they just wander around the woods, waiting for Colony scouts to follow and kidnap?" Sam said, laughing. He was starting to feel a little nauseous, but he didn't care. "That must be a strange life. I mean, how? And why?"

"All lives are strange, when you think about it," Abigail said, tugging hard at the stitching, causing Sam to wince. "You don't think that hiding yourselves away behind your high walls and hoarding all the Old World tech, and all the wealth, is strange?"

"What are you talking about?" Sam asked. Though he had already begun to wonder; had been, in fact, contemplating what Vincente had told him about the outlanders staying far away from the Colonies. What was the relationship between the Colonies and the rest of the world? Or even between one Colony and another? Sam knew they talked to one another — how else could they have known the Jackson Colony had gone dark? But those messages only went through the Elders. A troubling thought popped into his mind. "You think I'm some sort of bad guy, don't you?" he said.

"What?" Abigail said with a scoff. "No. You would have to be a threat to be a bad guy, first of all."

Sam barked out a laugh. "I am threatening," he slurred.

"Sure you are," Abigail said. She tugged on the stitching, harder than Sam thought was strictly necessary. "What I think you are, Sam, is naïve. You don't question the nature of your Colonies because you've had no reason to. You haven't known anything else."

"And you have?" Even as he said it, Sam knew she was right, and he was wrong. There was a whole world out here, one in which Abigail lived every day of her life, and he knew nothing about it. Did his Colony really hoard tech? He found it hard to argue the point, even knowing as little as he did. The Wilds looked like a combination of a prehistoric Arcadia and a post-apocalyptic hellscape. Compared to the world out here, his Colony was an island of humanity and civilization. *Were they really living inside at the expense of the people — the Uninfected — on the outside?* He didn't want to believe it. It had to be more complicated than that.

"I only know what I've seen, and what I've heard," Abigail said. "People out here don't trust the Colonies, and they don't like Colonists. You need to remember that, by the way, when you get to our new destination." She pulled the stitching tight and snipped off the excess with her knife. "All done," she said. "See, not so bad. And you will even have some manly new scars to show off to your little Colony girls."

"Great," Sam said. He put his hands on the roof below him and spun to face Abigail. It took him a second to stop the suddenly spinning world, and another to fight down a fresh wave of nausea. *The shotgun scar* would *make a good story,* he thought. *If I ever get back home.* "What do you mean our *new* destination?" he asked. "Where are we going?"

Abigail's face, in the faint light of the glow sticks mounded between them, was a dull chemical green striped with long black shadows. She looked dangerous, yet difficult to take his eyes off of, like a picture of a tiger from one of the Colony archive files.

"Deacon and his Ravagers have blocked our path back to your Colony," she said. "The way I see it, we only have two choices. We can run north, toward nothing but cold, empty wilderness and more damned Infected. All the while we'll be watching our backs for the hunters and war parties that Deacon will never stop sending."

"And the second option?"

"We stop the Ravagers from looking for us," she said. "There is only one good way of doing that. We kill Deacon."

*Now we're talking.* Sam clapped his hands. "You're finally seeing things my way," he said. Since Vincente had fallen to his death, Sam had wanted nothing more than to strike back at the Ravagers responsible for killing his friend. His original plan had been to get away from this strange girl holding him hostage, and after that, to kill Deacon himself. After seeing Abigail in action, however, he wasn't ashamed to admit that he stood a far better chance of getting his revenge with her on his side. Plus, he was growing increasingly used to her company.

"What do we need to do?" Sam asked. Despite his excitement at the news, he was suddenly very tired. He lay down next to the glowing lights and stared up at the slowly churning black clouds above.

Abigail reached over and took the half-empty vodka bottle from him. "The first thing you need to do is get some rest," she said. "In the morning, we'll work on getting outfitted for a real fight."

"What does that mean?" Sam asked, his voice slow, his eyes fluttering open and shut.

"We need to make some trades. For that, we need to head for a settlement. Tomorrow, Sam, you get to see how the other half lives."

"Goody," Sam mumbled as he began to doze off.

"I thought about it more, Sam. What you asked," Abigail said, after a few minutes of silence. Sam had mostly gone to sleep, but her voice roused him slightly.

"What's that?" he whispered, unable to find the strength to open his eyes.

"I don't think being a Reaper would be the end of the world. I guess that's what I would choose, if I was to be infected. A Reaper, I mean. I think I could live with that."

"I wouldn't want you to be a Reaper," Sam whispered, fluttering now in and out of sleep. "A Reaper killed my parents. I wouldn't want you to be a Reaper, Abby, because I like you. Because I wouldn't want to have to kill you."

After that, Abigail let him sleep.

# 13

SAM WOKE UP THE NEXT MORNING with a splitting headache and a shoulder that felt like it had been through a wood-chipper. Abigail already had their supplies packed up and had found new clothes, and though Sam would have liked nothing more than to continue to lie there for the rest of the day, he gathered himself up and followed her down off the store roof, back out into the Wilds.

The truck they had stolen from the Ravagers was out of gas, so they traveled on foot. All day. Sam threw up twice during the first hour of travel, and then two more times before they stopped for lunch. He told himself, more than once, that he was never drinking again.

After a lunch break that was over far too quickly, they resumed their travels. They walked mostly in silence. Abigail knew where they were going, and Sam was too queasy to ask questions. They continued west, through rocky plains, steep hills, and eventually thick forests. Abigail struck a fast pace early, and kept it up all day. Sam had no choice but to try and keep up, despite protest from pretty much his entire body. By the time they stopped at sundown, Sam was convinced he was actually going to die. He had never walked so far in his entire life. Irrationally, he was sure he had taken more steps in that day than he had in the sum total of days since he'd been born.

He was starting to think he liked Abigail more when she was keeping him prisoner.

The next morning she woke him even earlier, this time before the sun had even finished rising. Once again, she had repacked their bags and broke their camp, her face already re-wrapped in her ninja-cloth. She handed him his breakfast — a roasted squirrel on a stick — and told him he could eat it on the road.

They stopped earlier this time, though what Sam thought was a lunch break turned out to be something else entirely. Abigail said she was looking for a tree. Sam didn't have the heart — or the energy — to tell her that they were in the middle of the forest, and she could take her pick. But apparently it was a very specific and (from how long it took her to find it) well-hidden tree.

Abigail led them in what seemed like a circle for a good hour before finally stopping at the far edge of a steeply-sloping mountainside. When they reached their elusive destination tree, she handed Sam her bag, got down on her hands and knees, and began to dig.

"Should I even ask what you are doing?" Sam said, trying to conceal just how out of breath he was. Truth was, he didn't much care what she was digging for; he was just happy to have a small respite from her seemingly endless march.

"Look at the tree," she said, pointing up with a single, dirt-crusted finger. She continued to dig with the Bowie knife in her other hand. The ground here was apparently softer than it looked; she had already dug over a foot into the earth.

"What am I looking for?"

"Two sets of branches up, there are three small horizontal lines."

Sam craned his head upward and squinted his eyes. "Okay, sure. So what?" he said. He didn't see anything.

"That is the marker, obviously." When he didn't respond, Abigail stopped digging and looked up at him. "We are going to get supplies," she said. "What do you think we're going to pay for them with? Our winning personalities?"

Sam had been wondering about that, but since about an hour into their two-day death march, he had been too exhausted to think about it, or anything else, with much depth. It took most of his effort, even now, just to keep himself from keeling over.

In truth, he just kind of assumed Abigail knew what she was doing. *Anyone who walks with as much purpose as she does must know what they are doing,* he thought, *right?* He certainly hoped she did.

"I hope you have a better idea than piles of dirt," Sam said.

Abigail rolled her eyes at him and resumed her dig.

"So you…buried something here," Sam said. "And what would that—"

Abigail pulled a shiny rectangular object out of the ground and handed it to Sam. He took it, not quite believing what he was seeing.

She had dug up a bar of solid gold. And she was still digging.

✝

Franklin had been bounty hunting the Wilds of the former U.S. of A. for nearly the entire twenty years it had carried the name. Before that, he had worked as a conservation officer in woods not far from where he now stood, chasing down poachers and cartel drug farmers and quarantine runners. And before that, he had been a Marine, seeing some of the worst fighting that Afghanistan, Pakistan, and Kyrgyzstan had to offer. He woke from nightmares every morning, and his hands still trembled from time to time for no good reason at all.

In all those years, all that exhausting, terrifying, dirty, tedious, disorienting, soul-shredding, fatalistic, and terrible work, he couldn't think of a single job he'd had a worse feeling about than the one he was working now. Maybe he was getting sloppy in his old age, taking on contracts he shouldn't from people he'd have been smarter steering clear of. Maybe his standards were just slipping.

He hiked the last few steps to the crest of the hill, feeling each footfall in his joints like they were crammed full of ground glass. When he finally reached the top, he leaned against the sticky bark of a broad-trunked pine and sighed. His breath quickly turned to a hacking, burning cough, and he pulled a stained, gray cloth from his pocket and brought it again to his mouth. When he finished, he didn't bother to check the rag for fresh spots of blood. He knew they were there.

"Hiking uphill is a young man's game," a low, gravelly voice called out from somewhere ahead of Franklin. "Still, can't beat the view from the top."

Wick. If taking a job from a Ravager war chief wasn't fool-minded enough, Franklin had been thick enough to go in with that fire-minded madman. Wick sat with his back against a tree a few yards ahead of him, looking out across the wooded horizon and rolling a dimly-glowing ember expertly across the back of his gnarled, scar-coated knuckles. The instructions had been to remain hidden and assume the area was being watched. Franklin shouldn't have been surprised that Wick had disregarded this piece of direction and made himself a campfire. Discipline; control; following orders; these weren't qualities Wick was known for. He was more reputed for destruction and collateral damage. Not typically the kind of man you hired to bring in a bounty alive. He wouldn't have been Franklin's first choice on a job like this, or even his tenth choice. But then, he hadn't done the hiring. A damned Ravager had.

Wick wasn't wrong about the view, however. Stretched out before him in the late afternoon light were wavy hills thick with trees, greens slowly — almost indiscernibly — flowing and swirling beneath a perfect blue sky. Here and there a tiny crag of slate-gray rock jutted upward, and behind one of the ridges he could barely make out the ethereal white mist that marked a hidden waterfall. Birds called out to one another, all around him. For a moment, Franklin was almost able to forget why he was here and who he was with.

Then Wick noisily cleared his throat and hocked a great clumpy wad of phlegm to the side, forcing Franklin back to reality. He was here to somehow catch a Reaper — alive — and he was partnered up with one of the most cracked-brained and violent men he had the deep misfortune of knowing. And Wick wasn't even the partner that frightened Franklin most.

A twig snapped, gunshot-loud, a few feet to his left. He and Wick's heads swung toward the sound as one, and Franklin for a brief moment was certain that his heart had finally stopped beating. A slight figure, dressed all in black, stood silently a few paces away, his arms folded behind his back. He regarded them both with eyes the color of dirty ice, and his expression was unreadable.

The third member of this strange team of bounty hunters had finally arrived.

"I take it this is the right hilltop, then," Wick said, poking at the ground between his outstretched legs, not looking up. "Took the pair of you long enough."

"I don't know what astonishes me more," the man in black said. "That you somehow found the correct rendezvous point, or that your ill-advised fire didn't lead to your capture and incarceration by the valley's inhabitants. Nevertheless, here we are."

"Here we are," Wick spat.

Franklin grunted his assertion, trying his best to avoid the eyes of the man in black. There was something in those eyes that turned his bones cold, something Franklin had seen many times before. They were the eyes of someone who thought nothing more of killing a man than of swatting a mosquito. Wick might be a madman, and Franklin himself was certainly no saint, but this man — Null was the name he had given — was something else entirely. A man to avoid, and certainly a man not to cross. The sooner this fool job was finished, the better.

"I trust the two of you have carried out your respective assignments adequately," Null said. "If so, I can begin to outline our final preparations."

Wick spat out another yellow wad of mucus and pushed himself up to his feet. He kissed the now-black ember and let it fall to the ground, and began to walk toward Null.

"Aye, I've done my job, boss-man, just like I said I would. Though I admit, I've been starting to wonder about the division of labor in our little triad here. To wit, just exactly when did we decide you were the one giving the orders?" Wick stood now about a foot in front of Null's face, his arms crossed, his mouth curved in a sneer. "Because I don't recall," he continued, nodding his head toward Franklin, "the three of us ever agreeing on that part."

The two of them stood staring at one another for a long moment, neither moving. Wick's face was covered in undulating, bone-white burn scars that contorted his face into a nightmare mockery, even when he wasn't twisting his mouth into a crack-lipped grin. Combined with his reflective welding glasses, which gave his stare an empty, dead-eyed look, he wasn't an easy man to face down. But Null did, without a hint of anger or contempt or respect. Without anything at all.

Finally, after a seemingly endless stretch of silence, a slight, mirthless grin formed on Null's lips. "I give the orders because the plan is mine. Because without me and my plan, you have little chance of surviving this assignment, and less of actually succeeding. And, because you still entertain the foolish notion that you might be able to double cross me after the work is done and take the entire bounty for yourself." He raised his eyebrows, and for a moment actually smiled. Even with the man's gaze on someone else, Franklin felt himself shudder.

Null turned away from Wick and strolled casually around the top of the hill, seemingly lost in thought. He removed what Franklin took to be one of his cigarillos from a pocket and rolled it back and forth in one hand. "I trust you've brought your little menagerie of Plagued Ones?" he asked suddenly.

Wick watched Null as he walked, looking somehow even more angry than he had moments ago. "The Plague-Heads? Yeah, I've got them corralled a few hundred yards south of here. They've been stuffed and secured. Just like I had planned, before I got roped into your dead-fish-eyed service," he said. "I know my own work. Don't go worrying about old Wick."

Null nodded. He turned to Franklin. "And you, hunter? You've kept your eyes on the eastern approach? You've detected their trail, I trust."

Franklin nodded, staring at the man's feet. "I did. It was like you said, they passed by the ground to the east. I haven't seen them with my own eyes. But they're heading the direction you guessed."

Null again smiled, briefly. "There was no guesswork involved."

Franklin heard the sound of a hammer being pulled back. Null turned, and as he did, Franklin saw that Wick was standing behind the man, holding a sawed-off shotgun in one hand, its barrel inches from Null's head.

"So you were right, weirdo," Wick said. "We know where they're headed. You've done your part; pulled your weight, small as it was, for this little partnership. Don't get me wrong, I'm grateful. Saved me a whole load of work. But now, for the life of me, I can't think of a good reason why this bounty shouldn't be split two ways, rather than three. In fact— "

Franklin didn't see Null move. He was still trying to wrap his mind around what Wick was trying to pull — though he was far from surprised at the burned man's betrayal — when it happened. One moment, Wick had the shotgun poised at Null's head; the next, the weapon had been knocked aside, and Null was holding Wick by the neck, a good foot off the ground, with a single hand.

Wick clawed at Null's outstretched arm and tried unsuccessfully to free himself. Null, for his part, looked no less relaxed and unconcerned than he had since he'd appeared minutes ago. Franklin watched speechlessly, frozen in some combination of fear and disbelief.

"Because, partner," Null said, "we still have work to do. And your assistance will make things easier for me. Please do not make them more difficult. I assure you, neither of us would like that." He opened his hand, and Wick fell to the ground, coughing and gasping for breath.

After taking a moment to regain some composure, Wick sat up and raised his hands in surrender. "Okay. We do things your way," he croaked, as casually as Franklin believed one could given the circumstances. "Just one request."

"I'm all ears," Null replied, folding his hands behind his back.

"Maybe you might be able to spare me one of those cigs, eh? Haven't had one in years."

Null smiled. "Of course, I am nothing if not polite. Just make sure you savor it. You never know if you'll get another chance at one."

"Oh that I will," Wick groaned a few moments later, sitting up and rubbing his throat. "That I will."

Null nodded toward Franklin, the motion so slight Franklin wasn't sure he hadn't imagined it, and turned away, looking out toward the horizon. "Soon, gentlemen," he said, "the real work begins."

A few heartbeats later, Franklin remembered to breath.

☦

Sam did not think it was fair that he had to carry the gold. Abigail was, after all, the one with the freakish stamina. Instead, he was now trudging along with four heavy gold bars in his pack, along with the few cans of food and bottles of water they had scavenged from the Wal-Mart's rotting shelves. And that was on top of the fact that the ground they traveled over continued to become more steep and rocky, the thick forest all around them only broken up by the occasional multicolored hot spring. Even with the pack slung over his good shoulder, every step sent a fresh, new wave of pain through his gunshot wound.

As they reached the top of the latest steep forested hill, Abigail stopped short and raised a fist, and the two of them froze. Sam saw what she did a half second later: two people, walking slowly along the ridge at the far side of the shallow valley in front of them.

The two figures wore brown, white, and green camouflage, and were only barely visible against the background of trees, bushes, and fallen leaves. Each one carried a rifle, and they walked the hill like they knew the ground well. Luckily, they didn't seem to have noticed Abigail and Sam.

"That's the outer patrol," Abigail said. "To be honest, I expected to see them before now."

"Is that good, or bad?" Sam asked. He and Abigail had ducked behind a large bush; Sam hadn't pointed his rifle at the new pair, yet, but he was holding it in their direction. He didn't know what 'outer patrol' meant, but he did know that since he had been outside the Colony, everyone he had met either wanted to rob him, kill him, or both. Still, these were *people*, real ones, not Ravagers or other Infected, and he didn't relish having to shoot at them.

"Neither," Abigail said. "For us, at least. It does mean Mae's people are getting sloppy. They're letting their security get lax."

"Mae's people?" Sam asked. "Please tell me Mae's is the place we've been walking toward. I really can't take another all-day hike."

"Mae's settlement is where we're heading," Abigail said, nodding. "Now, we just have to get the patrol's attention, without them spooking and taking a shot at us."

"Without them taking a shot at us?" Sam said. "Let me ask you a question, Abigail. Just how safe is this 'Mae's' settlement for us?"

"As long as you don't piss her off, Mae's place is perfectly safe," Abigail said. "It's when you get on her bad side that things can get a little dicey."

"But you have been here before? Please tell me you're not on her bad side."

"I wouldn't say I was on her bad side."

"So, just to be clear, you're not?"

"Not exactly," Abigail said. "But to be clear, I would never say I was on her bad side. You'll never get anywhere with a pessimistic attitude like that. Think positive, Sam. Besides, I'm sure once I talk to her, she'll see the whole thing was just a big misunderstanding."

"You're not exactly filling me with sunny thoughts," Sam said, "and you could have—"

He heard a twig snap, just a few feet to his left. A moment later, another snapped to his right. Beside him, Abigail swore. She put a hand on the top of Sam's rifle and gently pushed the barrel down toward the ground.

He dropped the weapon, and he and Abigail slowly stood up, raising their empty hands carefully up and into the air. Camouflaged riflemen and women stood around them in a half-circle, each with weapons raised. As he turned, Sam caught sight of the pair on the far ridge — the asses were waving at him.

"So much for the lax patrols," Sam said.

Abigail just growled under her breath, to no one in particular.

One of the riflemen stepped forward, his face barely visible between a camouflaged ball cap and a bushy brown beard. He had a thick wad of tobacco wedged under his bottom lip.

"Hello, Abigail," he said, lowering the tip of his rifle slightly. "I thought Mae told you she'd kill you if you ever came back here."

## 14

MAE'S RIFLEMEN WALKED THEM the rest of the way to the settlement. It laid tucked back against a barrier of heavily wooded cliffs, cordoned off from the Wilds with a circle of high, camouflaged metal walls. The settlement was well hidden; despite its considerable size, Sam could imagine walking right past the place if he didn't know what to look for.

Once they marched him past its creaking metal gates, Sam saw the settlement was laid out not unlike a real Colony. The buildings were older, and the materials that composed them were more mismatched and ramshackle, but all the familiar components were there.

But at the same time, there was no mistaking this place for Sam's home. Instead of a motor pool, they had a stable; instead of automated sentry guns, they had riflemen in wooden crow's nests; and instead of a fabricating lab, they had an honest-to-God blacksmith, complete with forge and anvil and a large bearded guy wearing a black apron and hefting a hammer. The biggest difference, however, was despite the presence of a waterwheel and a small bank of windmills, much of the camp seemed to be operating entirely without electrical power.

Sam wondered just how worried he should be about this Mae character and her ominous-sounding history with Abigail. He had any number of questions he wanted to ask, but since the ambush, Abigail hadn't been interested in talking, much less answering questions. *I guess I'll just have to ask Mae herself,* Sam thought, trying to summon a confidence within himself that he in no way felt.

The riflemen brought them to a stop in front of a long, thin building that in a past life may have been a mobile home or a government emergency trailer. Sam and Abigail were patted down again, and once the bearded rifleman was satisfied — apparently the third pat-down was the charm — he stepped back and left them to stare at the building's door, and whoever was presumably inside.

They didn't have to wait long. The door swung outward, and a short, gray-haired woman stepped out, wearing a wry, lopsided grin on her weather-worn face.

"I had to see it to believe it," she said, hopping down from the trailer and walking over to Abigail. "I was sure we had seen the last of you, girl."

"Mae," Abigail said, stone-faced. She gave the older woman a slight, almost imperceptible nod. "I can't say I expected to be back here, myself."

Mae wore an ancient leather duster over a pleated, ankle-length blue dress. Her hair was worn up in a pile of messy braids, and tiny silver hoops pierced her brow, nostril, and ears. A gun belt hung low on her hip, weighed down on one side by an oversized revolver. She took a step forward, toward Abigail, and a chorus of surprised shouts came from the riflemen, along with a half-dozen raised weapons. Mae shook her head, clicking her tongue disapprovingly, and gestured for the riflemen to stand down.

"I think we can all relax, can't we?" Mae said. She directed her words toward the other settlers, but her eyes remained locked with Abigail's. The same crooked grin remained on her face, friendly yet hard, inscrutable to Sam. "The girl is a lot of things, but she ain't stupid. She knows better than to attack a woman right in front of her sworn guns. Don't you, child?"

Abigail sighed, but otherwise remained silent. The guns lowered back down, and Mae leaned forward and took Abigail in a grandmotherly embrace. She held the younger woman for a few moments — she might have been whispering something in her ear, but Sam wasn't sure — before she stepped back and patted Abigail on the arm.

"See," Mae said, to the settlers, Abigail, or both. "That wasn't so bad."

Mae looked over at Sam. "It appears you have a new traveling companion. I hope he's an improvement over your old one."

*Who, now?* Sam wondered.

"He is dead, Mae," Abigail said. She turned and spat. "You know that, as well as anyone does. You saw him die."

"I saw him burn," Mae said. "I didn't see him die. Your father is a hard one to kill, girl. You know that better than anyone."

"He was *not* my father," Abigail said, her voice suddenly hard and full of barely-contained rage.

Mae shrugged. "Well, whatever you want to call him. I'm just glad he's not darkening my door. And if he truly is dead, well, then we're all better off. Now, to the next order of business—"

In a flash of movement, Mae had her pistol off her hip and in her hand, its barrel pressed to Abigail's forehead.

"Why don't you explain to me, nice and clear like, why I shouldn't just do both of us a favor and pull this trigger."

Sam's heart jumped into his throat. "Let's just everyone slow down," he began. "I'm sure we—"

"Quiet!" both Mae and Abigail yelled, not taking their eyes off of one another.

"I came back here for two things, Mae," Abigail said. Her voice was calm and even, like she was talking over tea, and not a loaded handgun. *How does she do that?* Sam wondered, and not for the first time. "The first is supplies. We're running low, and we need to stock back up. I'm sure your men have looked through my bag, and can see I didn't come empty-handed."

Mae shrugged. "So you brought some gold," she said. "The way I see it, those bars are already in our hands. Doesn't seem like a very good deal, trading for what I already have."

"So you're a robber now, Mae?" Abigail said.

Mae laughed. "I don't think you want to get into a name-calling contest with me, little girl. We both know where that leads." She tilted her head at Sam. "Does this one know about you, Abigail? About what you did? About what you are?"

"You're right, Mae," Abigail said. Sam thought he heard the slightest hint of fear creep into her otherwise cool voice. "I don't want to get into a name-calling contest. And you're also right about the gold. It's yours. Call it a gesture of good faith. But that's not all I brought."

"Now, that's the Abby I remember," Mae said, her smile widening. "What else have you brought me?"

"I've brought you something you'll want," Abigail said. "I've brought you an offer."

✝

The settlement became a bit less hostile after Abigail presented the framework of her offer. The settlers hadn't put down their guns, but at least they were no longer pointing them at Sam and Abigail.

Mae was whispering over her shoulder to one of her hunters. Sam noticed that even though she turned her head away from Sam and Abigail, her eyes never left them.

"Why do these people keep threatening to shoot you?" Sam asked, whispering in Abigail's ear.

"It's a long story," Abigail said, talking out the side of her mouth. "If we live through this, maybe I'll tell you."

"If we live through this?" Sam said. "I thought you had settled things with—"

"Alright kids," Mae said. "The decision's been made. You can stay the night here while me and my people discuss your offer."

"Great," Abigail said. "I knew we could come to an understanding."

"The understanding here," Mae said, stone-faced, "is that you still might be of use to me, and that's why I've temporarily lifted your ban here. But don't get things confused, girl. You and your little Colony pet are on a short leash. Step out of line — even a little — and you become more trouble than you're worth. That happens, well…bullets, brains, all that. I might be forgiving, but that don't mean I'm forgetting. Anything." She smiled, crinkling her face back into that of a friendly hippie grandmother. "So do please try and behave yourself. Are we clear?"

Abigail spit to the side. "Crystal, Mae," she said.

Mae stepped forward and put a hand on Abigail's shoulder. "That's good, dear. We'll set up a couple of beds for you in the bunk house. I trust you remember where that is. And maybe smile for once. After all, you might yet make it out of here in one piece."

She turned and walked away, parting the line of hunters as she passed. They fell in behind her, and the group headed away from Sam and Abigail, toward one of the larger buildings at the settlement's far side.

"So, that went…well?" Sam said.

"Far better than I expected," Abigail said. She began to walk off, in the opposite direction from Mae. Sam chased after her.

"We're still alive," he said. "So a deal's a deal. What the hell happened between the two of you, anyways?"

Abigail continued to walk her too-fast walk. She didn't look over at him, but she did crack just the hint of a smile. "You mean, why does Mae seem so particularly friendly with me? I would have thought that was obvious by this point."

"Maybe I'm just slow."

"No maybe about it. Look, it's simple. Mae tried to kill me, and then I tried to kill her. Neither one of us finished the job, obviously, and so now here we are."

*A bit anticlimactic,* Sam thought, but it did seem to track with what little he knew of the two women's personalities. Mae looked to be pretty quick on the draw, in a very literal sense, and she seemed like the type of person who took absolutely no crap from anyone. *And Abigail was…well, Abigail was Abigail.* A veritable legion of dead Infected behind them testified to her ferocity. And her temperament? *She wasn't exactly a people-person,* Sam thought.

"You've got to give me a little more than that," Sam said. "You said it was a long story, and we've still got plenty of time."

Abigail rolled her eyes.

"Come on, Abby, I—"

She stopped abruptly and turned on him. Sam nearly tripped over his own feet as he came to a halt.

"Don't call me Abby," she said, poking a finger at Sam's face. "My name is Abigail. I don't like it when people call me Abby."

"Okay, okay," Sam said, raising his hands in surrender. "I didn't mean anything by it. Abigail it is."

"Good," she said. She turned and resumed her walk, slower now. More the pace of a normal person. "Fine. Okay."

Sam walked silently beside her, wondering what that had been all about. Mae, he was certain, had called her Abby, and Abigail hadn't exploded on her. But still, there was something about that name which obviously struck a nerve with her. Maybe something having to do with that person Mae had called her father. Sam was immediately deeply curious about what the name meant to Abigail and her history. He had the feeling he was treading on dangerous ground, however, and with Abigail he was becoming increasingly aware that the word 'dangerous' was nearly always literal. *Still, maybe if I approached the whole thing from a diff—*

"It was a little over a year ago," Abigail began, looking out into the middle distance ahead of her. "When things happened, I mean. Between me and Mae."

She sighed heavily. "Turn around," she said, "and lift up your shirt."

"What?"

"Your wound. Your bandage needs to be changed. Its hard enough looking after you when you don't have gangrene. And I can tell you this story without you looking at me with that confused puppy stare."

"Puppy dog stare," Sam began. "I don't think I do that…"

"If you could see yourself right now, you might think differently. Now, come on, turn around." She twirled her finger in the air in front of his nose. Sam decided arguing with her was useless, and he turned around and lifted his shirt without further complaint.

"You have to understand," she began, pulling free a bandage from the small amount of supplies Mae had returned to them, "—that you're not from out here. Things in the Wilds, they work differently than things in your precious Colonies. You don't have someone up on high, tucked away in their dark rooms in their fancy white towers telling everyone what to do. You figure it out for yourself, and usually you don't get it right the first time, or the second."

"I guess that makes sense," Sam said, wondering how she knew so much about how the Colonies worked. He winced as she tore free his old bandage, and then again when she slapped a palmful of alcohol on his wound.

"And there's not always enough to go around. In fact, there usually isn't. So you take what you need. That's how things work out here. That's how they've always worked in this world. Even before the Horsemen came stampeding. Out here, there just isn't any time to fancy it up, to trick yourself about how the world works.

"Mae's place, and most of the other settlements around here," Abigail continued, "they have to specialize to survive. They find a niche, and then they fill it. People come here because they know what Mae has, and what they can trade for it. Mae's specialties are weapons and hunting. Pelts, meat and the like. People from the other Uninfected settlements come from miles around for her guns and bullets, and other supplies."

She pressed a fresh bandage onto his back, and held it until she was sure the adhesive would stick. "There we go," she said, patting the bandage — and Sam's wound — harder than he thought was strictly necessary. "Good as new." She stood up and waited for him to do the same.

Sam laughed to himself and got to his feet. *I hardly think a fresh bandage over a bullet-wound constitutes good as new*, he thought. Instead of saying that out loud, however, he simply stood up without a word. When Abigail began to walk, he fell in beside her, waiting for her to resume her story.

"Other places, they have different specialties," Abigail said. "Vegetables and grains, for instance. Or heating oil and gasoline. Fabrics. Or medicine and blood."

"Blood?" Sam asked.

"People get injured, they bleed. You lose blood, you've got to get re-filled. Plus, some people have…other uses for it. The point is, it's not easy to keep blood useable out here in the Wilds, and those people who can, they can charge a premium for it. That's what my…that's what the settlement I was staying at specialized in. And we did a lot of business with Mae's place. Guns and blood, they kind of go together."

"And things went south?" Sam guessed.

Abigail scoffed. "You could say that. You could also say a small misunderstanding spiraled into a full-blown war. People died, and people killed. I did a good bit of it myself."

"I'm sorry," Sam said. "That must have been…tough."

Abigail shrugged. She continued to keep a laser focus on the middle distance ahead of her, and her voice remained as hard and steady as ever. "I've done plenty of killing," she said. "And everyone dies. I've always understood that. It's Mae that had such a problem with it."

They walked for a while in silence after that. Finally, Sam decided he was just going to ask. He knew he probably should keep his trap shut, but he had to know. Abigail had spoken to him more in the last five minutes than in the last three days, but he was still no closer to knowing the person that he traveled with, whom he had entrusted with his life. He needed to know more about her. *And why is that?* Sam wondered. *Why do I even care, so long as she continues to put down Ravagers so effectively?* But he did care, and he did want to know more. He did want to know her.

*Screw it.*

"And Mae, she...killed your father?" Sam asked, mentally wincing from the fury he knew was coming his way.

Instead of raging at him, Abigail sighed.

"Solomon was never my father," she said. "He was just some guy I followed for far too long."

Sam nodded and remained silent.

"And Mae didn't kill him," Abigail said. "I did. Find somewhere else to walk, Sam. I'm through talking with you."

And with that, she turned away from him and began to walk faster. Sam stopped and watched her go, understanding Abigail less than ever.

# 15

SAM WALKED THE GROUNDS of the settlement for a little while, not entirely sure what to do with himself. For some time he stood by a group of barrels outside the blacksmith's forge, watching the man at work. The smith moved cherry-red blocks of hot metal from the fires to the black iron of the anvil, hammering them into various utilitarian shapes. As the smith finished with each piece, Sam tried to guess its eventual use, and he wondered how and when this man had come to learn this ancient trade. Certainly, blacksmiths existed in the Old World, but how many could there really have been? Most metalwork had been done by machines, by assembly lines or by 3D fabricators, like they had in the Colonies.

Maybe the man had been an artist, or a historical reenactor. Or perhaps he had simply been an accountant, or a bank robber, or something else entirely unrelated to his new trade. He might have learned how to smith from a scavenged book, or an old video (unlikely, since the settlement had no electricity). Or...maybe he'd just figured it out because someone had to. It was interesting to Sam, thinking about this new, hardscrabble world rebuilding itself out the ashes of the old. In the process, it was becoming something that seemed to exist both in the past and the future at the same time.

Eventually, Sam grew bored with watching the man swing his hammer, and his thoughts returned to Abigail. After she had left him, he had respected her wishes and let her go, let her be alone. It was the least he could do given how he had pried into her past, which had obviously upset her. He wondered if he should apologize, tried to imagine what she would say if he did. She'd probably just laugh at him, tell him she didn't care about him or his apologies, and that he should worry far less about what she thought of him because she didn't think of him at all. He could actually picture her standing in front of him saying the words, and he scowled. I'm *not going to apologize for anything,* he decided. Of course, that didn't mean he wasn't curious what she was up to.

He found himself, almost without thinking about it, walking in the direction of the stables. The same stables toward which Abigail had earlier stormed off. *She's probably in there yelling at a horse for not being tough enough,* he thought. *Or in the middle of a fistfight with one.*

As he crossed the camp, he noticed the settlers shying away from him. It was subtle: a small change of direction here, a head turning away there, but he wasn't imagining it. He wasn't sure whether it was fear or hatred driving the bubble of isolation around him, but its effect was the same. Mae's people wanted nothing to do with him. He wondered if he would have thought differently, being in their place.

It was surprisingly dark inside the stables. The ceilings were low, and though it wasn't entirely enclosed, enough of the long, hay-strewn building was comprised of windowless horse stalls that the interior was covered by thick, crosshatched shadows. There were maybe twenty horses inside the building, along with four or five people, either tending to an individual horse or occupied with general cleaning. He didn't see Abigail at first, and Sam wondered if she had walked straight through and out the back door of the stables to throw him off her trail. Of course, that assumed she thought he would follow her, which he hadn't, till now. Just as Sam was about to dip back outside, he spotted her - about three-quarters of the way down the rightmost of the two aisles, with her back to him, gently stroking the nose (or was it snout? he had no idea) of a black-and-brown spotted horse.

Sam leaned against a pillar near the stable's center, watching Abigail intently. She looked relaxed; almost at peace with the beast. *That's probably why it took me so long to see her,* Sam thought. *I didn't realize she was capable of relaxing.* She patted the horse on its cheek and fed the animal a carrot, which it eagerly munched from her hand. She leaned forward a bit and rested her head against the animal's forelock. *It was like seeing an entirely different person,* Sam thought.

"She almost looks normal, doesn't she?" a gravelly voice spoke from beside Sam. It was one of Mae's hunters; the lead one with the bushy, gray-flecked beard. "You almost forget just how dangerous she is, when you see her like this."

"Yeah. I guess," Sam said, confused and unnerved by the hunter's sudden presence.

"Name's Ray," the hunter said, nodding toward him. Sam noticed that he was still carrying his rifle, strung behind one of his boulder-like shoulders.

"Sam," Sam said.

"If you're wondering if I followed you, Sam, the answer

is yes. You're an unknown quantity here, and we aim to keep things safe. Doesn't mean we have to be rude about it, though, so I thought I'd come and say hello." He leaned against the wooden railing next to Sam and picked at one of his thumbnails with a small utility knife. "Plus, I got tired of skulking around in the shadows."

Sam shrugged. "Understandable, I suppose," he said. He was trying to think of the most polite way to extricate himself from this conversation when he had an idea. "How well do you know Abigail?" he asked.

Ray worked at his wad of tobacco as he thought over the question. "I know her well enough," he finally said. "As well as anyone can know someone like that, at least."

Sam nodded. "I know what you mean," he said.

"Do you?" Ray said, turning his head to look Sam in the eye. Between his formless camouflage jacket, heavy brown stocking cap, and barely-kempt beard, Ray reminded Sam of a grizzly bear. But from this close distance, his eyes shone with an all-too-human mixture of pain, fear, determination, and rage, forcing Sam to look away. "I've seen some hard men over the years. Violent men, and ruthless men. Hell, I've been one, for most of my life. But that girl, and the man she traveled with...they were something else. Something I barely understand, even now."

"She told me about the fights you had," Sam said. "Her settlement and this one. She said it was bad."

Ray shook his head and laughed. "Bad. That's one way of putting it. We used to have twice as many hunters here, back before Mae decided to make a deal with Solomon Smith. Worse men than we've got now, harder men. Stone killers, dozens of them. This place used to draw them like flies. Mae took them in, tamed them — some, at least —

and she built us into an army. We had the guns, and we had the soldiers. We owned all of the Yellowstone and the surrounding plains."

Ray fell silent, staring blank-eyed straight ahead, lost in memories. Abigail continued to stroke the mane of the horse in the corner stall, seemingly oblivious to the presence of either Sam or Ray.

"We grew foolish, overconfident," Ray said. "We made the deal with the blood-peddler."

"The blood-peddler?"

"Solomon, Abigail's keeper. Creepiest bastard I ever set eyes on. Abigail told you it was a fight between settlements, but that's not what it was. Solomon didn't run a settlement; he ran something else. It used to be a settlement, years ago. One of Mae's old rivals, a man named…I don't remember what his name was. It's funny, I actually fought against that old boy - it was the longest and most bitter fight we ever had, but I don't remember his name now. I just remember that he brought in a hired gun, a man traveling with his young daughter, a man he thought might give him an edge. It didn't. Solomon won that old boy a couple of skirmishes with our people, but something happened, and Solomon turned on him.

"After that, the place wasn't a settlement anymore. It became an empty place, a place that sold things, but didn't make them. Things came to Solomon, and he sold them, and he became rich. But there were always rumors, ghost stories. Stories about disappearing folk, and people that went there to trade and were never heard from again."

Sam suddenly felt very cold. "And this Solomon, he came for you next?"

Ray laughed. "No," he said. "Then Mae made a deal with him. Blood for bullets. The ghost stories were just that, stories. We had the numbers, and we had the guns. Whatever thieving trickery he worked with everyone else, it wasn't going to work with us."

"But it did, obviously," Sam said. "That's why you fought, right?"

"I'll tell you this, boy," Ray said. "I don't know what deal you have going with Abigail over there, but don't try to cheat her, and don't underestimate her. That's what Mae did with Solomon — she tried to strong-arm him, change the terms of the deal. She told him if he didn't like it, he could come up here and take his bullets himself." He closed his utility knife and put it one of his many pockets. "He didn't come himself, though. He sent that girl over there. Mae laughed when she first saw her; hell, we all did. That was when things turned south for us, though. Hunters started disappearing, and others returned without their weapons or with broken arms or legs. Sometimes both. And every time we cornered her and forced a real fight... well, you've seen what she can do. By the time Solomon was burned alive, our army was a shadow of what it was. As many had run off as had gotten killed. The girl did put Solomon down, though. Probably why Mae didn't just kill the both of you when you first showed up."

"Hooray," Sam said weakly.

"Just don't expect anyone else to be as warm and cuddly with you as I'm being now. People around here don't like that girl, and they're not going to trust anyone travelling with her."

Ray nodded toward Abigail. "And don't you forget, boy, Abigail might look like a little girl, but she is death walking. You best remember that." He sighed and shook his head. "I sure hope Mae does."

Sam stared at Abigail and tried to reconcile Ray's story

with the young women in front of him. She was certainly capable in a fight, and she was gruff. But was she really as frightening and merciless as this Ray made her out to be? Sam was having trouble believing this bear-like man, who was probably just spinning an elaborate tale to cover up the shame of past losses in battle. *But if he is lying, he's damned good at it*, Sam thought. The man seemed to believe every word he said, and by the looks of him, he wasn't exactly someone who relied upon his cunning conversational skills to get by. But as he watched Abigail, Sam had to admit that out here in the Wilds, people weren't always what they appeared to be.

A horn sounded from somewhere outside the stables. One long, low blast. Sam looked toward the door, bothered by Ray's last words.

"What do mean when you call her 'death walking'?" Sam asked.

Ray shook his head. "You know why I told you that whole story, Sam? All those details it's probably best not to share with strangers? It's because you're a sheltered Colony boy, and you're too dumb to know what to do with the information. Like confessing your sins to a donkey. But now we've got new arrivals, and I've got real work to do, so I'll bid you good day. Thanks for letting me unburden myself, Sam. It feels good to say that story out loud."

He slapped Sam on the shoulder hard enough to knock him off balance, and then he turned and walked away. Sam watched him go and looked back to Abigail. She had turned around and was staring directly at him, her arms crossed over her chest and her face expressionless as a death mask.

# 16

"YOU ARE AN IDIOT, YOU KNOW THAT?"

"That seems a bit harsh," Sam said. "I prefer to think of it as I'm at the bottom of a learning curve, out here. And to be honest, I think I'm climbing said curve at an exceptional rate."

"You're an exceptional idiot, more like," Abigail mumbled.

Sam and Abigail stood just outside the entrance to the stables and watched as Ray and the rest of his hunters brought in the party of traders. Each of the traders — there were three men and one woman, along with a single heavily laden ox — was wearing a black bag over their head. Even the ox was wearing blinders, as if the beast was somehow capable of memorizing and revealing to others the route it had taken into Mae's settlement. The high outer doors swung shut behind them, and one by one the bags were pulled off the traders' heads.

"How come we didn't have to do that whole head-in-a-bag thing?" Sam asked.

"Because I already knew where the settlement was," Abigail said. "Idiot."

"You know, for a hardened killer, you are remarkably sulky," Sam countered.

"Maybe that's because you were dumb enough to believe what Ray-fucking-Durand had to say about me. If you had questions, you should have come to me. Believe me: Durand doesn't care about you one bit. He's not a man to trust."

Sam smiled. "But I thought you didn't care about me. One bit."

"Idiot. This place survives because it remains hidden. Keeps it out of the path of Ravagers, and prevents it from becoming too tempting a target for other settlements. The forest itself is much more the outer walls of this place than those flimsy pieces of metal."

Sam looked up at the walls, with their ugly, uneven lines of welding and their decaying patches of rust. This place might be set up similar to his Colony, but life within these walls was far different. "It's really that bad out here, huh?" Sam said. "Just constant fighting, constant struggling. How do you stand it?"

"What other choice do I have?" she said.

Sam thought about that. He didn't have an answer for her. Life out here in the Wilds did seem objectively terrible, and yet, he didn't miss being back at the Colony. He felt like he should. He should miss his warm, soft bunk. He should miss the high, impregnable walls keeping him safe. He should miss the defense cannons keeping watch, and the fabricators keeping him in comfort. He should be chewing his nails down to nubs worrying about the survival of the only home he had ever known.

But he didn't miss any of it. His worry for the Colony was a dull, far away thing, a concern in the back of his mind that only bubbled up on rare occasions.

Of course, that didn't mean he liked Mae's settlement any better, because he certainly did not. And it didn't mean that the Colony wasn't worth saving, because it certainly was. Sam was as committed as ever to retrieving the drive from Deacon and avenging Vincente, but a sense of duty was different than a sense of home.

He'd make sure that the Colony lived on. He just didn't think it would live on with him.

While he stood lost in thought, Abigail had begun to walk away.

"Wait up, dammit!" Sam called after her. She looked back at him over her shoulder, and laughed. "I'm hungry," she called back. "Stay out here with your worries, Sam."

He stood there, unsure what to do.

*And what else is new?*

"Or, come with me and eat some dinner," Abigail added, lengthening her stride.

Sam's stomach growled. *Yeah,* he thought, *dinner sounds good.* He ran after her.

✝

In the Black Hills Colony, Sam's home, the residents ate at a communal mess hall. It was a brightly-lit room with three lines of long, clean tables, and it was staffed by a trio of white-clothed chefs who handed out trays of food from a behind a brushed steel counter. The residents ate during their prescribed shift, ate quietly, and cleaned their trays, before leaving in a similarly orderly fashion. The mess hall had always reminded Sam of the lunch room from the Beverly Hills teen drama entertainment the Colony girls liked to watch on the big television most evenings.

The dining hall in Mae's settlement was a fair bit different from what Sam was used to.

Rough-carved wooden tables, each bearing years worth of knife gouges and food stains, were arranged haphazardly around a central, circular bar. Laughter and shouts and clinking glasses bounced off one wall and then another, tangling with the rest of the noise into a snarled din of barely-controlled chaos. Someone played a piano in the corner, poorly. A drooped, elderly bartender poured beers from a single tap and liquors from the multi-colored bottles ranged behind him, the settlers imbibing drinks as fast as he could pour them. Thin diagonal lines of dancing dust motes glowed in the rays of white sunlight peeking through the cracks in the walls, illuminating thin slices of the room far brighter than the dim glow provided by the fluttering kerosene chandeliers overhead. Somewhere on the other side of the room, Sam heard someone swear, and then glass breaking on what could have been someone's head. From the lack of reaction, he deduced this was a fairly commonplace event.

Sam thought the place was awesome.

Abigail took a seat at a half-cleaned table, and Sam joined her. A heavy-set, surly looking woman appeared and asked them what they wanted. Sam was going to ask what they had to eat; Abigail answered before he had a chance, ordering something called 'still-water.' Sam said that was fine, and that he would have one as well. He had been walking all day, after all, and he was parched. Abigail said they would have 'food, too,' which was apparently the only dinner option available.

The waitress returned a minute later with two clay mugs filled with surprisingly clear water, before disappearing back into the raucous crowd of dining — or simply drinking — settlers.

"Stop smiling like that," Abigail said. "You look like you've been kicked in the head by a horse."

Sam ignored her. "Look at this place," he said. "It's like something out of the Old West. I half-expect someone to be challenged to a duel in the middle of the street."

"This is place is nothing like the Old World," Abigail said. "The Old World was more civilized, not less. And a dispute here would likely end with a knife in the belly, not in some kind of bladed duel."

"What are you talking about?" Sam said, before realizing that Abigail hadn't grown up like him, surrounded by an entire library of Old World entertainments. She probably had no idea what the Old West *was*. For all he knew, she had never watched an entertainment program in her life. "The Old West," he said, "not the Old World. Or, I guess it was the *really* Old World. Back before cars and the internet, when cowboys rode around with six-shooters and fought bandits, and all that."

Abigail looked at him like he was speaking Mandarin. "Yes," she said dryly. "The Old West. Of course."

"It's just…the place is interesting, is all I'm saying," Sam said. He took a large sip of his water, and then nearly threw up. His mouth was suddenly on fire, his sinuses numb, his eyes choked with tears. "What the-" he coughed, the vile liquid spilling out of his mouth. About half got back in the cup; the other half went all over his chest.

This earned a smile from Abigail. "Still-water," she said. She raised her own cup and gulped down its contents. "Mae's specialty. 195 proof. I was surprised you chose to order it."

"I thought it was water," Sam said, scraping his tongue against his teeth, trying to remove the remains of the horrible taste. "I thought it meant, like, no bubbles."

"Why would water have bubbles in it?" Abigail asked. The sour-faced waitress reappeared with two plates of steaming root vegetables and burnt hunks of meat, dropping them down on the table with a clatter. Abigail asked for a glass of water for Sam, and the waitress grunted a reply and again promptly disappeared.

"Never mind," Sam said. He looked over his plate of food. It didn't look — or smell — particularly appetizing, but it was warm. *And it was, you know, food.* He grabbed his fork, hoping it wasn't too dirty. Everything else here seemed to be. "So what is our next move?" he asked, digging in.

"We get our weapons from Mae in the morning, and then we leave," Abigail said. "Then, we go and kill Deacon."

Sam listened, nodding as he shoved the mushy, over-salted vegetables into his mouth. They were delicious. He looked up a few moments after Abigail finished talking.

"That's it?" he asked. "That's the whole plan? Get guns, shoot bad guy?"

Abigail shrugged. "That's what I told Mae. And that *is* what you wanted, isn't it?"

"Well, yeah," Sam said, his mouth still half-full of potato. "But there's got to be a little more to it than that. Shouldn't we, I don't know, hire some of Mae's people to help us out? Come up with some sort of battle strategy beyond just 'kill Deacon?'"

Abigail smiled and shook her head. "You do remember those hunters brought us in here at the end of their rifle barrels, right? And you remember Mae pointing her own ridiculous pistol in my face? The silly story Ray Durand told you? What makes you think we could possibly trust these people?"

*She does kind of have a point,* he admitted silently. *Still, though...* "We can appeal to their self-interest," Sam said. "Mae knew the name Deacon, and she obviously wants him dead, or she wouldn't have agreed to deal with us. He's got to be as much of a threat to them as he is to us. More even. I mean, sooner or later he'll find this place, and what then? I doubt these people can throw off a full Ravager assault force. Mae will have to listen to reason."

"We can't. Trust. Them." Abigail pounded her fist on the table, emphasizing each point.

The combined noise of impact and exclamation was loud enough to quiet the room, if only for an instant, and to draw a few dozen pairs of eyes. Then, as quickly as then din had faded, it resumed, as loud as ever. Sam did notice that the room felt a few ratchets tenser than it had a minute earlier, however. *Or maybe that's just me being paranoid.*

"Come on, Abigail," Sam said. "Be reasonable. We're eating their food. We're sleeping under their roof. If they wanted to kill us, they have all the opportunities in the world to do it now. We need more fighters to take on Deacon and his Ravagers. Maybe we can convince Mae to—"

"I won't fight alongside people I don't trust," Abigail said. She threw back her still-water and slammed the mug down on the table. "You can't trust these people, Sam. You can't trust anyone."

Strangely enough, her words made Sam feel warm inside. "But you've fought alongside me," he said, a smile forming on his face. "So that means you trust me, don't you?"

"Don't read too much into things, Colony boy," she said, scowling at the wall. But while Sam couldn't be certain in the tavern's low light, he swore he saw her cheeks redden slightly, and even a tiny hint of a smile tug at one side of her lips.

Suddenly she was looking back at him. Or rather, about a foot above him. "What do you want?" she said. Sam felt the heavy breaths of the person behind him, blowing down on his neck.

"We know who you are, devil-girl," the man standing behind Sam said. Sam turned his head, just a bit, and looked behind him. The man was large — tall and thick, with wide shoulders and a heavy, round belly. He had at least one other man standing behind him, possibly more. Sam could smell the alcohol — and the simmering anger — coming off of the men in waves. Moving as slowly and as smoothly as he could, Sam grabbed his heavy clay mug in one hand, and his two-pronged, bent fork in the other. Visions of people being tossed through front windows and dragged, belly-down, along the length of bar tops danced through his head. He gripped the dish and the utensil tightly, ready to move if this turned into some sort of saloon brawl.

Abigail saw what he was doing. She gestured for him to stand down. "I'm already forced to deal with the blandness of this food; I don't care to add the blandness of your predictable, ineffective threats to my evening," she said to the man, tone dismissive. "You say you know me? That's great. I don't know you. So if you don't mind, kindly be on your way."

Coughs of shock and confused fury sounded behind Sam as the men processed Abigail's retort. Across the table from him, Abigail took a bite of her meat, and seemed to forget the men were there.

Finally, after Sam thought the wordless tension was going to explode his heart, somebody spoke.

"How about if I told you that if you don't get out of this room right now, girl," the lead man, the fat one, said, "I'll come over there and twist that pretty little head of yours right off your shoulders? How predictably ineffective would that threat be?"

Behind him, the man's friends laughed. Abigail cut off a section of carrot and put it in her mouth, chewed, and swallowed before setting down her fork and looking up at the man behind Sam. She smiled faintly.

"I would say it's a slightly less bland threat than I expected, fat man. But still not terribly effective."

She spoke brightly, conversationally. Friendly even. It terrified Sam.

"A threat is supposed to scare its recipient," she continued, "and we both know I'm not the scared one here." She shook her head. "Plus, we both know you don't mean it. Sure, you might try to beat on me, given the chance, but you wouldn't actually rip my head off. You don't have that kind of horrible, over-the-top violence in you."

Her smile disappeared in an instant, replaced by the stone-faced expression she wore during a fight. "But I do," she said. "So I'll turn it around on you. Take one step toward me, and I swear by everything I believe that I *will* remove your head from your shoulders. One step forward, and you die. Simple as that." Her easy-going smile returned. "Maybe that's more of a promise than a threat, but who knows. So make your move or leave quickly please, because I wasn't kidding about how much you are boring me."

She returned to her food. Sam sat, frozen against the chair back, every one of his muscles clenched. Behind him, no one spoke. At first, he imagined that the men were trying to batten down their rage at Abigail's casual insults before attacking, rallying their courage before making their move.

Finally, after nothing had happened for nearly a minute, he risked turning his head to see what the men were doing.

They were gone.

Abigail finished the last of her bread and drained her mug. "What's taking you so long to finish your food, Sam?" she asked. "I thought you were the hungry one."

# 17

"RAVAGER HORDES, as far as the eye can see. One smashing up against another like some kind of...thing, with a bunch of people, all in a group."

"An army?"

"No. More like a horde."

"That's what you just said. Hordes, Ravager hordes. I thought you were trying to use some kind of flowery metaphor to describe it, but you just kind of trailed off."

"A what now?"

"Never mind."

After Sam had finished eating, Abigail had led them to the bar, where she sat down next to three of the caravan traders that had arrived earlier that day. She had said she wanted to see what news they brought with them from outside. Sam was eager for any information at all concerning this wild, strange world he knew nearly nothing about; unfortunately for both of them, the only one of the traders who seemed interested in talking was the one that was already exceedingly drunk.

"What he's trying to say is that to the south, it's pretty much open war between the various Ravager hordes."

One of the other caravan traders had finally spoken, either out of pity for Abigail and Sam or simply because he was tired of listening to his drunken fellow talking himself in circles.

"Something has them all riled up," the middle trader continued. "The whole of the high plains south of here is too dangerous for travel, all the way up to the foot of the Mountains."

Sam remembered the black smoke that had constantly lined the southern horizon while he'd been on the road with Vincente. He had wondered what it meant at the time; it appeared he now had his answer.

"What kind of numbers are we talking?" Abigail asked.

"I couldn't tell you," the trader said. "Thousands."

Sam nearly spit out his water. "Thousands?" he said.

All three of the traders, as well as Abigail, turned to look at him.

"Those are the Ravager's lands," the middle trader said, looking at Sam as if he had expressed surprise that water was wet. "It's where their so-called 'King' makes his home, where they can tear around in their fleets of old cars and on the few horses they still haven't cooked and eaten. Thousands ain't unheard of; everyone knows that."

"It's just...high, is all," Abigail said, distracting the traders away from Sam. "My friend is just a little excitable, is all."

"Fraidy-cat, is ya?" the drunk said, nearly leaning into Abigail to stare at Sam, his mouth hanging open in a slack-jawed smile.

"Sure, whatever," Sam mumbled, rolling his eyes.

There had been four travelers in the caravan when it arrived that afternoon. Sam and Abigail sat next to three of the four, their party a regular on the supply routes as far north as Old Billings and as far south as Nuevo Cheyenne.

All three were on the older side of middle age: the drunk was the oldest, with parchment skin and white, greasy hair. The other two were probably in their forties. The man in the middle seemed to be what passed for their leader; Sam guessed the woman at the far end of the group was his wife or girlfriend. She had been silent since he and Abigail had approached. Other than to occasionally look over at Abigail and scowl, she made no indication she even realized their party had company. The fourth traveler sat at a small table on the other side of the room by himself, staring into his drink through his reflective welding glasses, his cowl drawn up tightly around his face.

"Is it a full war," Abigail asked, "or just heavier than normal activity? I only ask because we've seen some of that closer to here."

"The great and powerful Deacon, you mean," the drunk said. "The wily one, everywhere and nowhere."

"Could be that one," Abigail said. "Mostly, I just wonder if whoever is operating around here might be connected to this Ravager King."

"Couldn't say," the middle trader said. "I could say, however, that everywhere seems like it's getting more dangerous every day. Two kids like you probably shouldn't be going out into the roughs at all."

"I appreciate the advice," Abigail said. "Any other news?"

"Just the usual rumors, most of it lies and less. Talk of Free City militias to the west, clearing news lands of Plague-Heads and Howlers, pushing out their borders. Probably heard that before, though. It's always on the tongues of naïve fools, tall tales of civilization returning to the world. Anyone who's been to the Free Cities knows 'civilized' ain't a word much used."

"Of course not," Abigail said. "Anything else?"

"Nothing worth talking about. Talk of Colonies dis-appearing- good riddance to them. Strange tales coming from the far east, but that's nothing new."

"Strange tales like what?" Sam asked. "What is that about Colonies disappearing?"

Abigail turned back toward him. As soon as her face was out of sight of the caravan traders, she shot Sam a look like she wanted to kill him. *Well, screw her if she thinks I'm embarrassing her,* Sam thought. *The Black Hills Colony is to the east.*

"One near Jackson, and two south of here," the middle trader said.

"The stories from the east, boy," the drunk said, "are the same as they've always been. Old World ghost armies, crossing over the Dead River and killing everything in their path. Spook stories; heard 'em a thousand times before."

"Ghost armies, huh?" Sam said. "I mean, why not? We already more or less have zombies and werewolves and vampires. Plus, whatever it is Ravagers are. I don't know... crazy fury-monsters?"

"You two sure have a lot of questions," the far trader said, the first words she had spoken. She watched Sam, her expression wary.

"Where did you two kids say you hailed from?" the middle trader asked, seemingly catching his companion's suspicion.

*Stupid,* Sam thought to himself. *Abigail was right, no more talking.* He looked down at his water and waited for her to answer.

"There you are, little girl!" a new voice exclaimed, before Abigail could answer the trader's questions. It was Mae.

"I've been looking all over for you. Should have figured you'd be in here." Mae took Abigail's mug from in front of her and sniffed its contents, before throwing back the still-water in one gulp. "Liquor, huh? I would have guessed something…warmer. Maybe a little more color."

"What can we do for you, Mae?" Abigail asked. Sam could hear the irritation in Abigail's voice, but for his part, he was relieved for the interruption in the trader's sudden interest in them.

"Just wanted to let you know," Mae said, "we can go over final discussions for your little plan at first light. My office. I take it you remember where that is, Abigail. Though feel free to use the door this time, rather than the side window." She patted Sam on the back. "We'll do it over breakfast. I'm sure this growing boy will be hungry."

"That's fine, Mae," Abigail said. "Thank you. We will be there. Anything else?"

Mae smiled, the same part-grandmotherly part-trickster half-grin she'd given them earlier. Her ear and face rings seemed to glow red in the reflected light from above the bar. Two of her hunters, both enormous, trailed after her like baby ducks. "There is just one more thing," she said. "I thought I'd like to tell you myself. We're overbooked on sleeping arrangements this evening, so the two of you will have to share a bunk. I'm sure that won't be a problem, of course."

"That *is*, *in fact*, going to be a problem, Mae," Abigail said, standing up from her chair and facing the settlement's leader. "We agreed on two bunks."

Mae just smiled wider. "Plans change, dear. It's only a single, unfortunately, but you can make it work."

"Dammit, Mae" Abigail began, raising her voice.

"The lady can always stay in my bed," the drunk said, laughing.

Abigail, still staring at Mae, calmly grabbed a handful

of the drunk's hair and jerked, sharply cracking his head off the bar. His head bounced back up, looking dazed, but apparently with enough wits gained to remain silent.

"There's got to be something-" Abigail said.

"These are my halls, and my word goes," Mae said. "You can go along, or you can sleep outside the walls. But if you leave, you aren't coming back in." She actually pinched Abigail's cheek between her thumb and forefinger and squeezed; Sam thought Abigail was going to kill her right then and there. "Have a good night, dears. I'll be seeing you in the morning."

She turned and left, laughing, and Sam could swear he heard her say something along the lines of 'seeing at least one of them in the morning, anyways.' Sam didn't quite understand what had just happened, but he knew his heart seemed to be fluttering somewhere around his Adam's apple, and he felt a strange mix of embarrassment, excitement, and terror. It was all very confusing. This whole evening had been confusing.

Abigail made a noise somewhere between a growl and a muffled scream and turned back to the traders at the bar. "You asked where we're from. We're scavengers from north of here, mostly around Old Buffalo." She spoke quickly and with barely-contained fury, and Sam found himself trying to make himself as small as possible, while also trying to lean as far away as possible from her without tipping over in his stool. "Any more stupid questions?"

The trader's recent suspicion was gone, replaced by a quiet fear. Sam was beginning to see that this was the smart reaction to have to Abigail when she became angry.

"Good, because I need to get out of this filthy hall, and I don't have time to play twenty questions."

"But you were the one asking us-" the middle trader

began, then fell silent as Abigail's stare fell upon him. "Never mind," he muttered.

"Good. Then tell me about your friend, sitting over there by himself, and I'll be gone for good. You can get back to… whatever it is you were doing."

The drunk barked out a laugh, then instinctively cowered his head away from Abigail.

"We met him about a day out," the middle trader said. "He saved us from a Plague-Head attack."

"It's the only reason we let him travel with us," the far trader said.

"Why?" Abigail said, leaning in, over the drunk's cowering head.

"No real reason," the middle traveler said. "Better not to travel with strangers."

"No," Abigail said. To Sam, it sounded like a challenge, not an agreement. She pointed at the third trader. "You wouldn't have been so quick to dismiss him to me if that was the case. What is it about him?"

"He's off-putting," the third trader said, a note of defiance entering her voice. "You say you want to leave, then go. I'm getting tired of talking-"

"Why is he off-putting?" Abigail said. "Exactly."

"Why don't you ask him yourself?" the third traveler shot back.

"He's just…he doesn't talk," the middle trader said, trying to calm the rising tension. "Sits by himself, staring into space when we would stop for the day. I would wake up in the middle of the night and he would just be gone, disappeared, and by morning he'd be back, without word one of explanation. And he never takes off those glasses, or his hood."

"Don't know what he's covering up," the third traveler

said, "but whatever's wrong with him, it starts inside his head. I think the two of you would get along, girl."

"He's a damn Reaper, just like I've been saying for miles," the drunk chimed in, before immediately hiccupping and then burping. "Only explanation that fits. Man like that, don't survive by himself otherwise."

"A Reaper?" Abigail said.

"You listen to old Jared there, everyone's a Reaper," the middle trader said. "I told you, Jared, if we had met a Reaper on the road, we wouldn't very well have made it here alive, now would we?"

"Bah," the drunk said, waving a dismissive hand at the middle traveler.

But Abigail had suddenly stood up very straight. She was looking at the fourth traveler now as if seeing him for the first time. The expression on her face was strange. If Sam hadn't known her, he would have sworn part of that expression was fear. The other half was clearly hate.

"Relax, girl," the third trader said. "He's nothing but a weirdo. He's not a bloody Reaper."

But Abigail was no longer listening. She was striding over to the lone traveler's table, having drawn a curved knife from the small of her back. After a second of surprised hesitation, Sam followed.

The hooded man looked up from his drink just as Abigail reached his table. Abigail grabbed his circular, reflective glasses and ripped them upwards, removing both them and pushing the heavy cowl back from the man's head, exposing his face.

One half of it was covered with bubbly, red and boiled-egg white scar tissue, the legacy of some sort of severe burn. The skin on the other half of his face was the color of teak, which gave him the look of two different faces stitched together.

Abigail pulled his head back and slipped her knife under his chin, pressing the blade against the half-burned skin of his neck. The man's one good eye went wide, and he raised both his hands off the table in a gesture of surrender.

"No, please," he said, his croaky voice trembling.

Abigail leaned closer to his face, turned it one way and then the other, inspecting its features.

"Please, don't hurt me," the man said. "I don't know what I have done."

Abigail let him go and abruptly straightened up. She ran her fingertips through her hair, her breath coming in quick, ragged bursts. "Never mind that," she said. "Go along with your drink. I thought you were someone else."

She turned away and looked around for the door. She looked disoriented and frightened; for the first time, she seemed to Sam more like a teenage girl than a hardened Wilds killer. He reached a hand out for her, not entirely sure what to say.

"Abigail," he said, putting a hand on her shoulder.

"*Never mind*, I said," she spoke, just short of a shout. She looked over at Sam, now with an expression of anger that he didn't think was entirely genuine. "Just drop it, Sam," she said. "Leave me alone."

She pushed him away and stomped out the door of the tavern dining hall. Sam stood there, in the middle of the room, as the settlers drank and ate and laughed and fought, and he felt more alone than he had since he'd left his Colony.

# 18

OUTSIDE, NIGHT HAD FALLEN. When Sam had entered Mae's dining hall-slash-Old-West saloon, the sky had still been a pale, almost-white blue, streaked with red-gold clouds, only fading to ultramarine in the very east. Now it was pure black, everywhere he could see.

That wasn't really true, though. He'd seen pure black under that mountain, back when he had lost Vincente and gained Abigail. A thick, oppressive blackness like a physical thing, one that seemed capable of choking the life out of you and overtaking your very soul.

It wasn't like that tonight, but it felt nearly as unreal, nearly as unworldly, as that horrible darkness. The moon was out, and at least near-full, because despite hiding behind the clouds, it bathed the grounds of Mae's settlement in a kind of ethereal, silver-gold light. Outside, on nights like these, Sam had always felt like he was walking across an alien planet, in the middle of the day while a black star shone brightly above.

It was quiet out here, after the racket of the saloon. He could still hear the shouts and the laughs and the music. Clearer now were the familiar sounds of the woods at night, cicadas and frogs and the odd hoot of a lone owl, somewhere in the trees towering all around the metal walls that kept the Wilds at bay.

It took him some time to locate Abigail. In that time, he wondered what had caused her to storm out, what he was going to say to her, and if he should even be looking for her at all. Maybe she just needed some time to herself; maybe he needed to give her some space. Since they had met, they had barely been out of sight from one another. If anything, he should relish the brief respite from her hovering presence. *She's been more my jailer than my companion, hasn't she?* Sam wondered.

But one foot kept finding itself falling in front of the other. Sam wandered deeper into the open spaces of the settlement, looking around the corners of buildings and inside the open windows of the various utility structures. A hollow feeling had taken hold of him, even in the few minutes of being alone, but it was more than that. He was worried about the damned girl, as silly as that sounded, considering who that girl was. Still, he needed to make sure she was all right. Maybe she did want to be alone, maybe the last thing she wanted to see was his stupid face, maybe he was walking toward nothing but a stream of curses and a punch in the nose...

That was okay. If she wanted to be alone, and told him that, he would leave. He would find his bunk — hell, he didn't even want to *think* about what Mae had told them about their revised sleeping arrangements, whatever that meant. He would find his bunk and lie down and bury his face under whatever this place had for pillows, and he would wait for sleep and hope his keeper was in a better mood in the morning. But he couldn't do that until he knew Abigail was okay. As it was now, he felt... he didn't know how he felt. Maybe something like how he felt when he knew he was leaving Vincente behind. It was a feeling he couldn't bear.

He found Abigail standing beside a stream that ran alongside the westernmost settlement wall. Past her, a large wooden waterwheel turned slowly under the current, creaking softly with each herky-jerky rotation.

And among the creaks of the wheel and the distant revelry of the dining and drinking settlers and the wild sounds of the forest, Sam heard the last noise he ever expected to hear.

Abigail was crying.

Well, maybe not *crying*, exactly. But there were sniffles, at the very least. And by Abigail standards, that was practically inconsolable, hysterical screaming and garment-rending. *Or was it?* Sam tried to remember he had only known this girl for a few days. Really, he didn't know her at all.

"Abigail," he said, softly.

In a flash she had turned 180 degrees and unsheathed the same small, curved knife she had earlier used to threaten the burned traveler. Before Sam had even registered the movement, the tip of her blade was hovering a millimeter in front of his face, just above his nose.

*It's not a particularly large knife,* Sam thought, *but it sure is a whole lot more menacing from this distance.*

After one terrifying second, Abigail recognized that it was him, and she lowered the blade. She sniffed and wiped her nose with her free hand, turning away from him.

"I should have known it would be you," Abigail said. "You follow me around like a freaking puppy dog."

"It's not like I've had much of a choice," Sam said. "Have I or have I not been your prisoner since you pulled me out of that underground Colony?"

Abigail scoffed. "Prisoner? Please. More like your protector, your keeper. If it wasn't for me, you'd have long ago been dead."

"Maybe," Sam said. "Probably. But which one of us was it that shot those Ravagers out of that water tower? I'm not completely useless."

Abigail laughed, once. It wasn't a lot different than her scoff, but Sam heard the difference. *That's something,* he thought.

"Still," he said, "that's like plus one for me and about plus fifty for you since we started this stupid journey. So, I'd say you weren't completely useless either."

She laughed again, longer this time. It looked like she was wiping some tears out of her eyes. Sam took a chance and stepped up to stand next to her.

"It's been a strange day," he had, staring straight ahead. He put his hands in his pockets and then, deciding it would look more natural, removed his hands and folded his arms across his chest. "This is a strange place, and that's just for me. I can only imagine what it's like for you, considering your history with these people."

"These people are arrogant fools, deceiving themselves if they think they can survive like this," Abigail said. "They are living on borrowed time."

"Well, if we can help them with this whole Deacon problem, maybe they'll survive a bit longer."

"Deacon is *our* problem, and that's why we need to deal with him ourselves," Abigail shot back. "Without help from that old bitch Mae, or Durand, or any of the rest of them. I wouldn't spit for them."

"Yeah, okay," Sam said, nodding. "Deacon is our problem, and we will solve it. 'Our.' It's funny...saying *our* like that, meaning the two of us. It doesn't sound nearly as bad to me as it did a couple of days ago."

She scoffed. "It's just a word. I should have said *my*. That's why I do what I do, not for you. Not for anyone but me."

"Sure," Sam said. "Everyone for themselves and all that." He drew in a quick breath, and he took another chance. He turned to her. "What happened back there, Abigail?" he asked. "What's wrong?"

Her teeth showed, for just an instant, as she growled, before turning slightly away from him, crossing her arms noticeably tighter over her chest. But she didn't turn completely away, Sam noted. He forced himself not to smile a little. *Small victories,* he thought.

"It's nothing," she said. "It was nothing."

"You know, Abigail, you are pretty much the most composed person I have ever met," Sam said. "Well, except for the occasional outburst of angry, homicidal anger. But that wasn't anger, back in the saloon. That was something else."

She half-laughed, half-sobbed, a single laugh. "The saloon? The dining hall, you mean?"

"I decided I'm going to stick with saloon," Sam said. "The Old West, like I said before. It fits, and I don't care if I'm the only one who calls it that."

She laughed again. "The saloon. I like it."

"What was it about that guy back there?" Sam asked. "The half-burned guy with the welding glasses? You acted like you expected to know him."

Abigail was silent for a long while, and Sam waited. Once, it looked like she was opening her mouth to talk, but she just sighed. Finally, she screamed a brief, frustrated close-mouthed scream and turned back to Sam.

"I thought he was…I thought he was someone he couldn't have been. Someone dead. The last person on this entire dead rock that I wanted to see."

She again went silent, and again Sam waited quietly.

"I thought he was the man who raised me," she said. "I thought, right up until I saw his ugly, scarred-up face, that he was Solomon."

Sam remained silent.

"The...the piece of crap is still with me, and he's been dead for over a year. I see him out of the corners of my eyes, I hear his voice in my head, and I hate it."

"That Ray guy told me a little about him," Sam ventured, "but, like you said, he's not telling me the whole story. Or even half of it."

Abigail laughed bitterly. "Ray might have met Solomon twice. He didn't know him. I lived with him. Ray's just lucky that Solomon sent me after him, back during our conflict, rather than come himself. This whole place would be a forgotten pile of ash right now if he had."

She went quiet after that. She kicked at the dirt with one foot.

"He sounds...quite capable," Sam said. He wasn't sure what else to say.

"Mostly, he was boring. I mean, he didn't talk a lot while I was growing up, didn't even seem like he noticed I was there most of the time. But he had a philosophy, and when he got going on that, he wouldn't shut up about it. Survival this, and kill-or-be-killed that. If I laid it all out for you now, you would say it was all so simple and rote, but for most of my life, I believed it. And even now, I tell myself that I don't believe it, but it keeps coming back to me. His stupid lessons, repeated just as repetitiously as the knife motions he made me spend so many hours practicing.

"Maybe I'm lying to myself," she continued. "Maybe I'll never really be free of him."

"I think," Sam said, "that we choose every day who we want to be. If you don't want to be this person you think he made, then make that choice tomorrow morning. Make the choice to be who you want to be. And then, do it again the next morning. Until it sticks."

It was a version of the advice Vincente had tried to teach him over the years. Sam had nodded along while Vincente spoke, but he had never really thought too deeply about what he meant until just that moment. Now that he said the words out loud, he realized that he really did believe them, and he was glad that he did. He only wished Vincente was still around for him to thank. It was funny, just what parts of people stuck with you after they were gone.

Abigail had done it silently, but Sam could tell she had begun to cry again. She had certainly gotten more angry.

"So that's it?" she said, staring him down with hard, watery eyes. "Just *decide*, like that, to stop being Solomon's sword. Just decide to get his damned, evil voice out of my head? Can you just decide that your parents weren't killed by some filthy, worthless Reaper? Can you just *decide* them back to life? Can you, Sam?"

"It's not the same thing," Sam shot back, his voice rising despite his efforts. "I can't bring back my parents, but I can decide how I remember them. I can decide how I live today. It might not be easy, but I can at least try."

"And when you do meet a Reaper? Are you going to decide to kill them, too? Because it's a little more complicated than that, Sam."

It occurred to Sam for the first time that Abigail might have some sort of history with the Reapers as well. She certainly got angry enough when they were mentioned. Most people spoke of Reapers with a sense of quiet fear, but one tinged with excitement, or at least interest. For reasons Sam never could understand, the other kids of the Colony had always thought Reapers were cool. *Probably because the things hadn't killed* their *parents.*

"What happened before this Solomon?" Sam asked. "What happened to your real parents?"

She brushed away the question. "Dead, before I could remember. Solomon found me in the remains of a destroyed caravan when I was an infant. Or so he said."

*Well, so much for that,* Sam thought. He had hoped that, if Reapers had been behind her parents' deaths as well, he might be able to help her by telling her how he coped. He had far less common experience with being raised by a psychopathic knife-master, or whomever this Solomon was.

"Solomon may have lied," Abigail continued. "He might have killed my parents himself and taken me, for all I know. He was certainly capable of something like that. It doesn't matter. What's done is done. And he's dead. He's dead. I killed him myself, for God's sake. Or at least I may as well have. But I just feel like I can't get his stink — his evil — off of me. I don't know if I ever can."

Sam smiled. "Abigail, you are the one person who I wouldn't be exaggerating to by saying that I believe you could truly do whatever you wanted."

She scoffed. "You don't know me," she said. "I can't do this."

"How do you know?" Sam asked. "Why not just try? For one day, at least. If you can't you can at least laugh at me one more time, for how big of an idiot I am, and how wrong I was."

She laughed. "Just like that," she said. "Just try?"

"Why not?" Sam said. "It's easier than taking on an entire Ravager camp, led by a deranged genius-Ravager, all by ourselves."

She laughed again, but this time kept laughing. She sniffled again, and again wiped her nose with the back of her hand. She sat down at the creek's bank laughing and sighing and looking up at the sky. After a moment, Sam sat down next to her.

"Do you know what the worst part is, Sam?" Abigail said. "Part of me, no matter how much I hate him, and no matter how much I hate myself for feeling this way, actually misses Solomon. If it wasn't for him, I'm sure I would have died a long time ago."

"Well," Sam said, "I guess that's one good thing this Solomon did."

They sat there, side by side, and listened to the quietly babbling creek. Overhead, the clouds had begun to break, and the full moon hung heavy in the sky, bathing them both in silver.

"I miss Vincente," Sam finally said. "You probably guessed that already, but I do. He was my only real friend, back where I come from. It's still hard to believe he's actually gone."

Abigail turned to face him, her eyes dry now. "You don't talk about him much," she said. "I wasn't sure if he was a real friend, or just your commanding officer."

Sam sighed. "Vincente was the only person I've ever really been close to. He was older, but we both came to the Black Hills Colony at about the same time. My father had died on the road, and my mother…she was taken not long after we arrived. A woman named Shayla took us both in — she had just lost her husband — but she died too. After that, Vincente was old enough to be on his own, but I was still a kid, and there was nobody that wanted to take me on. Not long term, anyway. I bounced around from house to house, adult to adult, but I never really knew any of them. But Vincente was always there for me. Always checking in on me, always showing me things — teaching me things — that most kids probably learned about from their parents. He taught me how to shoot, and I went out every day, between the inner walls and the outer ones, and I practiced. And when Vincente became a scout, I knew that's what I wanted to do as well." Sam laughed, almost feeling light-hearted at the memories. "And he didn't even mind when I became a better shot than him, and then a much better shot. Without him, I'm not sure where I would be right now. Who I would be. And now he's gone." He sighed, the moment of reverie broken.

Abigail leaned in toward him, nearly imperceptibly, and her shoulder brushed against him. Sam had no idea whether it had been intentional on her part, or accidental, but for a single instant, his body felt like it had been filled with electricity.

"You two did seem like you were close," Abigail said. "For what it's worth, I am sorry. For your loss, that is. I'm sure losing a friend is difficult." She laughed, once. "I would only be able to guess, though. I've never actually had a friend, as stupid as that sounds." She shook her head and stared into the slowly moving creek, studying the somberly dancing reflection of the moon on its surface.

"I'm your friend, Abigail," Sam said. "Whether you believe that or not. I am."

Abigail laughed softly to herself and continued to stare into the creek. A moment later she leaned in to rest her shoulder against Sam's.

He moved before he realized what he was doing, or he would never have been able to work up the courage. He worked his arm back and draped it over her other shoulder, and they sat there, each staring into the gentle waters, each, for the moment, no longer alone.

After a while, a thought occurred to Sam, and he laughed.

"What?" Abigail asked, turning her face toward him.

"It's nothing," Sam said. "Its just…well, just when I think things have gotten as strange as they can get out here, they just get stranger."

"The world is a strange place," she said softly. Sam turned toward her, and their eyes met, and Sam felt another surge of electricity. He had another thought, one that seemed almost suicidal. *There are a thousand ways this can go wrong,* he thought. *A thousand painful ways.* He was terrified, but he didn't care. He tilted his head and leaned in to kiss her.

He watched her close her eyes a split second before he shut his own. *This is really going to happen,* he thought. He didn't care that he had no idea what he was doing.

Just as his lips should have been brushing hers, something jabbed him in his shoulder. Hard.

The impact pushed him to his back on the dew-wet grass. A thousand thoughts were bouncing around his skull, and not a single one made any sense.

Abigail swore and got to her feet.

"Bastard," she said. "I knew it. You don't care about me, you're just trying to exploit my feelings to your own ends. To your…carnal thoughts."

"Carnal thoughts?" Sam said from his back. *I stand by my earlier statement,* he thought. *Just when I think things can't get any weirder…*

"I am a fool," Abigail said.

Sam started to get to his feet. "Abigail, I-"

"You're an even bigger fool if you think to stand near me

right now, Sam," Abigail said. "After what you've done to me."

"After what I've done to you?" Sam said, sitting back down. "I don't know what you think I've done, or was trying to do, Abigail. Really, if I'm being honest, I don't really know either. But...that doesn't matter. If I did something wrong, I'm sorry."

"Pretending you care, the oldest trick in the book," Abigail said. She barely even seemed to be talking to him directly anymore.

"I do care," Sam said, raising his voice to her volume. "Why wouldn't I?"

She shook her head at him, pacing back and forth. "You," she said, pointing a shaking finger at him, "you're good, you know that? You're good."

"Well, now I'm certain I'm completely lost," Sam said. "I shouldn't have tried to kiss you, okay. That was stupid of me. I obviously...I don't know, read the mood wrong. I've never done something like that before."

Abigail continued to pace, looking at Sam occasionally. From her expression, it looked like she was trying to believe him, but maybe that was just Sam's wishful thinking.

"I need to go for a walk," she finally said. "Go back and go to bed, Sam. And don't get any ideas. I'll sleep outside. I'm used to it."

Sam opened his mouth to argue, to say that's not what he expected, that he would sleep outside, and that obviously, they both wouldn't share the single bed. But there wasn't any point. "Fine," he said. He didn't want to argue. He got up and, after a final look at her, turned toward the bunkhouse. He hoped Abigail would stop him, but she did not.

Sam slumped down outside of the bunkhouse and leaned back against its wall. Despite what she'd said, he had decided he would sleep outside. *And she can damn well take the bed,* he thought, with both less anger and conviction than he was hoping for.

Despite his agitation and his confusion, he was incredibly exhausted, and he fell asleep almost as soon as he closed his eyes. He slept through till morning, only half-waking when someone sat down next to him and leaned into him, resting her head against his own.

# 19

SAM AWOKE to someone kicking him in his side.

He lurched awake, frightened, looking all around. He had somehow fallen asleep on his bad shoulder; practically that entire side of his body now ached.

He blinked the last bit of sleep out of his eyes and took in his surroundings. Everything seemed to be as it should. Settlers were moving this way and that along the various paths, carrying supplies, sipping from steam-trailing cups, beginning their day. He looked toward the source of the kicking and recognized a now-familiar pair of mud-caked boots. He looked up and saw the silhouetted form of Abigail, peering down at him, the sun shining from just beside her head. Her hands rested on her hips and one foot tapped impatiently on the ground.

"Get up," Abigail said. "It's time to make a deal."

She turned without another word and stalked away. Sam wondered if he had dreamt last night. A settler looking backward bumped into Abigail as she walked, and Abigail shoved the settler back and onto the ground without breaking stride. *I don't think my mind is capable of dreaming up the version of Abigail I spoke to last night,* he thought.

He got up and, as was quickly becoming a habit, ran after her.

✝

Two plates were dropped down in front of them on the table. Each had small portions of mashed potatoes, green beans, and carrots, thin wisps of steam rising from both plates. A moment later, Mae stabbed a fork into Sam's potatoes, and then a second in Abigail's. She then sat down across from them and rested her elbows on the table, watching and smiling.

Sam instinctively reached for his plate and pulled it close. He wasn't that far from road rations and charred squirrel that he'd turn down real cooked food.

Abigail grabbed his plate and pulled it back, signaling him to wait. Sam's stomach growled in protest.

"Now Abby," Mae said. "Don't keep the lad from his meal just because you kept yourself from yours. Growing boys need their food, after all." She nodded toward Abigail's plate. "You too, Abby, eat up," she urged.

Abigail's only move was to raise an eyebrow. Mae laughed. "You think I'd poison you? Seems like an awful lot more trouble than just shooting you. Plus, it wastes good veggies. I've never liked to waste things, you know."

Abigail, after seemingly trying and failing to think up further objections, finally relented. She let go of Sam's plate, took up her fork and began to eat. That was all the permission Sam needed, and he took up his own fork and began to wolf down his breakfast with abandon.

"Now," Mae said. "Once you two finish stuffing your faces, we can begin to talk strategy."

"What strategy?" Abigail asked. "You give us the supplies

we talked about, and then we go kill Deacon. Your Ravager problem is solved, and so is ours. There's your strategy, conversation over."

"If it was that easy, girl, you really think we wouldn't have done it ourselves by now?" Mae asked.

"Like how you took care of Solomon by yourself? No, you needed me for that, and you'll need me again if you want to take out Deacon. If that's not reason enough to jump at the chance I'm offering you, consider this: now you have something better than just me," Abigail said. She pointed to herself, and then to Sam. "You have us."

Mae laughed. "And what is this wet-behind-the-ears Colony child going to do that any one of my sworn hunters can't?" she asked.

"Hey," Sam protested, his voiced muffled by half-chewed potatoes. "I can do stuff, too." It was probably good the words were indecipherable; they weren't his most eloquent.

"A few days ago, I watched Sam take out two Ravagers at over 800 yards. Two shots, he put them both down," Abigail said. She had embellished Sam's accuracy, as well as the distance. *It couldn't have been more than 750 yards, and it took me way more than two shots*. But Sam wasn't going to choose now to split hairs. *Besides, those were* hard *shots*.

"Sam can take out their perimeter guards before they see us, and can get us close enough for me to finish off Deacon," Abigail said. "Now that is something I know none of your hunters can do."

"Maybe. Maybe. Though last time I took your help I traded problems with Solomon for problems with Deacon. I almost wonder what I might be trading for this time." Mae tapped at her teeth, considering Abigail's words. "No," she finally said. "It won't work."

Sam threw down his fork, which was easier than he

expected considering how hungry he was. "What do you mean, it won't work?" he said. *I've already come too damned far to have some Podunk settlement leader simply say 'no, you can't do that,'* he thought.

"It can work," he continued, "and it will work. Just because you—"

"You're going to want to stop talking, right now," Mae said, all congeniality sudden gone from her voice. "If you think I've got hard feelings toward our little friend Abby, well, they're nothing compared to how I feel about your kind. So you sit there, and you eat your food, and you let the adults talk. Okay?"

Sam didn't know what to say to that. So, choking down his anger, he retrieved his fork and returned to his food. *Abigail can handle Mae,* he thought, *at least for the time being.*

"That's a good boy," Mae said. She looked back toward Abigail. "Now, what I was *going* to say is that you two won't succeed on your own. This Deacon, and his war party, they aren't like normal Ravagers. They are something new, something special. All the fury, all the strength and the animal fearlessness of regular Ravagers, but none of the reassuring stupidity we've grown so accustomed to."

"We've noticed," Abigail said. "It's troubling."

"It's more than troubling," Mae said. "It's damned terrifying. Ravagers used to be little more than an inconvenience: like faster Plague-Heads, or Howlers without the hunting instincts. But Ravagers that can think? That can plan?" Mae whistled and slowly shook her head. "That sounds like the end to me. The end for us all." She took in a long, tired breath, and after a silent moment she let it out. "I never thought I'd say this, my dear little Abby, but in this Deacon,

I think I've finally found something that scares me more than you do."

"Who, Abigail? Scary?" Sam asked, trying to ease the mood. His quip earned him a fresh glare from Mae and yet another irritated head shake from Abigail. *Wrong crowd*, Sam thought.

"Here's what I'm going to do," Mae said. "I'm going to give you the supplies you asked for. The bullets, the explosives, the silencers, everything. But what I'm also going to do is send four of my best hunters with you. I'll tell them to follow your directions, but they stay by your side. Their participation, that's not something that's optional, understand?"

Abigail looked surprised. Sam certainly felt surprised. Not only was Mae going to give them everything they asked for — and not kill them, which was a definite positive in Sam's book — but she was going to send help along with them. It seemed too good to be true.

"That is… it's awfully generous of you, Mae," Abigail said.

"Well, this Deacon is a threat to all of us. I'd be foolish not to use you if I've got you. And before you think I'm getting too generous, keep in mind that I'm giving the hunters orders to shoot you if things go south. Can't have you falling into Deacon's hands, knowing like you do where we live."

"That's the Mae I know," Abigail said.

"Don't tear up on me now. And we're keeping your gold; hopefully that goes without saying. My other concern, little Abby, is that you go in at your best. Frankly, from what I've seen, or rather, haven't seen, since you got here…well, it gives an old woman pause. I never thought I'd say something like this, but I think you need to top yourself off. You're no good to me in a fight if you're running on empty."

Abigail stared daggers across the table at Mae. "You don't know what you're talking about, Mae," she said. Sam looked from one hard woman to the other, but like he had been for much of this conversation, he was lost.

Mae smiled a mirthless smile. "I know what I know. And if you aren't going to take the initiative your own self, I think I have the answer." She pulled a tiny silver key from the pocket on the front of her overalls and waved it at Abigail. "See, Abby, I never totally believed you wouldn't come back. Not really. And if you never did…well, sooner or later someone like you was bound to come along. So, we've kept the bones you like. I don't like thinking about it too closely; the whole thing is…well, it's off-putting. They're in the icehouse, as cold as we can manage. So, the last part of the deal is you go into that icehouse, and do what you do. Once that's done, I'll point out Deacon's base on the map, and we'll look to head out."

"Mae…" Abigail said, shaking her head.

"That's the deal, girl," Mae said. "We can't have you fighting such an important fight on an empty stomach, now can we?"

"What are you two talking about?" Sam said, too confused now to remember he wasn't supposed to talk. "What bones?"

Mae smiled at him. "What bones indeed? Abigail?"

"It's nothing, Sam," Abigail said. "Mae's idea of a joke. A bad joke."

"Oh come on now, little Abby," Mae said. "There's no sense keeping him in the dark. After all, how long do you—"

Outside, a siren began to whine. Mae was on her feet in an instant. "Were you followed?" she demanded, her eyes wide with either anger or fear.

Before Sam or Abigail could answer, the first explosions started.

✝

Sam and Abigail followed Mae outside, chasing the source of the explosions. Just as Sam came outside, another detonation sounded, causing him to wince back and then look toward its source.

"Fireworks?" Sam asked. Overhead, bright red and green trails of light streamed down toward the settlement, their last embers crackling and smoking against the deep blue of the early dawn sky.

"Why are you setting off fireworks?" Abigail asked Mae.

"We're not," Mae said, shaking her head. "What in the damn hell is going on up there?" she called up to the nearest sentry.

"I'm not sure, Ma'am," the sentry called back. "It's not us."

"Of course it's not us," Mae shot back. "Where is it coming from?"

"I can't tell, Ma'am."

Above, another set of fireworks burst deafeningly.

"Shit," Mae said. "Everyone up on the walls. We're under attack."

One of the riflemen — the one with the hat and the bushy beard — jogged up to Mae.

"What's the word from our rangers?" Mae asked him.

"That's just it, Ma'am. I can't get any of the eastern rangers on the horn. Nothing but static. We've got a serious problem, here."

Another set of fireworks went off, lower this time. "You think?" Mae said.

Sam stepped over to Abigail. "Whatever's happening, it isn't good," he whispered. "We need to get out of here, now."

Abigail nodded.

"We've got Plague-Heads!" the sentry yelled from his tower. "I'm counting five to ten. Check that; twenty Plague-Heads, coming in fast."

"Well, why don't you start shooting!" Mae called back, furious.

Sam heard a shot, but the sound was wrong. It had come from too far away.

The sentry took a step back from the wall's edge, staggered for a heartbeat, then tumbled down to the ground in front of them, a single gaping red hole in the center of his forehead.

Shots lit up along the wall as the rest of the sentries opened up with their weapons.

"Let's go," Sam said, grabbing Abigail's sleeve. They turned to run, but froze when they heard the sound of a pistol's hammer being cocked into place.

"Wait right there," Mae said, her voice cold and hard.

Abigail and Sam turned slowly as one, each raising their hands.

"This is your doing," Mae said, staring daggers at Abigail. The pistol shook slightly in her hand

"My doing?" Abigail said. "What possible reason could I have for bringing a bunch of Infected here behind me? And not only that, how could I? I've been with you this entire time."

"They're at the wall!" one of the sentries screamed.

"That's why we have a wall," Mae yelled back, keeping her eyes locked on Abigail. "Plague-Heads aren't getting through that."

"Mae, whatever is going on, we can help," Abigail said. "Just put the gun down, and—"

"I should have shot you the moment I saw you," Mae said. "I should have never let you in here at all."

"This. Isn't. Me," Abigail said. "Don't be stupid, Mae."

All around them, settlers ran from building to building, either grabbing weapons or looking for shelter. Sam watched the chaos all around him, wanting to flee but held in place by Mae's tremoring gun-barrel. Everyone else in the settlement seemed to be on the move except for their group. No, that wasn't true: Sam saw one other person standing still. It was the lone traveler from last night, the one with the half-burnt face. He stood alone, leaning against the wall of the saloon with his arms crossed over his chest. He had a short cigarillo in the corner of his mouth and a small black box in one hand.

"Umm, guys," Sam said. Everyone ignored him.

"It's too late for your secrets and your lies, Abigail," Mae said. "You might not have done this yourself, but you led them right to us regardless. You've gotten sloppy, dear. The Abigail I knew would have never let someone tail her."

Abigail was silent for a moment. She shook her head. "Shit," she said. "I should have known."

"Yes, you should have," Mae said. "They wanted us, and they used you to find us."

"No, Mae," Abigail said. "You've got it backwards. They knew we would come here, so they got here first, set up, and then they waited. You were never the target, Mae. You were the bait."

"Impossible," Mae said. "If these people knew we were here, they would have hit us long before now."

Abigail shook her head. "No Mae. You're just a backwoods settlement, barely scraping by. You're not important enough to these people. Not even important enough to Ravagers, apparently."

"And you are?"

Another firework streaked toward them. Sam saw it first, and the arc was way too flat. It wasn't going to explode overhead. He dove into Abigail, tackling her to the ground and covering her a moment before the blacksmith's hut exploded into flames.

Pieces of wood and metal and bits of dirt rained down around them. Sam heard a sentry atop the wall yelling that there were too many Plague-Heads, and another telling the first to shut the hell up. Sam raised his head and looked to the saloon. He met the lone traveler's eyes just as the man raised the black box and moved his thumb to the top of it. Sam understood, finally, what the box was. It was a detonator. The traveler smiled at Sam, and he pushed down the button.

One section of the wall, where moments ago two of the sentries had been exchanging curses and warnings, turned to fire.

Plague-Heads immediately began to stream in through the newly-blown gap. A handful of riflemen jumped down from the battlements, engaging the Infected on foot. For the moment, they seemed to be holding them, but anyone could see that the situation was rapidly deteriorating.

"Now can we go?" Sam asked Abigail, pulling her to her feet.

"Not yet," Mae said, her pistol trained on Abigail.

"What is it going to take, Mae, to make you see reason?" Abigail shouted. "This place is coming down around your ears, and you're still worried about me. We can *help* you, damn it."

Mae shrugged. "I guess I'm just stubborn," she said. She pulled the trigger and the pistol roared.

Abigail snapped her head to the side as the bullet caught her in the neck. Blood immediately sprayed out, cutting across the air in a flat arc as Abigail spun around, splattering Sam's face in the process.

Sam's heart dropped. It was like seeing Vincente fall all over again. The horror and the hurt washed over him. It was even more difficult to process what he saw next.

Abigail staggered a single step to the side and slapped a hand against her wound. But she didn't fall. From the amount of blood she had just lost, she should already be dead, and she certainly should not still be standing. But she was.

Mae swore and fired again, but Abigail had already dodged to the side and dashed forward, closing the distance between the two of them in a heartbeat. Her hand came off her wound and smashed Mae in the temple, then her other hand cracked Mae in the jaw with an uppercut, actually taking the older woman off her feet.

The bushy-haired rifleman had turned back toward them, his attention drawn by the gunshot and the scuffle. He swung his rifle around toward Abigail, but she had already begun to move toward him. She ducked under the rifle barrel and around to his back, pulling the knife from his belt as she did so. Before he could begin to turn back around, she had already raised the knife and brought it back down, burying it in the base of his skull. As he fell forward, she came down on his back; when he hit the ground she was kneeling on top of his dead body.

She looked up at Sam, panting, her skin an ashen, nearly transparent white. Sam stood frozen, not able to understand what he had just seen. Abigail had gone from certain death to incapacitating one person and killing another, in what couldn't have been more than 10 seconds. And the gunshot wound, the one that had taken a golf-ball sized chunk out of her neck, was now a lump of angry pink scar tissue. It had healed itself.

He took a step back from her. "What are you?" Sam asked, feeling suddenly very lightheaded.

"I'm sorry, Sam," she said. And then she twisted the knife in the dead rifleman's neck and buried her mouth into the wound.

Sam immediately knew what she was, even if he didn't want to believe it. Abigail was a Reaper.

The color — what color she normally had — returned to her face almost instantly. She sat back up and looked at Sam, her mouth rimmed with scarlet blood and her eyes wet with tears. "I can explain, Sam," she said.

Sam didn't know what he could possibly say to her, so he turned and ran.

All around him, the settlement was burning. Riflemen were running back and forth, some toward the encroaching mass of Plague-Heads, others away in fear. The fire from the blacksmith's shop had spread to the dining hall, and from there to the barracks. Sam had to get out of here; the entire place would be ash and death before nightfall.

But first, he was going to get what he'd come here for. He had lost the two people he cared about: first Vincente, and now Abigail — the Abigail he thought he knew, not the monster she actually was. The only thing Sam had left was the mission, and he was going to see it through. He may never have really felt a part of the Black Hills Colony, but there were good people there, and some he might have even considered friends. Sam was the only thing left between them and annihilation. He would save them, and he would kill Deacon.

But for that, he needed weapons.

He took advantage of the chaos around him to locate and dash to the settlement's armory undetected.

The armory door was hanging open, and inside was everything he could have hoped to find. He grabbed a canvas supply sack and began to stuff it with all it would hold — bullets and pistols, knives and bandages, explosive charges and detonators. This place might not be much for comforts, but they were exceptionally well-armed. The bag full, he looped its strap over his shoulder and grabbed a rifle. The weapon wasn't a long-range model like his old one, but it came with both a silencer and a grenade launcher mounted on its jet-black body. It would do.

He turned to run, stopping short when he remembered the rifleman and his radio. He needed to call back to home; he should have done so long ago. He grabbed a radio from the supply rack and stuffed it in the bag. He remembered something Abigail told him, and he grabbed a small knife and stuffed it in his boot. Just because she was a Reaper didn't mean he couldn't take her survival advice.

He turned back to leave and nearly ran into another of Mae's men. Sam tried to raise his hands and explain he meant him no harm, but the man only pulled out his pistol. Sam ducked as the man fired. The shot passed safely over his head. Sam grabbed one of the pistols from his bag and raised it up, firing as fast as he could. Three of the rounds caught the man, two in the stomach and one in the shoulder, and he collapsed to the ground. Any other time, Sam would have been horrified by what he had just done, but now he simply did not have the time. He turned away from the dying man, and he ran.

Sam turned in a circle, trying to locate the settlement's front gate. It was the only way out that wasn't blocked by Plague-Heads.

*Except that one.* One of the Plague-Heads had broken through the mass at the breach point and had locked onto Sam. He raised the pistol, aimed, and put a round in its head, just before it reached spewing distance. *Too close,* he thought. He wished the armory had contained a few plastic face masks.

Past the falling Plague-Head, he caught a glance of Abigail, fighting three Plague-Heads with her bare hands. She was covered in plague-spray; for a brief moment, he was worried she was infected, before realizing in a wave of chill that she had been infected long before she had met him. And she had lied to him.

Though what else could you expect from a Reaper?

He shook his head and ran toward the now-open gate, shocked by how empty the area was. Plague-Heads didn't think, however; they were simply attracted by bright lights and loud noises. That had been the point of the fireworks, Sam realized with a shudder.

He passed under the gate, trying to figure out where to go next. He would continue to make his way toward Deacon — once he figured out how to find him, of course. Abigail had known his location, but now Sam would have to find the Ravager leader on his—

A low thump sounded behind him, and something punched him between the shoulder blades. *Not again,* he thought, as he collapsed to the ground in pain.

Steps crunched in the leaves as someone approached.

Sam tried to reach for the bag, and the weapons within, but spasms of pain wracked his body, and he was unable to extend his arm. A steel-toed boot dug under his chest and flipped him over.

"Bean-bag rounds are a bounty hunter's best friend," Sam's assailant said.

It was the bomber. He wore those same round, reflective welding goggles over his black-and-white scarred face. At some point during the chaos, he had exchanged his detonator for a black combat shotgun. At the moment, Sam was just glad the weapon hadn't been loaded with more birdshot.

He leaned over Sam, looking him over with his hidden-away eyes. "Damn," he said. "I was hoping you were the Reaper." He withdrew the detonator from his pocket and thumbed the button, triggering another explosion within the settlement. "C4 stuffed Plague-Heads," he said through a cracked chuckle. "No one ever expects them. No one ever expects me either. 'Course, hiding an old-fashioned bomb-in-the-wall does help things get started."

Sam reached again for his bag, uninterested in the details of goggle's nefarious plan. He got a little further this time. The bounty hunter stepped across him and kicked the bag away, clicking his tongue disapprovingly at Sam. "Deacon might want you alive, boy, but don't think dead won't work," he said. He grabbed Sam's collar and hauled him, groaning, to his feet. "Now, come along easy and let's us figure out how I can keep my two special partners from cutting me out of the lucrative half of this bounty."

Sam reached for his boot, hissing against the sharp pain of the movement.

"What's that?" the bounty hunter said, laughing.

Sam's fingers found the knife, and gritting his teeth, he brought the weapon up and stabbed the bounty hunter twice in the unburned side of his neck.

Sam stared at his reflection in the man's goggles. "I said, I think I'm going to have to decline your offer," Sam said.

The hands holding Sam relaxed. The bounty hunter made a gurgling sound, and Sam stabbed him a third time for good measure. All he could think about was the sight of Abigail stabbing that rifleman, and what had happened afterward. He felt a wave of nausea and choked it back down. There would be time for that later.

For now, he had to get out of here. Feeling good enough to move, he grabbed his bag and his rifle, took a final look back toward the burning settlement, and ran off into the woods.

# PART 3

## The New Plan

DURING THE DAYS now referred to as 'The Fall,' the exchange of information and research among the world's scientists became increasingly fragmented. As a result, different parts of the world reached different conclusions regarding the Infected now colloquially referred to as 'Ravagers.' Doctors in Shanghai believed the phenomenon was simply as new stage in the lifecycle of the infection. Military leaders in the quarantine zones of the U.S. eastern seaboard were certain that these 'Ravagers' were not Infected at all, but simply normal people driven to extreme violence by the collapse of society. Once a third type of Infected, the so-called 'Howlers' emerged, this thinking was revealed to be incorrect.

*The Origins, Structures, and Effects of the Horseman Virus; Official Colonial Records.*

# 20

ABIGAIL SAT AT THE TOP of the high, rocky hill and watched as the last tufts of black smoke rose from the final embers of Mae's settlement. *How had things gone so wrong, so fast?* she wondered. And more importantly, when had she started to *care* about things? When had she started to care about people?

It was that boy, Sam. What was it about him that caused her to feel so...so attached? She didn't even want to think about what almost happened last night. And even discounting her...moment of weakness, under the moon, her behavior as of late was disturbingly atypical. Up till now, she had never cared about anything, much less another person. And much, much less a simple Uninfected person like Sam.

Abigail had always assumed she was simply incapable of caring. Just as a matter of biology. She had been a Reaper as long as she could remember. If it were possible, she would have assumed she had been born a Reaper. And Reapers didn't feel things like loss, or regret, or sadness. They were predators, nothing more, and nothing less. Solitary, and completely independent. A tiger didn't feel guilty about how another tiger looked at it when it fed; a shark didn't feel ashamed at what it was. What was happening to her?

She cracked another femur, and then she scraped the marrow into the soup pot simmering over a small camping grill. She had found Mae's stash of bones and brought them up here with her, along with a water bottle filled with three dead Plague-Heads- worth of drained spinal fluid and one can of condensed chicken soup. The slowly-simmering concoction wasn't pretty, and it sure wasn't going to taste good, but she didn't have much of a choice but to choke it down. Mae was right, she had gone days without medicating, and what little strength she still had she had used up healing from that damned gunshot. She needed to recharge. And this was the only way. Part of her was glad Sam had left. She didn't want him to see this.

Over her travels, Abigail had listened to countless stories about Reapers, told by all sorts of Uninfected that hadn't the slightest clue that Reapers sat among them. One of the most persistently-expressed myths was that Reapers were essentially vampires, undead demons who fed off of living human blood in the night. For the most part, this conception was equal parts ridiculous and inaccurate, but at times like this, boiling a pot of human remains, Abigail felt uncomfortably like one of the blood-suckers from the Old World tales.

Reapers didn't feed on human blood, at least not primarily. Abigail got hungry and ate normal food just like any other Uninfected. She had no aversion to garlic or crosses, and she quite liked silver. Sunlight made her itch, sure, but that could be attributed to her fair skin tone. It certainly didn't make her burst into flames.

Certain stories did have a kernel of truth to them, however. Abigail could heal quickly from all but the most serious wounds, and consuming human blood — or even better, bone marrow — did accelerate the process. She could also see at night as well as during the day, and she was far stronger and faster than a normal teenage girl her size would be.

Also, if she didn't consume human spinal fluid at least once every week, she would begin first to shake, then to seize up, her skin going ashen. If she persisted in denying herself her grisly medicine, she would eventually die in senseless, contorted agony. Solomon had taught her this shortly after he had taken her in.

Solomon, her savior and her tormentor. He was a Reaper like her, but considerably older. He liked to say he was one of the first, maybe even *the* first, but he did like to brag, and Abigail didn't put much stock in his tales. She did take his lessons to heart, though over the years she had wondered more and more about the cost of those lessons to her soul.

Solomon had found her in the ruins of old Salt Lake City, thirteen years earlier. He had discovered her, abandoned, starving, and twitching uncontrollably. He had fed her, given her a place to stay, and eventually taught her what it meant to be a Reaper, what it took to survive as one. When she had been younger, she had marveled at her luck: not only had she been found by someone who would take care of her, but he was another Reaper, like her. It was only later that she realized it had been anything but luck, and just how much of what Solomon had told her was lies.

Abigail sat back and ate her soup. Even after a single sip, she felt the tingling numbness that had settled over her arms and legs begin to recede. The wound on her neck stopped burning a few minutes later. She sighed in relief. She didn't know why the marrow and the fluid worked, just that it always did. Solomon had explained it to her long ago, telling her that the Horsemen Virus wasn't even a virus — it wasn't even technically alive — but that it still wasn't perfect. As though that somehow explained why spinal fluid kept her breathing, or why blood and bone marrow gave her vitality. Solomon threw out a lot of words like molecular reassembling, and bioengineering, and gray goo. *He did like to make himself sound wise*, she thought. He probably was making it all up, but she could not dispute the practical results.

*Just like he obviously lied about my ability to have emotions.* She wasn't cold and unfeeling because she was a Reaper, but because she had been raised and trained by a sociopathic maniac. She had felt something for Sam — whether it was simple friendship or something more, she didn't know — and now, he was gone.

And so too would her feelings go. Sam had made his choice, cast her away, and she had been a fool to think he would choose differently. Maybe she had felt something, but that didn't mean she had to keep feeling it. She would forget about Sam, she decided. She finished her soup and stood up, leaving the grill as she walked away. She didn't need it anymore. She didn't need anything. She didn't need anyone.

✝

Abigail heard her pursuer long before she made her move. She smelled him, though he was still over a hundred yards back, and she saw him, in a quick, casual glance backward, catching his slinking form despite the dead darkness of night. The hunt was on. The funny thing was, he thought *he* was still hunting *her*.

Mae couldn't have been more wrong about Abigail losing

her edge. If anything, her senses were stronger than ever. That could be because she had just topped herself off with her medicine — as she preferred to call it — or it could be because she no longer had Sam to distract her. In either case, the night belonged to her, and not the foolish Uninfected at her heels.

The wooded ground was uneven, covered as it was with streams and boulders, hills and cliffs. It wasn't hard to duck out of sight and double back around, or to reposition up on a rock face above where her pursuer would soon pass. She waited, breathing softly and evenly, watching him approach in the bright black and white of her nighttime vision. As he came closer, she silently pulled the knife from her back. *Not long now*, she thought.

The pursuer stopped, still back ten feet from her position, and slowly raised his rifle. *Had he seen her? Impossible.* She stayed still and waited as he peered forward through his weapon's scope, then turned back 180 degrees and looked back the way he'd just come. He knew something was wrong; that was evident, but he wasn't sure what it was. *Good instincts*, she thought. *Just not quite good enough.* He had not once looked up — he, like most Uninfected, tended to think in two dimensions. *Just a few more steps, you fool,* she thought, *and then I can put you out of my misery.*

But he did not come forward. Instead, he turned and began to run in the opposite direction, back the way he had come. *Shit,* Abigail thought. *Smarter than I thought.* She dropped to the ground and gave chase.

Her pursuer didn't get far. Even if she hadn't been a Reaper, she was young, and he was old. He heard her steps when she got close — she cursed her eagerness, she needed to remember caution — and he turned back, firing his rifle twice in her direction.

Neither shot came close. He unsheathed and swung a shiny chrome Bowie knife when she got near enough, but again, she was quicker. She dodged one way and raised her blade, and rather than cut her, his wild swing simply drove his wrist into the point of her knife.

His cry of pain was cut short by an elbow to the face. He crumpled to the ground, and Abigail came down on top of him, pinning his arms to the earth beneath her knees. She pulled her knife from his wrist and rested its blade against his neck, and he stopped the last of his struggles.

"You should have learned by now that the night belongs to the Reapers, old man," she said. She felt like her old self again — like a hunter, a killer — and she smiled.

The feeling didn't last. Neither did her smile.

"Yeah, following you didn't seem like the best idea I'd ever had. But, these are desperate times," the old man said, calmer than she expected him to be.

"I'd say your times just got as desperate as they are going to get," Abigail answered. "You are going to tell me everything you know, or you're going to bleed out here in the dirt. The choice is yours."

He sighed, seemingly reticent to talk. She pushed the knife a bit harder against his neck.

"Okay, okay. I'll tell you whatever you want," he said. "Though I don't rightly know what you expect me to say that will be of any use."

"How about you start with telling me who sent you?"

"Deacon, who do you think?" he said, spitting. "That crazy bastard said you'd know he'd be after you."

It was true: Solomon's last little gift to her had been bringing her to Deacon. After she had escaped, she knew it was only a matter of time before he came after her. And if she'd had any doubts, those Ravager patrols to the east had tidily put them to rest. Still, working with Uninfected bounty hunters was new. She didn't know the Ravager had it in him.

"I don't know what sort of world we're living in," the old man continued, "that one of his kind would send people like me after one of your kind. Humans hunting monsters, for different monsters. I really am getting too old."

*Join the club*, Abigail thought.

"How did you know I'd come to this settlement?" she asked. "Deacon had no way of knowing that."

The old man shook his head, as much as he was able to under the knife. "That wasn't the Ravagers, that piece of intel. That was provided by another one of the bounty hunters," he said. "I should have known better than to go in with him, but then again, I should have known better than to hunt Reapers. Figured with all three of us, we might stand a chance. It was a good price, even without the bonus of Deacon not smashing in my skull."

Abigail felt suddenly cold. It was happening all over again. "This bounty hunter," she said. "The one who knew where I would be: what did he look like?"

"Umm, he was short. Wore all black, like you, and a mask over his mouth. A hood. Called himself Null. Dead, black eyes. I don't know much more about him than that."

She put a little more pressure on the knife. A tiny bead of blood formed near its tip. "Think harder," she said.

"Okay, just wait. Please, just wait, and let me think." His eyes looked around wildly in the dark as he tried to recall details. "He had a real raspy voice. I remember that. Like his voice box was damaged, or he'd been sick. I remember that. Or it could have been those cigarettes he kept smoking."

*No*, Abigail thought. *No, no, no. It can't be.*

"These cigarettes," she said. "Tell me about them. What did they look like, how did he smoke them?"

"How did he smoke them? I don't know. I don't even know where he found the tobacco. Haven't seen it myself, not in years. I do remember that he rolled them himself, if that helps. Did it with one hand. It was kind of an impressive little bit of dexterity; I don't mind saying it."

Abigail raised her head and screamed. Solomon was alive.

To his credit, the bounty hunter kept his composure, despite having a knife to his throat and a screaming Reaper perched on top of him. At length Abigail calmed herself, and looked back down at her prey.

"Where is this bounty hunter, now?" she asked through grinding teeth.

"I wish I knew," he said. "Probably ran when things went south, like I did. Or maybe he's after the boy."

"Why would he be after the boy?" she demanded. "It's me that Deacon wants."

"If you say so," the old bounty hunter said. "All I know is, we come back with at least one of you, or we don't come back at all. Deacon won't accept failure." He sighed. "Maybe I should have left either way. Smart Ravagers. What is this world coming to?"

*Solomon couldn't be going after Sam, could he?* Abigail knew the answer was yes. He hadn't come after her, or she'd be talking to him right now, and Solomon wasn't one to simply give up. He had set his eyes on Sam.

*Sam might be able to handle Plague-Heads and Ravagers,* she thought, *but he wouldn't have a chance against Solomon.*

Abigail had to find him first.

Coming to this decision, she noticed for the first time the familiar howls that had begun echoing through the forest.

On the ground below her, the bounty hunter seemed to be thinking about them as well.

"If that raspy-voiced bastard wants the boy, he'd better hurry," the Uninfected said. "Because if I'm hearing them right, those Howlers are sounding mighty hungry."

Abigail pulled the knife away from his throat and slid it back into its sheath. "When you wake up, you start walking east, and you don't look back," she said. "I see you again and I'll eat out your guts while you're still alive. Understand?"

"When I wake up?" he asked, confused.

Her fist was already coming down.

She picked up the unconscious bounty hunter's rifle and slung it over her shoulder. Then she set out to find Sam, praying that she wasn't already too late.

# 21

SAM HEARD THE HOWLERS calling to one another. Each of the terrible, almost-human howls echoed off the mountains, each call sounding like it was everywhere at once. He thanked what little luck he still possessed that he had found the remains of this Old World lodge to take refuge in for the night. Maybe, if he was real lucky, he might be able to get a few hours sleep tonight, after he made contact with the Black Hills Colony.

Unfortunately, his stupid radio did not seem to want to work. He checked the frequency again, pointed the antenna out the door and up toward the open sky, and he again squeezed the call button.

"Sam Brennan, ID number 01-13-697, requesting call confirmation from home. Repeat, Sam Brennan, ID number 01-13-697, requesting call confirmation from home. Is anybody there; please respond."

His only answer was more static.

Sam cursed and stopped himself from throwing the radio against the half-rotted wall in frustration. He had no idea what he was doing; it was time to admit that. For all that he insisted he was ready for more time in the Wilds, that he was ready to be a full Ranger, now that he was out here, he finally understood how grievously unprepared he really was. He didn't even know how to work a stupid radio. One of the Colony radios would bounce a signal off the atmosphere — he thought — but he had no idea how one of these Wilds models worked. For all he knew, this piece of junk's effective range could be little more than a few hundred yards.

Vincente had been the one who knew what he was doing, and now he was gone. And then Sam had turned to Abigail — who he didn't even know, how could he be so stupid? And she'd turned out to be…well, she had been what she had always been. What he had been too blind to see. A monster.

A Reaper.

The image of her crouching over that dead man flashed through his mind for the hundredth time. The image of her…*eating* him. Sam wondered how he could have been so naïve, trusting the strange Wilds girl. *We first met because she kidnapped me, for God's sake.* And he had trusted her, despite himself. He had trusted her to lead him, and he had trusted her to watch his back. He had trusted a Reaper — the same kind of monster that had killed his parents — with his life. *I tried to kiss her.*

And why? Because she was pretty? Because he was scared, so soon after losing Vincente to those damned Ravagers? Because for some inexplicable reason he had felt like he could talk to her, like he hadn't been able to talk with anyone, not even Vincente, since he had lost his family all those years ago?

He knew the truth now. He knew it was because she had been manipulating him. That was what Reapers did, after all. They killed, and they manipulated. They didn't actually care about anyone besides themselves; everyone knew that.

They certainly didn't care about their…food. Sam didn't know what she was using him for, and he didn't care. He was just glad he was free of her, that he had seen her true nature before she could carry out whatever evil plan she had no doubt been plotting.

But he had survived, and he had gotten away. *And with any luck,* he told himself, *I will never see her again.*

Maybe the radio just needed higher ground. Sam grabbed his rifle and left the lodge, beginning a hike up to the nearest hilltop. It was a long shot, but he needed to do something. He couldn't just sit around all night worrying about what was going to happen next and reliving all his past mistakes.

He heard another howl as he was about halfway up the hill. *It's still far away*, he told himself. *They're still far enough away.* He had plenty of time to get up to the hilltop and back down to the safety of the lodge before any Howlers reached him. He hoped. Every fiber of his body wanted to turn back, to run and hide, but he set his jaw and ignored the flight impulse. Fear had become his constant companion, out here in the Wilds, and he was growing more used to it with every passing day.

The hill's peak turned out to be much lower than it looked from below. Sam could see the outline of the real mountains, dark against the bloody sky along much of the northern and eastern horizons. *I'm still not high enough*, he thought. But this was the best he was going to do tonight, so he might as well give it a try.

"Sam Brennan, ID number 01-13-697, requesting call confirmation. Repeat, Sam Brennan. Is anybody out there, for God's sake?"

As before, there was no answer over the radio. Not at first.

Sam heard a strange crackle against the static, and his ears perked up. He listened closer, as what sounded like a voice whispered faintly across the signal, fading in and out of decipherability. Sam adjusted the frequency dial, his heart rate picking up. Going up the band lost the voice, so he dialed back down, and the static died away.

"Repeat, is anyone there?" the voice, male, said. "Please repeat, caller, please acknowledge."

Sam fumbled for the call button.

"I'm here," Sam said. "I can hear you. Who am I speaking to?"

"Sam Brennan," the voice, now crystal clear, said. "I've been waiting to speak to you."

Sam's blood froze. "Who is this?" he said.

"I've been watching you, Sam," the voice said. "I know what you want. What you are looking for. Who you are looking for."

Sam's hand dropped down to the freshly recovered pistol on his hip. "Oh yeah?" he said. "Why don't you come out in the open, then, and we can talk face to face?"

"All in good time, Sam. All in good time. For now, I have something to tell you. Something you want to hear. Something you'll want to remember."

"And what would that be?"

There was a long bit of static silence before the voice spoke again.

"I can give you directions to our mutual friend. The Ravager you know as Deacon. Is that something you might be interested in?"

Sam heard more howls — closer now. He had to get back to the lodge. *But I also need answers.*

"And why would you want to tell me that, Mr. Mysterious?" Sam asked. "How do I know you aren't just trying to lead me into a trap?"

"To answer your first question, let's just say I would benefit from his elimination. And maybe I'm just curious to see if you are up to the task. In regards to your second question: the simple answer is that you don't. Trap, no trap, you have no way of knowing. You are right to mistrust me, after all. I'm nothing but a stranger on the radio. But I don't think you'll resist my offer. Finding Deacon, after all, is the only thing you have left. Now, listen carefully-"

The voice listed off a set of coordinates, and even an Old World city to use as a marker. Sam listened intently, and he committed the information to memory. The voice was correct, unfortunately: Sam could take precautions against a trap or ambush, but he couldn't ignore the chance to find Deacon and the information drive. More than that, he didn't have any other leads to follow. He had no other choice.

"Is that it?" Sam asked. "No more explanation of who you are, or how you know who I am?"

"Well, Sam, I'd like to talk more, but it appears that you have some visitors. If you turn your head approximately 120 degrees west from its current orientation, I believe you will see what I mean."

The voice was watching. And he was apparently not the only one. Sam slowly moved the rifle from his shoulder to his hands and turned to the west, unsure of what he was going to see.

At 120 degrees, just like the voice said, he saw them. Two sets of cat-like, yellow eyes, looking out from the gray darkness of the tree line. And they were both set, animal-focused and unblinking, on him.

The Howlers were here.

# 22

UP UNTIL THAT MOMENT, Sam had always wondered if a Howler would look as frightening in real life as they did in pictures. Now that he was face to face with one, he knew the truth.

In the flesh, the beasts were far more terrifying.

Ravagers and Plague-Heads both looked different from an Uninfected person, but the differences were relatively subtle. Plague-Heads had splotchy greenish skin and a complete disregard for personal hygiene; Ravagers had overdeveloped muscles and bulging, bloodshot eyes. Sure, if you were standing nose to nose with either variety, you would know something was very wrong with them, but they were still basically humanoid. And he knew now that distinguishing a Reaper from a human was harder still. Howlers were a different story. Howlers, once human like any other Infected, were twisted and transformed by the Horsemen Virus into something less, and at the same time something much, much more.

Each of the two Howlers standing in front of him was well over seven feet tall. Still retaining the basic shape of a person, their upper spines were curled sharply forward, so the tops of their heads were lower than the caps of their overgrown shoulders. Their front arms had become extended, so much so that they nearly dragged along the ground in front of them. Their fingernails had been replaced by things closer to claws, and their teeth by what could only be described as fangs, or maybe tusks. Coarse, bristly hair covered their faces and bodies. Sam could only describe them as a chaotic mix between orangutan, dog, and man; and yet that description hardly did them justice. On the whole, the Howlers were somehow even worse than the sum of their parts.

And then there were the eyes. Vertically slit like a cat's, oversized, and colored a bright angry yellow, they seemed to glow in the faint light of the evening. In those eyes, Sam could see both frightening intelligence and primal hunger. It was like looking into the very face of nature at its most brutal and pitiless.

Sam began slowly raising the barrel of his rifle to a firing position. So far, the Howlers had done nothing but stand there and stare at him, but any sudden movement could trigger their predator instincts, and then they would be on him. Granted, they would probably be on him soon, regardless of what he did or didn't do. Sam just wanted to make sure he was ready when they finally made their move.

Sam nearly had his weapon in position before he realized what the two staring Howlers were doing. They were distracting him.

Sam caught a flicker of motion at his side. It was a third Howler, a fourth; they had surrounded him.

In a way, this realization was a relief. There were no more decisions to make, no more chances to second-guess himself or make the wrong call. Because now, Sam had only one way out of this that didn't involve a stopover in a Howler's digestive system.

He had to attack.

Sam shot the first Howler in the head. His new assault rifle, courtesy of Mae's armory, spit out a burst of three bullets, killing the Howler instantly. The second Howler screamed in anguish and fury; from the right, a third Howler charged.

Sam snapped his weapon around just before the Howler reached him. He squeezed the trigger again and again, and bullets thudded against the Howler's wide, hairy chest in a syncopated, staccato beat. The mass of rounds slowed the beast's charge somewhat. Rather than impacting like a truck at full throttle, the beast only — only — hit him like an Old World linebacker.

He twisted the rifle around to brace against the Howler's fangs. Sam felt the monster's claws hit his shoulder, and he prepared for a rush of pain as they cut into him. The pain never came, as the strength ebbed away from the Howler.

Its body fell limp a second after it slammed into Sam, and with a final hot wheeze of carrion breath, the Howler died. Sam twisted and pushed the Howler away with his gun. He spun around wildly, breaths coming in heavy gulps, as he tried to locate the remaining Howlers.

One of the Howlers found him first. It slammed into his back, claws first, hissing. Sam's vest, another piece of equipment scavenged from Mae's, kept the claws from cutting into his flesh, but the impact was enough to knock the wind out of him and throw a wall of white stars onto his field of vision.

He rolled forward as best he could with the impact, and the Howler's momentum carried it, flipping head over feet, past Sam and onto the ground.

Unfortunately for Sam, as the monster passed it caught

a set of claws on his rifle, and with its bestial strength, it ripped the weapon from his hands and tossed it away.

Sam pulled his pistol. The Howler was back on its feet, faster than he believed possible, and it smacked the gun away before he could fire. The other claw ripped across Sam's chest. The vest again saved him from a potentially killing slash, but the oversized hand hit him like a baseball bat. The blow took Sam off his feet, threw him back onto the ground.

Right next to his rifle.

Sam rolled forward, grabbed the rifle, and raised it. The Howler pounced. Sam fired.

The shot went wide and the Howler smashed into Sam, slamming him back into the ground. The Howler roared and bit, its jaws snapping inches from Sam's face. He could smell rotten meat on the monster's breath; a bit of its slobber dripped onto his cheek. All that kept Sam alive was his rifle, held sideways between him and the Howler. Sam pushed with all his strength, fighting to stay alive for a few more precious seconds while he tried to think of a way out of this.

No ideas came to mind.

The Howler grunted once, a strange, surprised noise, and then its jaws suddenly relaxed. Its head lolled to the side, its muscles went soft, and with a final sigh, its ragged breathing ceased. And just like that, Sam found himself surrounded by silent, black night.

He waited for the next Howler to fall on him, but none came. The pack seemed to have dispersed. He wasn't quite sure what had just happened, but it appeared he was still alive. Now, he just needed to figure out how to get the gargantuan dead Howler off his body before it crushed him.

He needn't have worried. He heard a vaguely feminine grunt, felt the weight of the Howler carcass pulled off of him.

"I can't leave you alone for a moment, can I?" Abigail asked. She stepped over to the fallen Howler and removed her knife from the back of its head. She wiped the blood from the blade against her thigh and sheathed the blade at the small of her back.

Sam sat up and scrambled away from her. "Get away from me," he said, gathering his rifle to his lap.

"It's good to see you too, Colony boy," Abigail said. "You're welcome, by the way."

Sam wasn't having it. "You lied to me," he said. "You traveled with me all this way, and you didn't tell me what you were. You let me think you were a human."

Abigail rolled her eyes. "I am human, just as human as you are. As human as these three dead goons," she added, pointing to the deceased Howlers. "That is, if we're speaking strictly scientifically."

"You're a Reaper."

She nodded. "I'm a Reaper."

"What the hell do you even want with me?" Sam demanded. He rested one hand near his rifle's trigger, not quite pointing the weapon at her, but rather in her general direction.

Abigail ignored the weapon and crouched down, looking Sam directly in the eye. "If I'm being honest, Sam, I don't really know. But what I can tell you is that I don't mean you any harm, and that nothing I've told you, not since we've met, has ever been a lie."

Sam shook his head and laughed wearily. "Nothing you've told me has been a lie? That's a nice way of putting it. You may not have lied, but you didn't exactly tell me the truth. You didn't think that it was worth mentioning that oh, I don't know, that you're a *fucking Reaper*?"

"And why do you care so much?" Abigail asked, raising her voice in response to Sam's agitation. It was some of the first actual emotion Sam had witnessed from her. *At least since that strange, dreamlike night under the moon.* One he wished he could forget.

She sounded genuinely upset, and for a moment, Sam could almost again think of her as human. "What do you even know about Reapers, Sam?" she asked. "You said it yourself: you've never even seen one of them. Everything you know comes from rumors and old wives' tales, and most, if not all, of those stories are lies."

"I know Reapers killed my parents," Sam spat back. "That's a story I'm damn sure is not a lie."

"And I'm sorry that happened, Sam," she said, speaking quieter now, but no less desperately. "But it wasn't me that killed them. Uninfected kill every day, but I don't hold you responsible for their actions. Why can't you see that? Just because I'm a Reaper, doesn't mean I'm not also just Me."

Sam thought about her words for a long time. Around them, now, the crickets and the frogs again began to sound, confident that the fighting had ended. Overhead, a few white stars peeked through the gaps in the trees.

Sam wanted to believe Abigail's words. He did, more than anything. *But how can I?* he wondered. How could he be sure that every word out of her mouth wasn't another piece of careful manipulation? How did he really know she looked at him as anything other than food?

"I watched you…eat that guy," he finally said. "If I stay with you, I'll always be wondering when you'll decide to make me into your next meal."

She looked at him for a moment, then shook her head and let out a weary laugh, her hands on her hips. "It's not like that, Sam. At all," she said. "If you just let me explain—"

Sam shook his head. "I'm sorry," he said. "I can't believe anything you say, Abigail. Thank you for helping me, but I just can't. Please, just leave me."

"Sam…"

"Leave me!" he yelled, raising his rifle. "Or try and kill me. One way or the other, I'm done talking."

She took a step back from him, but she didn't look away. Her expression was unreadable, a hundred different emotions and none dancing across her face. Sam held his weapon as tightly as he was able. He hoped that in the low light she was unable to see him trembling.

"Sam, you stupid, stubborn fool," she said. "Go then. Go on your own, and get yourself killed. You won't be able to say I didn't try."

Sam said nothing. Abigail turned and walked away, disappearing into the night. Sam exhaled and lay back down, trying to convince himself that he had done the right thing.

# 23

HE OPENED HIS EYES, emerging from a blackness that seemed eternal, bottomless. It took him a few breaths to remember who he was. His name came back to him a moment later.

It was Vincente.

A hard-backed chair pressed against his sore back. His hands were chained to the chair's arms, his feet to its legs.

"Slow down, son," a man told him, leaning over and shining a penlight into his eye.

Vincente tried to duck away from the painfully bright light. The man firmly grabbed Vincente's head and pulled open his eye with a thumb.

The light clicked off. "The good news is that you're going to live," the man said.

He was inside a large, mostly empty warehouse. Stripes of pale sunlight painted the floor around him, slanting in from the broken and decaying roof high above.

"That's great," Vincente croaked. "Follow-up question. Where am I, and who the hell are you?"

The man gave him a weak smile. "Technically, that's two questions," he said.

Vincente narrowed his eyes.

"Okay," the man said. "I'm a doctor. The...man in charge brought me in to make sure you didn't, and I quote, 'finish shuffling off this mortal coil.' And it wasn't easy work, let me tell you. Bullet wounds, internal bleeding, subdural hematoma — really, when they brought you in you had more wrong with you than right. But I did it, and that's why they pay me the big bucks. So don't you go trying to thank me. A job well done is thanks enough."

"And the money, I guess," Vincente said. He shook the restraints binding his arms. "I'd shake your hand, but that seems to be a little tricky at the moment."

The doctor shrugged. A Wilds doctor, through and through.

"Yeah, well, I can't take all the credit," the doctor said, removing an infuser — itself attached to a familiar looking hanging bag — from Vincente's arm. "The truth is, without some of the tech those Colony mercs brought along with them, your injuries probably would be have been beyond even my skills. How did the commercial go, right before the Fall? 'Plasmamites get the job done right,' or something like that. It was a catchy little jingle."

"What Colony mercs?" Vincente asked, his mind suddenly racing.

"Some guys came in just after you, from the west. Montana by the looks of it. Mostly soldier, but a couple of scientists too. Of course, those uptight Old World lab coats just turn their noses up at folk like me."

"What did their uniforms look like? Did you catch any of their names? What are—"

The doctor winced and shook his head.

"I've already said more than I should. Like I told you before, I'm just hired help. Let me ask you this: do you remember what happened, before you got hit on the head?"

The thing was, Vincente didn't remember. He had no idea when, or how, he had come to be here. His whole sense of continuity was off. It was as if he found himself in a dream, the kind where you just sort of *appeared*, right in the middle of it. He tried to think back, to call up the last memory he had; he tried to *will* the blanks in his mind to fill themselves in.

And they did. He almost wished they hadn't. He remembered talking with Elder Jed and leaving the Colony with Sam. He remembered arriving at the Jackson underground research station and finding it already breached and invaded. He remembered the control room, the drive, the Ravagers, and the bridge.

And he remembered the bullets tearing through him. The bridge collapsing, and falling among the Ravagers, bloodied and broken. He remembered the large Ravager picking him up, raising the cleaver, and the gleaming block of metal coming down toward his face…

"Okay," the doctor said. "I can see it's all coming back to you now."

Vincente gasped, his heart suddenly pounding. He could feel cold sweat starting to bead on his brow. "You have to unchain me," he said. The man was a doctor, which meant he had to be an Uninfected. "I — we have to get out of here. Now."

"I'm afraid I can't do that," the doctor said. "Like I said before, I was hired to do a job, and that job only involved waking you up. And even if I wanted to help you escape, I wouldn't know where to begin. So, rather than staying here and debating the finer points of the Hippocratic Oath and the tenets of professional ethics with you, I'm going to leave, and I'm going to go and tell Deacon that you're awake."

"Please, man…"

"I'd say good luck, but I'm afraid you probably used up the last bit of that when you managed to peel open those eyes. But hey, buck up. You can take solace in the fact that you helped me earn a nice heavy bag of gold coins."

The doctor stood up and walked toward the warehouse doors. Vincente considered yelling after him, but he knew there wasn't any point. He had met countless men like the doctor, both out in the Wilds and back at the Colony. They were cowards and opportunists, and any sense of decency or responsibility toward their fellow man had long ago withered and died within their hearts. No, Vincente was on his own, he knew that now. He only hoped that Sam had gotten safely away.

Vincente didn't have to wait long for Deacon to arrive. The warehouse doors flew open and the Ravager leader came strutting in, trailing two smaller Ravagers in his wake — a tall female with half of her hair coarsely chopped off, and an even taller skinny male with a fist-sized ring of metal punched through the middle of each of his cheeks.

"If it isn't Rip Van Mother-Fucking-Winkle," Deacon said, his too-cheerful voice booming across the cavernous warehouse. "I was beginning to think you were going to snooze forever, sleepy head."

Vincente watched without expression as the three of them approached. He knew he wasn't likely to survive this, and he was okay with that. He knew this was a brutal world, and that every time he went outside the Colony walls, there was a good chance he wasn't coming back. He wasn't looking forward to whatever Deacon had planned, but he could take it. His only regret was that he wasn't able to destroy the drive. He should have done it as soon as he had found it, but he'd been worried it would have made too much noise — that it would have alerted the Ravagers. He could appreciate the irony of his current situation, even if he didn't particularly like it.

When the Ravagers reached him, Deacon grabbed a metal folding chair from a pile of debris to Vincente's right and dragged it over to him, the legs grating noisily against the concrete floor. The noise burned like acid inside Vincente's still very sore brain.

Deacon sat down and stuck a thick, dirty finger under Vincente's chin, pushing his head upward. Vincente stared into the Ravager's blood-red eyes, trying as hard as he could to betray no emotion, to give nothing away.

"How you feeling, precious?" Deacon said. "You know that you took a bit of a blow to the head, right? Not to mention a few bullets to the…well, pretty much everywhere."

Behind him, the two Ravager sycophants laughed. Vincente didn't react.

"It doesn't feel like I have a gash cutting halfway into my head, though I haven't had much of a chance to look in the mirror," he said in a cool, level voice. "I take it you hit me with the flat side of the cleaver?"

Deacon laughed. "Well, I couldn't just kill you, now could I? Then who would I have to talk to?" He gestured with a thumb at the Ravagers behind him. "This lot is good for smashing things up, but they're not exactly sparkling conversationalists."

If the other Ravagers were offended by their boss's comments, they didn't look it. On the contrary, they seemed to take pride in Deacon's words. *Those two are the kind of Ravagers I'm used to,* Vincente thought. *Dumb and proud of it.* Deacon was the strange one; more in common with a psychopath Uninfected than a homicidal Ravager. Mentally, at least. Physically, he appeared to have all the berserker strength of a Ravager. Vincente remembered the secrets that Elder Jed had told him before he and Sam had left on their mission. Seeing this Ravager close up confirmed every word of them. And that was very bad for everyone.

"I'm afraid I'm not really feeling up to talking right now," Vincente said. "I have a bit of a headache. Maybe you should come back tomorrow."

"Oh, we're going to talk right now," Deacon said, his voice low and gravelly. "See, I've been waiting for you to wake up for a long time, and I don't care much for waiting." He pulled a white, circular drive from his jacket pocket and waved it in front of Vincente's face. "You're going to tell me all about this little drive, or I'm going to let my friends here start cutting pieces off of you."

At this, the girl Ravager pulled out a large, serrated knife. Vincente looked over at her, making sure not to show any fear, and shook his head.

"You can cut off whatever you want, but it won't help me tell you things that I simply don't know," Vincente said. "Don't get me wrong, I'd prefer it if we could skip the whole cutting-things-off step, but the fact remains, I'm just a gofer. My bosses tell me to get something, and I get it. That's what I know about the drive. Somebody wants it. I'm guessing you already know this."

The female Ravager grinned. "It's cutting off time," she said eagerly. "I want an eye."

She moved toward Vincente and he turned his head away. Deacon let her knife flick against his cheek before he grabbed her by the shoulder and pulled her roughly back.

"Let's just hold on a minute, girl. We don't want to seem over-anxious in front of our guest, now do we?" Deacon said.

Her only response was to lurch, knife-first, at Vincente again. Deacon effortlessly held her back with one hand.

To Vincente he said, in a cooing voice, "Do you really want this to turn bloody? All you have to do is answer some questions. Just tell me what you know, and this doesn't have to turn into a mess."

Vincente shrugged. "Sorry, pal," he said. "I think I'd prefer to talk with the lady here."

The woman with the knife laughed maniacally. Deacon relaxed his grip on her, just a bit, and she inched closer and closer to Vincente. She waved the ugly, jagged weapon out in front of her; even tilting his head as far back as it would go, the swipes were close enough for Vincente to feel the breeze from the passing blade.

"So you're not afraid of a little pain," Deacon said. "I like that. If you don't want to talk about the drive, maybe you'd like to talk about your little friend Sam instead?"

*Shit*, Vincente thought. The mere fact that Deacon knew Sam's name was bad enough. If the Ravager had Sam here, or if he had already hurt the boy...Vincente was now scared in earnest. He couldn't help himself; he needed to find out if the kid was all right. But he needed to be smart about it.

"Keep the girl away from me, and maybe we can talk," Vincente said. "Just don't let her cut on me, that's all I ask."

Deacon rose and pulled back his arm, effortlessly hurling the female Ravager across the room. "Nice try, Vincente," he said. "But if I was a guessing boy, then my little guess would be you're more concerned about our mutual pal Sam than any of Roach's imminent knife-work. So how about a little of the quid-pro-quo, eh? You show me yours, and I'll show you mine?"

"Ugh. First thing's first. I want to see Sam."

Deacon thought about this, cracking the knuckles of one gargantuan hand, and then the other. "No," he said. "We can't bring Sam in here. We wouldn't want our two captives — pardon me, guests — exchanging any information, now would we?"

*Bullshit.* Vincente smiled. "You don't have Sam," he said. "You probably never did."

"And why are you so sure about that?"

"Come on, man. Everything about you is cruelty and self-entertainment. There's no way you would miss out on a chance to hurt us in front of each other. Hell, you probably wouldn't miss a chance to double the audience for your little folksy monologues."

Deacon's fist darted out like a snake, popping Vincente in the nose and cracking his head back. "We'll catch the little shit soon enough, don't you worry about that."

Vincente laughed. "You won't catch him. My guess is that you've probably been trying and failing the whole time I've been out. Sorry, Deacon. The boy is gone."

"Send me, chief," the female Ravager — Roach — said. "No more sheep-men. You send me; I'll bring you back his skin."

The walkie on the third Ravager's hip chirped, and he walked away to answer it.

Deacon patted Roach on the shoulder. "This is the kind of enthusiasm I like to see," he told Vincente. "If you love your job, you'll never work a day in your life." To Roach he said, "We don't need to worry about killing poor Sammy anymore, little girl. It's only a matter of time before his companion does that for us." He turned back toward Vincente, resuming his seat on the folding chair. "Oh, that's right, I forgot to tell you. Your little friend has taken to traveling with a real, bonafide Reaper. Now, how long do you think he can survive that? How long before that Reaper starts getting thirsty?"

The third Ravager walked back to them. He tapped Deacon on the shoulder.

"Chief," he said, "we got a call."

"I can see that, Bobbo. I'm a little busy right now. You deal with it."

Bobbo nodded and walked away again, whispering urgently into his walkie.

"Look, Vincente," Deacon said. "The way I see it, you've got two options. Option A: you tell me about this drive, and I kill the Reaper that has your boy. Option B: you keep this 'mums the word' act going, Sam gets turned into a juice box, and then I kill you anyway. And by the by, I've met this particular Reaper: if you think I'm bad, you have no idea. So why not do us both a favor, to make no mention of poor Sammy, and just choose option A?"

Vincente didn't know what to believe. Deacon could be lying about the Reaper, he could be lying about not having killed Sam, he could be lying about his ability to do anything at all. One thing Vincente was certain of was that Deacon was not sincere in his offer to help. No, he couldn't tell the Ravager anything, no matter how much he wanted to help Sam.

He shook his head. "Sorry," he said. "I can't help you."

Deacon suddenly stood up, violently kicking his chair behind him. "Tell me about the drive!" he roared. He stepped forward and kneed Vincente in the stomach, hard. "Tell me!"

Vincente was having trouble breathing. He felt like he was going to be sick, but he said nothing.

Deacon crouched down, grabbed a fistful of Vincente's

hair, and wrenched his head upward. "You know what I think?" Deacon hissed. "I think you know a lot more than you're letting on. I think you know exactly what is on that drive.

He let go of Vincente's hair and stood up, laughing. "Why do we have to keep secrets from each other, Vinny? Why do we have to talk in circles, saying everything except what we really mean?"

Deacon paced in a circle, rubbing his hands together and chuckling to himself, back to the sunny mood he had begun their conversation in. Vincente didn't know if the Ravager's rapid mood swings were an act, or if Deacon was really this unstable. Either possibility was frightening.

"I guess one of us has to take the first step, Vinny, and I'm just going to go ahead and be the bigger man here. You saw that Colony tech we had stuck into your arm, and you've heard me talk. You know — and don't pretend you don't, I can see it those big brown eyes of yours — that I'm not just a Ravager anymore. See I got my hands on the improved virus, the Horsemen 1.5 your so-called 'Elders' have been working on. I've got it running through my veins." He slapped Vincente on the shoulder and smiled wide, a few inches away from his face. "I guess you can call me the world's only Ravager 1.5, huh Vincente?"

Vincente had guessed as much by now. The Elders had told him of the improved virus, 'clandestine work by rogue scientists,' as they had put it, though Vincente had little doubt the work was being done on the Elder's orders.

"But the 1.5 isn't good enough, Vinny. No, what I really need is what's on that drive, because what's on that drive is the future. With what's on that drive, I can be the most powerful man in the world. I can rule the—"

"Where did you get the 1.5?" Vincente asked. There was

no point in playing dumb now. Deacon would get around to torturing him either way; and Vincente knew in his heart he was strong enough to die without giving him the codes."

"See? Now isn't it nice to just shoot straight with each other? Feels good, huh? Well, if you must know, I had my very own anonymous benefactor. Gave me the virus, lab equipment, even some know-nothing Uninfected to set the whole thing up. He was probably another one of your Elders, too, but it doesn't matter, because he delivered the goods. Of course, after he sent his little helper to me, things kind of got messy, but that's what happens when you deal with Reapers. But you know that, right Vincente?"

"I know what?" Vincente asked.

Deacon wagged a finger at him, clucking his tongue. "Come on, Vincente. It's too late to pretend that you don't know the truth about what's really going on in the dark centers of your precious little Colonies. Just give me the codes, Vincente. Please, just help me out. Help yourself out. We both know about the dark storm on the horizon, coming for us all."

"Chief," Bobbo said, holding out the walkie. "We got another call."

"Not now, Bobbo," Deacon hissed through gnashing teeth.

"Why do you still have the drive?" Vincente asked, smiling. "You should have sent it on south, to your so-called King, or whoever else is holding your leash." He laughed, though it now hurt to do so. "No, you're looking to make your own play, and you need whatever is on that drive for leverage. Leverage, Deacon; you know, that thing that I have all of here, and you have none?" Vincente relaxed his head back against the cold metal of the chair. "You can't kill me, Deacon. You probably can't even risk hurting me.

Because I'm the only one who can unlock that drive for you. Without that happening, you have exactly nothing."

Deacon clenched his fists as his face turned first red, then almost purple with rage. He slowly raised a giant fist. Vincente braced himself for the coming impact.

"Chief," Bobbo said again.

"What?" Deacon screamed. Bits of spittle splashed on Vincente's cheek and nose.

"We've got a problem, chief," Bobbo said. "Two sentries are down, shot from long range. I think we might be under attack."

Deacon's anger evaporated. "No," he said, a smile tugging at the corners of his lips. "It's just our long-expected visitor, announcing his presence." He reached out and patted Vincente on the cheek. "See, I never even needed to go hunting for little Sammy. He was nice enough to come straight to us. We'll have to continue this conversation later, Vincente. I'm afraid I have to go and collect our mutual friend."

Deacon laughed and walked away, the other two Reapers following closely after. Vincente listened as the warehouse doors opened and then groaned slowly shut. He worked again at the bindings that held him. *Sam couldn't really have come here,* Vincente thought. *He would have been smart; he would have left me behind and headed back to the Colony.*

But he knew Sam, and he knew that wasn't true. In his heart, he knew Sam was here.

# 24

IF SAM DIDN'T NEED HER, then she sure as hell didn't need Sam.

And yet, here she was, staring across Deacon's camp, watching as Sam set up traps and shooting positions and sight lines all along the basin's far ridge.

She had intended to abandon him, she really had. When he told her to leave — after she had saved his ungrateful ass from a pack of Howlers, no less — she had walked away. She had turned her back and strode out of those woods just as fast as her Reaper legs would carry her. She had moved faster than Sam would have possibly been able to, and subsequently, she had rapidly opened up a great distance between the two of them. The distance he had wanted; the distance she was now more than happy to give him.

But then she had come across the remnants of the Old World town, and she had stopped. The now-ancient ruins had been picked over, but not well, and there was still a great deal of scavenge to be found, as well as a fair number of good shelters still standing. She told herself that was why she had lingered there, why she had stayed, when any time before she would have quickly moved on.

She had transportation: sometime recently it appeared

another band of travelers had met their demise at the hands of the many Plague-Heads milling about town, leaving behind three working and gassed up motorcycles. She had brought the largest of the three to the bi-level motel where she had set up camp, and she was ready to move out at a moment's notice. She could travel a hundred miles in any direction; all she had to do was choose. Yet still, she stayed.

And after a couple of days, Sam had wandered into the town. Abigail told herself she was surprised, but really she wasn't. It was, after all, the logical direction he would travel. She watched him, unseen, as he found the remaining bikes and grabbed one, and it wasn't till after he motored away that she finally left the town.

And followed Sam here, to the very heart of Deacon's operations.

She didn't know for certain how Sam had found the place, but she had her suspicions. Which was why, for the first few hours, while Sam was working his way tentatively closer to the edge of the basin and a clear view of the actual base, she had circled the ridgeline, looking for the person she knew had to be close. Solomon.

If he was here, he was doing a better job of hiding than she had thought him capable. She rounded the ridge twice — each time coming undetected within feet of poor, oblivious Sam — and not only didn't find Solomon, but didn't see any evidence that he had ever been here. Was she going crazy? Was she imagining that her former Master was behind this? That he was behind what had happened at Mae's? Was she imagining that he was even still alive? All she had to go on were the words of an ancient Uninfected bounty hunter, a parasitic husk left over from the Old World. Just like Solomon, really — excepting the changed physiology, Solomon was Old World corruption personified. And she had seen Solomon die; she hadn't imagined that. Could she be simply jumping at shadows?

Ultimately, it didn't matter. Solomon was dangerous, there was no doubt of that, but he was no more dangerous than the growing mass of Ravagers and the menagerie of other people down in Deacon's camp. That was the real threat to her, just like it always had been. And that was the real threat to Sam.

But what could she, by herself, really do about it? Fighting a pack of Howlers, or a swarm of Plague-Heads, or even a war-party of Ravagers: that was one thing. Taking on a horde, that was something else entirely. And this was not her fight, was it? This entire thing had started because she'd wanted to get away from Deacon after Solomon had sold her out, because she wanted to get *away* from this place.

She turned away from the camp, away from Sam. She scanned the far horizon: flat ground and grainy sky in all directions, save for a few towers of red stone, a few scattered islands of stringy white clouds, and the fat dark tufts of dust kicked up by some far-away herd of beasts. She stood up and began to march away. She couldn't help anyone here. She couldn't keep Sam from throwing his life away. And she had decided, finally, that she wasn't going to try. There was nothing she could do here; not by herself.

†

Sam pulled the trigger, and then he began to count. *One thousand one, One thousand two...* the head of Ravager in his sights snapped back, and a moment later he tumbled down from the improvised watch tower like a marionette whose strings had been cut.

*That one seemed to get their attention.*

Sam was under no illusions: what he was attempting was crazy. However, despite the drunken caravan traders tales of thousand-strong Ravager hordes, he hadn't truly expected Deacon's outpost to consist of a significantly larger force than the one he'd encountered in the underground Colony. Twenty, maybe thirty Ravagers, tops.

Upon his arrival, Sam had found something very different.

Deacon's base, laid out among the sand and scrub grass in the basin below Sam's position, looked more like a small city than a camp. It had congealed and grown around the remnants of an Old World mining station, like a spreading rot. There were two large, half-decomposed warehouses and a collapsed drilling station at the camp's center, and around these permanent structures stood uneven circles of tents, trailers, and Old World vehicles in various stages of disrepair.

And spikes — lots of spikes. Walls of sharpened wooden poles, jagged and rusting metal beams, smashed and broken junk, hundreds of them jabbed into the ground in patterns of drunken spirals, with strands of barbed wire running from one to the next. It looked like a blind madman had been in charge of walling in the camp, if that was indeed what the spikes were intending to accomplish. But then again, based on what appeared to be mounted on many of the spikes, Sam considered that they might simply be there as a place to store excess decapitated heads.

Among the chaotic and gruesome infrastructure were at least a hundred encamped Ravagers. And, as if that wasn't bad enough, there were more than Ravagers down there. Sam observed a giant, improvised cage, filled nearly to bursting with Plague-Heads. He'd never seen so many in one place, well over a hundred. It was a full swarm, like the ones that had burned through the major Old World cities in the early days of the Horsemen Virus. Near the pen of Plague-Heads was a honey-comb of smaller cages, each containing the hunched-back, bristle-covered form of a Howler.

Then there were the Uninfected. Sam had spent a good deal of time watching the camp before he took his first shot. Much of that time had been spent trying to make sense of the side-by-side co-existence of a Ravager force with an apparently Uninfected one. But that was what he saw. A second, smaller camp — more orderly and far less gruesome — existed within the larger one. This smaller camp was occupied by smaller people; people that moved with purpose and organization, unlike the chaotic and often violent movements of the Ravagers in the outer camp. Most of these Uninfected looked like mercenaries or highwaymen from the Wilds, but not all of them. A single small and unassuming tent sat pitched at the far side of the Uninfected camp, tucked back against the rock wall at the edge of the basin. Sam saw two figures enter and exit this tent; both wore outfits that were as disturbing to him as they were familiar.

They wore the uniforms of Colony Elders.

Deacon had built up what looked a whole hell of a lot to Sam like an army. One composed of at least three of the four Infected, as well as Uninfected, including Colony leaders. This was a force built for war — for conquest — and only someone truly insane would try to assault it by themselves.

Or someone with nothing left to lose.

## 25

IT WAS THE SOUNDS OF THE BEASTS that gave him away. It was their movements, subtle but noticeable, moving back toward her, when earlier they had wanted nothing so much as to get away, that alerted Abigail to the presence of someone else. Someone other than herself and the cattle. Someone that frightened the herd as much as she did.

Another Reaper.

Deacon's camp was behind her now, nearly all the way to the southern horizon. She had stopped near the herd of cattle, and had just begun to plan out her next move, when her shadow finally made his appearance.

The herd of feral cows, like most animals, seemed to be able to smell the difference between the Infected and the Uninfected. They knew to fear Plague-Heads and the Ravagers, who would kill them for no apparent rhyme or reason. They knew to fear the Howlers, who knew nothing besides hunger and the hunt. And they knew, in the very core of their beings, to fear the Reapers, who were nothing less than death incarnate.

She spoke first, before Solomon had the chance.

"You're back," she said. There was really nothing more to say. She had long since expressed everything she'd wanted to say to Solomon, and she damned sure had heard every-thing from him that she was interested in hearing.

The only answer she received for a long while was silence. Maybe Solomon wanted her to doubt that he was really here, maybe he wanted her to doubt herself? Or...maybe he also simply had nothing left to say.

Abigail severely doubted that last possibility. She turned and strode around the edge of the herd, toward the spot from which cattle were milling away. Toward the spot where she knew he was waiting. She wanted desperately to be away from her former Master, but there was something that she wanted far more.

She wanted this to be over. And the only way that would happen is if she confronted him once and for all. So, she continued to walk toward him, when every instinct, every heightened sense she possessed was telling her to turn the other way and run as fast as her legs would take her. She walked forward, prepared to end things, one way or another.

Finally, just before she reached the far end of the herd, Solomon spoke.

"It's been a long time, daughter," he said. He spoke, as he always had, in little more than a whisper. If Sam had been here, he wouldn't have heard him over the din of the herd, their shuffling hooves and heavy breaths and brays of agi-tation. But Abigail heard him. As she had for as long as she could remember, she heard him just fine.

She found him sitting on a metal folding chair, one leg crossed over the other, working at an apple in his hands with a tiny knife. There was no way the chair had been here — they were in the middle of nowhere — so Solomon had clearly brought it with him. He'd carried it all this way in hopes of realizing some esoteric, unfathomable effect; Abigail had no idea what purpose he was hoping to achieve, but meaningless, empty gestures were something of a specialty with Solomon.

"I hope you don't mind that I decided to sit here and wait for you, child, rather than seek you out direct. It felt rather appropriate, as I always seem to find myself waiting for you to catch up."

"Well, I guess you can't win them all," Abigail replied, rolling her eyes. She took a quick mental inventory of her weapons. She had her blade, and a single pistol. Neither would likely serve much use against her former master. She also had the explosives in the satchel strapped to her lower back, and for a moment she had the crazy desire to set them off. Sure, it would kill her, but it would also kill him. Every time she had to listen to one of Solomon's patronizing little sermons, she had the overwhelming urge to kill both of them.

"You have been a very bad girl," he said, cutting free a slice of apple and putting it in his mouth. "I would have thought—"

"Save it," Abigail said, cutting him off. "I've heard it all before. What are you doing here, Solomon? I don't think I could have made things any clearer the last time we saw each other."

Solomon chuckled to himself, the soft laughs coming in short, ragged bursts. Even after all these years the sound still made Abigail shiver. "Yes," he said. "You did make your feelings abundantly clear. You, and that pathetic band of Uninfected. They're all dead now, I suspect. But I'm not upset that you tried to kill me, dear girl. I am only upset that you left."

"There's no reason to stick around with a corpse," Abigail said. "And, as I recall, you sold me like one of these cattle to Deacon."

"Is that what you think?" Solomon asked. "That I simply gave you over to him, to do with as he pleased? You were to be my eyes and ears within that filthy camp. You were to *oversee* the camp."

"Well, let's just say Deacon didn't get the message. He was about ready to start cutting me up, just like he had with the rest of his 'test subjects,' when I made my escape."

"Along with my lab equipment, as I recall. Setting back my work for months. Driving Deacon into the hands of that pathetic band of Colonist refugees from Montana. Honestly, there is simply no end to the problems you cause me, child."

"Same old Solomon," Abigail said. She pulled the knife free from her back and let it hang in her hand at her side. "I'm happy to end those problems for you once and for all, right here and right now. You just sit there quietly, and I'll finish what the fire started."

Solomon just stared at her, his face devoid of any emotion. He didn't look like much, sitting there. He was a short, slim man of indeterminate age, with close-cropped dark hair and eyes of jet black. There was nothing remarkable about his appearance; he was utterly forgettable. He always said it was one of the things that made him such a good hunter. People looked past him, ignored him until they noticed his unnatural calm, the hollow emptiness of his voice. By then, it was too late for them. But Abigail was ready for him, ready for whatever trick he was waiting to pull.

"I suspect you think I'm going to attack you," Solomon said, calmly cutting another slice of apple. "I can assure you that I mean you no harm."

"Good," Abigail said. She pulled a pistol from the back of her waist, pointed it at his head, and fired.

†

Sam led the Ravagers' car just a bit before he pulled the rifle trigger. The bullet exploded the vehicle's front tire. It veered one way, and then sharply back the other, before catching an edge and flipping over sideways. Another car followed close behind it, packed with well-armed Ravagers; seeing their compatriots taken out didn't seem to dissuade them from driving headlong at Sam. He gave them credit for courage, but then again Ravagers didn't actually feel fear like normal people did. Sam centered the driver in his sights and fired again. The bullet caught this one just below the left eye; the car went careening sideways as the Ravager in the passenger seat struggled to grab the wheel.

It was time to move.

Taking out the two lead cars bought Sam a little breathing room; the next set of Ravagers were piled onto a modified fire engine several hundred yards back. Sam still had a few moments before they got high enough on the hill to spot his position, and he didn't plan to be here when they did.

Deacon's camp was set into a depression surrounded on three sides by a horseshoe of ridges and jagged red cliffs. Sam had spent a good deal of time before he took his first shot locating, planning out, and preparing a series of firing positions that would hopefully allow him to stay one step ahead of the Ravagers' counter-attack. Now, he was about to see if all the prep work had been worth it.

Hugging his rifle to his chest, Sam slid down a short steep slope. Slinging the weapon over his back, he then set to climbing an uneven wall of rust-red rocks, his hands finding easy grips in the pockmarked sandstone. He grimaced as he pulled himself up, the pain in his shoulder wound flaring up for the first time in hours. Reaching the top, he crouched behind a small stone rise that shielded him from the camp below. This wall would serve as his makeshift battlement, and his second firing position.

He looked through his rifle scope, first back in the direction that he'd come — the fire engine was still heading toward his original position. Swiveling, he turned his attention to the camp below. He scanned the entire camp as quickly as he could, looking for Deacon. All he needed was one clean shot. Once Deacon was down, Sam was convinced the other Ravagers would fall into chaos. Chaos and infighting were a Ravager's natural state, after all; it was only Deacon's strength and intelligence that held this group — this army — together. *At least I hope so.*

Unfortunately, Deacon was staying out of sight. Sam wondered if he was even here. After all, what did he have to go on besides a set of directions given by a creepy anonymous voice on the radio? It was possible this was just some random Ravager encampment, wasn't it? Sam had spent much of his journey to the base pondering these very doubts, and even now a part of him wondered if he wasn't dangerously misguided in coming here.

But a larger part of him didn't doubt at all. Once he had seen this place, the sheer horrific scale of it, Sam had known at once that this was Deacon's home. This was where things were going to end.

Sam ducked back from the rock wall as a burst of gunfire erupted from the camp below, striking nearby. He shook his head in frustration. Where was that bastard? Deacon didn't seem like the type to cower in some bolt-hole while his home base was under attack, yet he still hadn't appeared.

In fact, many of the Ravagers and all of the Uninfected had taken cover below — the base was under better discipline than Sam had expected. For about the thousandth time, he wondered if he should simply abandon this mad plan, return to his scavenged dirt bike, and make a break for it.

*Though it might be too late for that,* he thought. The fire engine skidded to a stop at Sam's first firing position, and a dozen Ravagers hopped off either side. *This better work,* Sam told himself. He unclipped the detonator from his belt, armed it, and squeezed together the leads.

The explosion threw Sam back and into the air. He shook the cobwebs from his head and scrambled back up to see the results — hearing nothing but a high-pitched ringing in his ears — and watched as what was left of the fire truck slowly slipped back down the side of the bluff toward the camp. Much of the ridge around it was simply no longer there. The blast had cut a half-moon crater into the cliff face, and had reduced all the fire engine's resident Ravagers to body parts.

There were still more Ravagers in pursuit, however. Sam grabbed his rifle and made his way to his next firing position.

# 26

SOLOMON MOVED FASTER than any person should have been able to, Reaper or no. He was out of his chair before she had finished squeezing the trigger; he had knocked the pistol out of her hand and was at her throat before she could begin to readjust her aim.

"You never should have left," he hissed, pressing the tip of his knife against her throat.

"And you should have stayed dead," Abigail answered, raising her leg and smashing down on his foot as hard as she could, and then driving an elbow into his solar plexus. She spun 360 degrees and connected a roundhouse kick to his chin.

The kick propelled Solomon up into the air, then down onto his back. On hitting the ground, he rolled backward in one smooth motion and sprang to his feet, smiling.

"You can never just make things easy on yourself, can you, Abigail?" he said. "That's why you headed out on your own. That's why you took that pathetic boy under your wing, and that is why you're still fighting, even now." He feinted one way and then darted in another, hooking an arm under Abigail's knee and flipping her airborne as he passed.

She raised her arm up in time to cushion part of the impact, but her head still knocked against the ground hard enough to make her see stars. She scrambled to find her footing and stand back up, a great deal less elegantly than Solomon had a moment earlier.

He clicked his tongue in disapproval, circling around to her right. "Still too slow," he said. "I'm beginning to think you're never going to be quick enough. Certainly not if you continue to insist on living out here, among the dead and the forgotten. I gave you a chance to be part of the future, part of a new world, and you threw it back in my face. Tell me, Abigail: did I waste my time in keeping you alive?"

Abigail grabbed a fistful of dirt and threw it in Solomon's face, following behind with a series of lightning-quick punches and elbow strikes. Techniques Solomon had taught her, many years ago. He was able to block most of them, but a single fist got through his defenses and struck him in the nose, forcing him back and at least temporarily shutting him up.

"What would you have me do, Solomon? What is your future? More skulking around in the shadows, more killing travelers and destroying settlements? That doesn't sound like much of a future to me."

The cattle had begun to back away faster from the two fighting Reapers. Their snorts and moos were becoming more agitated. Abigail could empathize. Solomon, however, was as infuriatingly calm as ever.

"You saw the future," Solomon said. "You just came from it, after all."

He lunged forward and kicked at her knees and her thighs, trying to incapacitate her. It was one of the first fighting techniques he had taught her, back when she was still a little girl. Abigail danced backward, away from the flurry of blows. She knew that even if she blocked them, they would still bruise her legs, still slow her down.

"Where I just came from?" she said, trying to understand. "Where, Deacon's camp? Even for you, Solomon, that is crazy. Deacon is a madman; you know that as well as I do."

Finally Solomon kicked too high, and Abigail stepped forward and grabbed his heel. She wrenched it upward and pulled him off his feet.

He should have slammed down onto his back. Instead, he jumped with her pull, launching himself into a back flip and catching Abigail under the chin with his other foot as he did so. He landed light on his feet, like a vampiric cat, and then smiled as Abigail shook the cobwebs out of her head. *This isn't working,* Abigail thought. *He's too fast, and too strong, to beat in a straight fight.*

"You are right, Abigail," Solomon said. "And at the same time so, so wrong. Deacon is a madman, but he is *my* madman. He is one of the many tools in my belt, a weapon in my arsenal for the war that is soon to come."

"What war, Solomon?" Abigail demanded, her voice cracking mid-shout. She was finally losing what little cool she had left in the face of her former Master's cryptic insanity.

"Why, the only war, my dear. The last war. The one that was started twenty years ago. The war for what we will become."

He stepped forward in a flash and struck her twice before she could react. Once in her stomach, and then once directly between her eyes. Abigail stumbled back and collapsed to the dirt, her ears ringing and her vision going blurry. She did the only thing she could, and crawled away from him.

"You were always behind this," she croaked. "You never stopped holding Deacon's leash, this whole time." She saw her pistol, several feet away, lying near Solomon's discarded switchblade knife. "That's why he's still here, why he hasn't taken that drive back to his Ravager king in Colorado." She crawled toward the gun: it was her only chance, even if it wasn't a good one.

"Yes, well, in a manner of speaking. Deacon still believes he is the one in charge, and of course his new Colony allies have forced me to take a more subtle tact. We have to work behind the scenes, child. It's the only way we win this war. Whether it's some petty Ravager lord or a band of rogue Colonists, or even if it's you, child, the trick remains the same. You give your orders in a way that makes your subject think she's the one making the decisions. Or did you think you arrived here, with me, by accident?"

"Talk like that reminds me just why I burned you alive, asshole," Abigail said, slowly continuing to make her way toward the weapon. All his talk of manipulation, and of being in control, it was just talk: talk she had heard from him too many times before. Now, here, she only hoped that Solomon's monologue would help distract him from her true purpose. That all he would see was her beaten and trying to escape him; that his pride would blind him to anything else. "So it's what, you against the Uninfected? Against the Colonies? Your strength and speed against their tech? Even you can't be so far gone that you think that's a fight you can win, Solomon."

"Wars within wars within wars," Solomon said. He walked casually past her, his arms folded against his chest. He kicked the pistol away, toward the cattle. "But nothing so simple as you might think, my dear Abby. I mean, honestly:

Reapers vs. Uninfected, do you really think my master plan could be so trivial?" He crouched down in front of her and tilted his head, silently posing her the question.

"There were Uninfected down there," Abigail said, more to herself than to Solomon. "In Deacon's camp. Colonists, high ranking ones."

"Yes. My enemies have their armies, and I have my own. They have scientists and technology, and I also have my own. What I needed was my second in command, someone I had groomed for the job their entire life. Someone who would take orders without question, execute them without pity. Someone who would obey!"

He shouted the last word, spittle flying out of his mouth and his cheeks turning crimson. It was the first time Abigail had heard Solomon raise his voice, even after knowing him for more than a decade. It confirmed what she had always suspected: that beneath his cool, contemptuous façade surged a deep well of rage and hatred. He was no better than Deacon, really. He was just slightly more polished.

"Sorry to disappoint you, *Master*," she said, curling her hand into a tight fist. She gripped the weapon she had really been crawling toward, the tiny knife Solomon had thrown away and forgotten. She formulated one final, insane plan. *I'm only going to get one chance at this,* she thought. "It looks like I won't be able to help you in your mad campaign against the Uninfected."

Solomon stood up and let loose a booming laugh. "You still don't understand what this war is, little girl. Let me ask you this: How long did it take your little friend Sam to figure out what you really were? The Uninfected can't tell us from one of their own, not like they can the rest of the Improved." He gestured toward the cows. "These simple animals can see the truth plain, whereas the pride of the old humans makes them blind. Their lack of vision allows them to be deceived and to be killed. It allows them to be disposed of, to be made meals of. To be wielded, without their better knowledge. Now tell me, Abigail: who do you think leads the various Colonies of this great new world? What do think each and every Colony Elder is?"

"No..." Abigail said, her voice cracking. Her left hand, hidden by her prone body, palmed the knife and turned in so she was holding the blade flush against her wrist. She rolled over onto her back, feigning weakness, while the other hand went to the satchel on her back.

"Yes, Abigail," Solomon continued. "Every one. Even your precious Sam was sent out here by a Reaper, to find the last weapon any of us will need to purge the final remnants of the Unimproved. The weapon, my dear, that an oblivious Deacon now possesses. The weapon I will use to finally defeat my enemies, and take my rightful place as the ruler of this new world. You could have been a part of that, Abigail. Even today I had hoped to change your mind, to put you back on the path. Now I see that was a foolish hope. All you have left to do for me is die."

This was the best chance she was going to get. She rolled toward him and buried the blade in the meat of his calf. *Maybe that would shut him up.*

She was back on her feet in an instant, raining blows down on Solomon's hunched over body. He recovered his wits quickly, and after no more than a few free punches Abigail found him again blocking and dodging each of her attacks.

He sent a punch her way, aimed square at her nose, and she ducked underneath it and darted close in to Solomon, her chest pressed against his stomach. She reached around him and grabbed him by the belt with her free hand, the one that had earlier been holding the knife. She bent her knees and lifted with all of her strength, moving to pick up Solomon and slam him down to the ground.

He easily countered her, putting a leg between her own, stopping the lift. He brought an elbow down viciously into her shoulder, and her arm went numb. The next thing she knew, he had turned and flipped her into the air with a hip throw, and she was again flat on her back on the ground, looking up at him. Of course, this time both of her hands were now empty. She reached again into the satchel at her back

"Such a slow learner," Solomon said, smiling ruefully. He looked down at her and shook his head. "I wonder what I ever saw in you."

"We all have our blind spots," Abigail said, her fingers finding the last object still in the satchel. The detonator. "We all miss things. Things that might seem obvious in retrospect."

Solomon's smile died just as Abigail's appeared.

"Like why an apprentice would try on the master a throw that has never once worked before," she said, as Solomon realized what she had left under his belt.

She squeezed the detonator and Solomon disappeared with the blinding bright ball of the explosion.

It took a second for the ringing in her ears to cease, and for her vision to unblur. Solomon's body may have shielded her from any of the explosion's shrapnel, but its concussive blast had hit her hard and good. When she felt steady enough she stood, walked over to what was left of Solomon. The charred pieces of him stared back up at her, lifeless and indifferent. She took one last look at what was left of her master, and then she turned away.

"Good riddance. Father," Abigail whispered.

She smiled, satisfied with her work. Then she jogged back to her bike and fired up the engine. She still had one more job to do today.

# 27

THE EXPLOSION RATTLED THE WALLS and the ceiling of the warehouse. There was a loud, long groan, and then a tearing sound as an enormous section of the roof paneling came loose. It fell end-over-end, trailing a comet's tail of dust and dirt and rust down to the floor, where it flattened one of Vincente's Ravager guards like a shoe squishing a caterpillar against the pavement.

Roach, the female — and now the sole uncrushed Ravager guarding him — was silent for a long moment, her face covered, as was Vincente's, in the other guard's blood. And then she laughed, a loud, ragged and maniacal cackle that almost made Vincente wish Deacon was back with them. As much as he hated and feared the Ravager leader, at least he seemed almost halfway sane. Vincente had no such confidence in Roach's mental health.

It turned out he didn't have to wait long for the Ravager leader's return.

Deacon yanked open the door — the sounds of distant gunfire becoming for a moment much louder and more immediate — and slammed it shut behind him.

"Get three more mooks and start wheeling out the shield-wall," Deacon shouted. He eyed the remains of the roof paneling and the male Ravager — Bobbo — squished beneath it, and made a sour face. "Four more mooks, I guess. It looks like this whole 'taking Sammy alive' plan is going to be a big hassle, and frankly I'm sick of waiting."

Roach stared at Deacon for a long moment before uncertainly pointing to herself.

"No," Deacon said, shaking his head. "I was talking to the Colony Jack tied to the chair. Obviously I want our hostage to escape, go out and grab reinforcements. Dammit, Roach, sometimes I really do wonder about you."

"Why don't you just send me after this Sam?" Roach asked. "I'll bring the boy back here. Mostly alive, even."

Deacon pulled out a revolver and cocked back the hammer. The weapon's loud, metallic click bounced off the warehouse's remaining intact walls in a series of pinging echoes.

"How's about you go and do what I say, quick-like?" he growled. "I'd hate to have to splatter what little brains you've got all over poor Vincente, here."

"Right, chief," Roach said nervously. Turning on her heel, she practically sprinted for the exit.

Deacon walked up to Vincente and struck him hard in the shoulder with the heel of his hand. Vincente spun in his chair, felt himself jerked backward as Deacon grabbed the backrest just above Vincente's head. With a lurch, he began pulling Vincente toward the warehouse door, the chair rolling on its rear two wheels only.

"I have to do everything my own damn self," Deacon muttered. "Be glad you aren't a leader of men, my Colony-born friend. It's just one headache after another. I wanted to do things the easy way; but, well, you have to play the hand you're dealt."

As they reached the door, Roach and three other panting

Ravagers ran past. Vincente's chair was still facing back-ward, so he could watch as two of the Ravagers worked a vertical chain to slowly open the warehouse's enormous main doorway. The other two began to wheel what looked like a colossal section of fencing toward the steadily-wid-ening gap and the war zone beyond.

"Bring him out when I give you the signal," Deacon said, speaking with the Ravager nearest to him. He then leaned over Vincente's shoulder and looked him in the eye, smil-ing as he playfully ruffled his captive's hair. "Hope you're ready, pal. Because now, it's show time."

✝

Even Ravagers learned eventually. After being rebuffed twice — first by bullets and then by bombs — the latest three car-loads of Ravagers kept their distance from Sam. They had parked sideways, nose-to-tail, forming a make-shift barricade between themselves and Sam's rifle sights. For the moment, Sam and the Ravagers found themselves in a bit of a stand-off.

Sam knew this wouldn't last. Most likely, the Ravagers were simply pinning him in place with their gunfire while another group circled around to flank him. He hadn't seen any movement indicating that yet, but it was surely only a matter of time.

He looked down toward Deacon's camp again. Still no sign of the Ravager leader. Sam sighed. It looked like his plan had failed. He wondered, once again, just what Abi-gail would have done. Certainly something smarter than the idiot plan he'd come up with. He sent another burst of fire toward the nearest of the Ravagers, not really aiming, but just keeping them honest. He looked again toward the camp. There was movement, though it wasn't movement he understood.

Four Ravagers had left the safety of one of the camp's central warehouses. They appeared to be bringing something with them — two pulling at its front, and two pushing from the rear. Sam considered trying to pick off one or more of the Ravagers foolish enough to expose themselves, but then thought better of it. None of them were Deacon, after all.

Instead, he just watched through his scope and tried to figure out what the Ravagers were up to. The object looked to be some sort of wire wall. The metal was heavy, and each individual gap small, but the rolling wall wasn't so opaque that he couldn't see clearly through it. *What are they up to?* Sam wondered, wiping a band of sweat from his forehead.

And then Deacon emerged.

He strode, carefree, out from the warehouse and walked to the middle of the wire wall. As soon as Sam identified him, he was already lining up his shot. He pulled the trigger, leading Deacon slightly to account for his walk, and then fired three more times for good measure.

All four bullets pinged harmlessly off the wall. Deacon turned toward Sam and smiled. He raised his right arm in an exaggerated wave, his open hand swaying back and forth hypnotically.

The gunfire from the ridge abruptly ceased. Sam turned his head just in time to see the Ravagers scrambling back into their cars and, kicking up fat, circular clouds of red dirt, heading back down the hill toward the camp.

*Just what was Deacon getting at?*

The Ravager chief took something out of his pocket. It was a piece of paper, which he slowly and methodically unwrapped, before holding it up for Sam to read. On the paper were four numbers and a single dot: it was a radio frequency. With his free hand, Deacon unclipped a walkie from his belt and shook it in Sam's direction, in case Sam hadn't got the hint. Deacon wanted to talk.

Sam's response was another three bullets.

Again, they had no effect. Sam watched as Deacon shook his head and gestured toward the warehouse from which he had just emerged. A second later, another Ravager appeared, pulling a rolling chair to which a person was tied. Sam gasped as he recognized who it was. It was Vincente, still very much alive.

Sam scrambled for his radio and switched it on.

# PART 4

## The Last Chance

WHILE THE BIOLOGICAL STRUCTURE of the microbe commonly known as the Horsemen virus is unique from previous known infectious agents, the assertions that the disease was in any way engineered, or that its origins were in any way unnatural, are nothing more than dangerous and seditious propaganda, rooted in either fear or traitorous lies. Stories of the virus being not wholly organic, or any tales of nano-technological aspects of the virus, are similarly ridiculous and dangerous.

*The Origins, Structures, and Effects of the Horseman Virus; Official Colonial Records.*

# 28

SAM DECIDED THAT HIS PLAN, which had been marginally crazy under the best of circumstances, was looking worse and worse with every step he took. If his original plan had been nuts, his new plan was downright idiotic.

Deacon's camp looked far more foreboding down here on ground level than it had from the ridge above. While he could see less of it from this perspective — walking toward the front gates, trying hard not to piss himself — the features he did see were all the more strange, violent, and terrifying.

It was these details, the ones that didn't come through in the telescopic view of his sniper scope, which stuck most in Sam's mind. The contrast between the brick red of dried blood below the impaled heads and the burnt orange of ancient, sun-bleached rust on twisted metal; the jagged, uneven camp walls and palisades, wreathed in barbed wire. Also, it was the smell: spilled motor oil, stale beer, even staler vomit and gore, all slowly cooking under the mercilessly beating sun. Sam's nostrils twitched at the stink of roasting, burnt meats of unknown and dubious origin, at a dozen different rank body odors, their tang so ripe and rotten and sickly-sweet he could almost taste it in the back of his throat.

But above all, it was the sound that really unnerved him. The camp — which by all appearances should be filled with the sounds of chaos and primal revelry and the brutal, violent clangs of a war-machine buzzing with destructive potential energy — was all but silent. As Sam walked beneath the empty sentry towers and the open, abandoned gate, the only sounds that greeted him were the low, groaning creak of metal slowly twisting in the high-plains breeze and the far-away, almost plaintive call of a vulture high above, in the cloudless blue sky.

But there was no turning back now.

After Deacon hailed Sam over the radio, the Ravager boss had offered him a deal. If Sam would stop shooting and come down to talk in person, Deacon would release Vincente in exchange for the drive codes, and the two Colony scouts could then, in the Ravager leader's words, 'high-tail it back to your little teched-up hideyhole back east.'

Sam had immediately pointed out that Deacon's offer had all the hallmarks of an obvious trap. Deacon had laughed and cocked his pistol, leveling it at Vincente's head. 'We're all civilized folk here,' he'd said. 'Now why don't you hop on down here like a good jackrabbit, before I kill your friend for a second time?'

It had been a compellingly visceral argument, and one that Sam had reluctantly agreed to, on the condition that Deacon pull back all of his Ravagers and leave the three of them alone. Deacon, after a particularly colorful listing of his numerous qualms with this condition, had agreed, and the two of them came to terms.

Of course, Sam didn't for one second believe that Deacon *wasn't* trying to lead him into a trap. That was why he was currently wearing the remainder of his C4, lifted from Mae's armory, taped around his waist. It was wired to a detonator in his pocket; a quick click and a push, and everything within a 50-yard radius of him would be blown to hell and back twice over.

He hoped there was a way he could avoid using it, but as he approached Deacon and the tied-to-a-chair Vincente, he was having a hard time seeing how that scenario would be possible.

"Sam!" Deacon said jovially, waving at him with a hand holding an oversized, chrome revolver. "So glad you could make it!" He then looked at the gun in his hand and made an exaggerated, open-mouthed mime of embarrassment. "Where are my manners," Deacon said, tucking the weapon into the front of his jeans. "Now you don't make any sudden moves, Sammy, and that blaster of mine will stay parked right there. This is a good faith negotiation, after all."

"You shouldn't have come here, Sam," Vincente said from his chair.

Deacon turned and wagged his finger at Vincente, clicking his tongue in disapproval. "We talked about this, Vinny. We speak when spoken to, and not before. I'm trying to keep a semblance of order to these proceedings. If everybody starts talking at once, we'll never get anything done."

"I'm here, Deacon," Sam said. "Let's get this over with, and we can all go our separate ways."

"Right to the point. I like that," Deacon said. He turned his head to Vincente. "How about it, Vinny? Access codes, and then you two can ride off east, into the…well, not exactly the sunset, but you get the idea. I'll head west, to take care of some unfinished business. You'll never see me again. Never the twain shall meet, and all that."

"You know I can't give you the codes," Vincente said,

looking up from his bound position, his jaw defiant. But his eyes, when he looked to Sam, said something else entirely. Sam saw sadness in those eyes, and defeat.

"Vincente, just tell him," Sam said. "It's just crop medicine. What's the harm in him having it? What is he going to do, start Ravager farms?"

Deacon began to laugh, a low, languid, and mocking laugh. "Medicine," he said. "Is that what you told the boy, Vince? Hell's bells, how many lies is little Sammy's head filled with at this point, I wonder?"

"I'm sorry, Sam," Vincente said. "He can't have what's on that drive. It's more important than either of our lives."

"Why?" Sam demanded. "What were we sent to recover? What didn't you tell me, Vincente?"

Vincente began to speak, but Deacon slapped a meaty hand over his mouth, silencing him. "I'll take this one, Vin.

"What I have on my drive, and what Vincente here is about to give me the tools to unlock, is the culmination of your precious Colonies' long campaign to tame our wild, wild world. To wipe out everyone they don't already control by doing to the world's crops what Project Horsemen did to the Old World's population."

Deacon looked forward, at Sam, for just a second, before turning his attention back to Vincente. Laughing, he removed his hand from his captive's mouth. "That's the long and short of it, isn't it, *Vincente?* Fighting the good fight, one scientific genocide after another."

Sam waited for Vincente to shout down Deacon's lies. He waited for his friend and his brother to tell him that the mission, which had caused Sam so much pain and hardship, had been to save their Colony, to save lives, not simply to retrieve a weapon capable of so much death and destruction. But Vincente did not protest. He didn't argue. He simply stared at the ground and shook his head slowly.

"I had hoped to tell you when the time was right," Vincente said. "When we were safe inside one of the Free Cities in the Rockies. I wanted to tell you the truth."

"The truth about what?" Sam asked, his hands tightening at his sides.

"About the Colonies. About what they really are. *Who* they really are."

"A bunch of little kids with magnifying glasses, pretending they're scientists," Deacon said. "And the whole world, and everyone on it, just a bunch of ants, waiting for the next blast of concentrated, cooking sunlight."

"I wanted to tell you, Sam," Vincente said. "I was never going to take the drive back to them, but I couldn't take your home away, not until we had a new one. Once we reached the Resistance, I was going to tell you everything. I was going to tell you the truth."

"But now it's too late, and blah, blah, blah, etcetera, etcetera, etcetera," Deacon said. "You see, boys, the three of us ain't so different after all. So, why don't you go ahead and give me those codes? Do it, and nothing has to get bloody."

But Sam had come to a different conclusion. Vincente, for all his lies and half-truths, was right about one thing. Keeping the contents of that drive from Deacon — from anyone — was more important than all of their lives. It had to end here.

It all had to end.

Sam slowly moved his hand toward his jacket pocket, intent on the detonator within. He knew without question that he was entering the final seconds of his life, yet he was strangely okay with that. He had been ready to die to kill

Deacon, and now he saw that destroying that drive, that weapon, was even more important than simple revenge. He had accepted his choice.

But that didn't mean he wasn't scared. He could feel his fingers twitching as they moved closer and closer to the detonator. Slowly, slow enough to not arouse Deacon's suspicions. Slow enough he could feel every pounding of his heartbeat in his temples and chest and fingers and toes, like a dozen different sledgehammer strikes. Each second seemed to stretch out in front of him, a moment of infinity.

He felt the very edge of pocket fabric on the tip of his thumb. He took one final breath. He was ready.

And then he felt the hot jab of a blade on the inside of his bicep. Immediately his whole arm went numb. Then, the pain was in his shoulder, as his arm was wrenched away from his pocket from behind. Finally, a kick in the back of his legs forced him to his knees.

"Sam, Sam, Sam," Deacon said, now walking toward him, unprotected. "That was a very big mistake."

# 29

"I THOUGHT WE WERE ALL FRIENDS here, Sam?" Deacon said, ambling over to him. Sam's arm screamed with pain; he remained balanced on his knees only due to the iron grip of the Ravager who had snuck up on him from behind. He could hear her mad, low giggle in his ear, smell the rotten meat stink of her breath in his nose.

Now towering over him, Deacon reached down into Sam's pocket and pulled out the detonator.

"A bomb, Sam? Really?" Deacon said. "I thought you might try to shoot me — try to go out in a blaze of glory. But I didn't think you would take the concept so…literally. Get him on his feet."

Deacon grabbed Sam's jacket and ripped it open. He let out a long, low whistle as he looked over the fat gray columns of C4 wrapped around Sam's torso. He cocked his head as he inspected the wiring closer, and satisfied he wasn't going to activate some sort of booby trap, Deacon yanked the detonator away from Sam, snapping the cord that connected it to the bombs.

"Well, you certainly weren't going to half-ass it, Sam. I'll give you that," Deacon said. "Those charges would have taken out half of my base." He tossed the detonator away and patted Sam on the cheek. "Normally I'd have to torture someone who tried to do that to my home; but damn it, kid, I like your moxie."

Deacon turned away for Sam for a brief moment; then he turned back and backhanded Sam across the chin with the side of his revolver.

Sam blacked out for a heartbeat, the blow lighting his whole head up with an electrical storm of pain. He tasted blood in his mouth, felt bees buzzing in his ear.

"We do have business to get to, however," Deacon bellowed, strutting back toward Vincente. "And it looks like I'm going to have to stop asking nicely."

Sam shook his head, trying to steady his swirling vision. His eyes came back into focus to see Deacon leaning over Vincente's shoulder, his pistol pointed right at Sam.

"Last, chance, Vince. I'll make it real simple: give me the codes, or I put a bullet in Sam. Right here, right now."

"Ummm, chief," the Ravager holding Sam in place said. "Can I get out of the way before you start shooting?"

"Can you move?" Deacon shouted back, incredulous. "No. You stand right there, and you keep your trap shut. What, are you afraid I'm going to miss?"

"No chief," she said, her raspy voice sounding less than certain to Sam. "It's just—"

"It's just what?" Deacon demanded.

"Nothing," she said. "I'll just stand here."

Deacon shook his head and rolled his eyes. "Well, I'm glad we've got that settled. So, Vin-*cen*-te: what's it going to be? Are we gonna have a happy ending, or am I going to turn Sam's head into a brain jack-in-the-box?"

"I'm sorry Sam," Vincente said. He squeezed his eyes shut and Sam prepared, again, for the end.

"Alright," Deacon said. "Have it your way."

He pulled the trigger and the gun roared.

A moment later Sam realized he was still breathing. He decided he must still be alive, because if he was dead and his arm still hurt this much...well, that would be a whole new level of unfair. He slowly opened a single eye and saw Deacon holding the pistol pointing straight up in the air, a tiny plume of gray-white smoke catching and fading into the wind above it.

"Oh thank God," he heard the Ravager behind him mumble.

"Damn it, Vincente," Deacon said. "You really were going to let me shoot the kid after all. Well bully for you, because this just became your lucky day. You get another chance to not be a complete damned idiot. What. Are. The. Codes?!"

"Screw you, Deacon!" Vincente screamed from his chair. "You may as well just shoot now; I won't tell you anything, never. Shoot me, shoot Sam, shoot yourself. Just end it!"

Deacon didn't speak for a long, hanging moment. When he finally did, his voice was soft, and again jovial. All his earlier anger was gone.

"We may come to that, Vincente," Deacon said. "First, I want to give you — and you too, Sam — a little demonstration." He put two fingers in his mouth and whistled loudly, and two Ravagers appeared at the Plague-Head pens. A wide, manic grin stretched across Deacon's face. "Ready boys? It's time for a little… science."

He gestured toward Sam. "Leave him, Roach. He's not going anywhere."

"You couldn't have told me that before you fired," Roach grumbled.

"Just get over here."

The Ravager — Roach — patted Sam on the top of his head hard enough to rattle his teeth, then hurried over to Deacon's side.

"I want you to see this, Vince," Deacon said. "Show you I'm not all bad. Show you it's okay to just quit throwing your obstinate little temper tantrum and TELL ME what I want to know."

He turned Roach around to face Vincente and put his arm around her shoulder. "Have a look at Roach here: Ravager through and through. Hunt, kill, smash, eat. Roach, like the rest of my Ravagers, has a basic mind; she's good at savoring the simple pleasures in life. To me: no problem there, I can dig it. But I know that to you sheltered Uninfected she's a little—"

He paused to let Roach growl at Vincente and snap her teeth at him.

"—a little frightening.'Mindless death-and-destruction machines' is how, I believe, you like to talk about them. But you can't say I'm mindless, Vinny, now can you? No matter how much you or little Sam over there hate it, you have to admit I'm more than your typical Ravager."

As he spoke, Sam watched as Deacon tucked his pistol into the rear waist of his jeans. With his now-free hand he took a thick syringe, filled with bright strawberry-red liquid, out of his pocket. He flicked the guard off the needle and placed his thumb on the plunger.

"Now, Roach. I like you and everything, but I think you could use a little upgrade," Deacon said. Raising the syringe, he jammed it into a surprised Roach's neck. She yelped in pain and looked up at Deacon, confused, before collapsing to the ground and beginning to convulse.

Deacon shrugged. "Well, it takes a minute, I suppose," he said. "But you'll see my point when she finishes her little shimmy. I'm creating something better here, boys. Once I crush my enemies, we'll all be part of a grand new world. One filled with people like me. Come on, man," he shouted, rubbing the top of his head against the side of Vincente's. "Why wouldn't you want to get on board this train?"

"All you're showing me is just how insane you really are, Deacon," Vincente said. "I won't now, and I never will, throw in with people — *creatures* - like you."

Deacon straightened and looked down at Roach's now-unconscious form for a few moments. "Well, you say that now," he finally said. "But we'll see what tune you sing once Sam is one of us."

Sam had almost forgotten the Ravagers Deacon had summoned to the Plague-Head's pen. Now he noticed them approaching, dragging along in front of them one of the monsters, a plastic half-mask wrapped around its mouth and its hands bound behind its back. It lurched — as much as it was able — alternately at Deacon, Vincente, Roach, and Sam. Sam was close enough to see into its clouded, milky eyes, to smell the fungal rot of the lichen-like growths splayed in all directions just under its skin. One of the Ravagers positioned himself behind Sam and held him tight, pulling him back to his feet.

"What kind of Infected do you think he'll turn out to be, Vincente?" Deacon asked. "The odds say he'll be just another Spewer, but hey — I'm feeling lucky. I think Sam has Ravager written all over him. I'm sure that, in time, he'll become a valuable member of my horde. Unless…perhaps you want to change your mind about those codes? We can still go our separate ways, all of us blessedly free of vomit. The offer is back on the table, for the next ten seconds only."

The Ravager holding the Plague-Head pushed the monster just in front of Sam. He unhooked the mask from the back of its head. The Plague-Head tried to vomit, but the Ravager held the mask firmly in place, dribbles of red-black sick oozing out around its edges.

Sam tried to move, to get free, to even just avert his face — his mouth and nose and eyes — a few extra millimeters from the shuffling ghoul. He hadn't realized till now just how primally-wired he was to fear these things, and how much more afraid his body, on an almost instinctual level, was of being infected than it was of simply dying. In that moment, Sam would have done anything, said anything, just to make the Plague-Head go away.

Vincente must have thought the same thing, because in that moment his will broke. Weepingly, he gave Deacon the codes.

"Now that wasn't so hard, was it?" Deacon said. On the ground in front of him, Roach had regained consciousness, though not all of her coordination, and was working slowly to sit up. In his chair, Vincente sat with his head slumped, defeated.

Deacon pulled out the drive and inserted it into a hand-held reader — Old World, probably Colony, tech. He typed in the codes, and a moment later let out a hearty, satisfied laugh. "Finally," he said. "Finally. Now I'm going to have myself a real war." He patted Vincente on the shoulder. "I was actually starting to think that you weren't going to talk. But I should have known better, Vinny. Everybody talks." Deacon pointed at Sam. "Spray him."

Vincente's head shot up. "No!" he screamed. Sam didn't fully understand what was happening, or maybe he just didn't want to accept it. It was like he was watching from somewhere else, from far away, as he saw the Ravager's hand flick the mask away from the Plague-Head's mouth.

The monster screamed and tilted its head back, shuddering. It then lurched forward and vomited profusely, soaking Sam's chest, neck, and face with infectious spray. The other Ravager let him go, and Sam collapsed to the ground in shock. He could feel the deadly liquid in his eyes and in his nose; he could taste it in his mouth. It tasted sweet, which made it all the worse.

He knew it took less than a minute for the virus to take hold, for the change to begin. Through a haze of fear, he wondered what it would feel like when he started to transform.

Deacon cackled maniacally, his voice echoing off the high basin walls like a chorus of insane ghosts. Sam looked up to see the rest of the Ravagers beginning to emerge from their various hiding places. He wondered if he would become just another one of them. He hoped against hope that he would simply die.

He waited. Deacon waited. Vincente waited, slumped in his chair like a deflated balloon. Roach waited, sitting on the ground with an expression somewhere between horror and disgust, completely devoid of the chaotic glee that had mere minutes earlier seemed her entire being.

A minute passed.

Then another.

"Huh," Deacon said, seeming genuinely stunned. He walked over to Sam, wrenched his head upward, and forced open his eyes.

"Not a Reaper," Deacon said, seemingly speaking to himself. He moved his head this way and that, inspecting every corner of Sam's eyes. "Not anything. Huh. I'll be damned." He pushed Sam back to the ground and pulled the pistol out from the back of his jeans.

"I really thought True Immunes were a myth," he said, pointing the pistol at Sam's head and cocking back the hammer. "You beat the infection, Sam, so good on you for that. Unfortunately, I can't have a True Immune running around out there, ruining all my plans."

*So that was that,* Sam thought. *Now, after everything else that has happened, I've beaten the damned Horsemen virus, and I'm still going to die.*

He wasn't scared. Just disappointed.

He worked himself up to his knees, as straight-backed as he could manage, and stared defiantly up at Deacon. Holding eye contact with the Ravager chief was surprisingly easy, now that he was resigned to his death.

Deacon pointed the gun at him, the end of its barrel looming cavernous and black.

"I'd ask if you had any last words," Deacon said in his too-friendly voice, "but I stopped asking that question a long time ago. The answers are always less interesting than you would expect."

In response, Sam turned his head and spat.

"Okay then," Deacon said, "I guess that's that. Goodbye, Sam. I can't say it hasn't been interesting. But I win."

Behind Deacon, at the edge of the high basin wall, a tiny stream of rocks caught Sam's eye. He could feel a slight rumbling in the ground, through his knees. Maybe it was nothing more than his own trembling muscles. He no longer cared.

He closed his eyes and waited for death to come.

# 30

THE BARREL OF THE PISTOL against his forehead was surprisingly cool, considering how warm the summer air around him was. He doubted the bullet would be nearly as cool. Sam let go of his pride and stopped glaring at Deacon, instead taking one last look at the sky. It was beautiful: robin's egg blue, with just a single white, cotton-candy cloud floating slowly past the high, yellow sun. As far as last sights went, it could be worse.

And then there was a cow. A brown-haired longhorn, tumbling nose over bull-ass through the air, looking more than a bit confused. Sam could understand how he felt. Cows weren't supposed to be up there.

The animal crashed to the ground like a bovine comet, smashing flat a half-torn-apart sedan and scattering the nearby Ravagers in surprise.

"What the-" Deacon said, turning his head toward the commotion. Sam continued to look up, awe-struck. Where there had, a moment earlier, been a single falling longhorn, there were now dozens of them, flowing over the edge of the ridge above them like a living, mooing waterfall.

It was a stampede.

Sam didn't need any more of a cue to start moving. He

slapped Deacon's pistol to the side and lurched forward, driving his shoulder into the front of the Ravager's knee cap. Deacon was knocked off-balance, but not off of his feet; turning his attention firmly back on Sam, he swung the pistol down side-armed, looking to cave in Sam's skull.

Sam rolled his head away from the incoming blow, catching it on his shoulder rather than his ear. It hurt, but not enough to slow him down. With all the strength he had left, Sam stepped forward, straightened, and drove a fist into the bottom of Deacon's chin.

Deacon's head snapped back with a satisfying crack. His pistol flew free from his hand, and Sam lost track of it in the background of falling cows.

Cattle were smashing down all around them now, and the emergent Ravagers, who had seemed so certain of their victory, were once again running for cover. Chaos, at last, had come for them.

Deacon didn't run, however. Unfortunately, Sam's punch only seemed to make him angry. He grabbed a fistful of Sam's collar and, snarling, began to rain down blows with his free hand. Sam was able to block most of them, but Deacon was far larger than him, not to mention freakishly strong. Sam quickly realized he wasn't going to last long in a fistfight. He needed a new plan, and fast.

A plan then fell out of the sky, quite literally.

A giant bull crashed horns-first just behind Sam and Deacon. Deacon's back was to the incoming cow, and the sound of one meaty impact was easily lost amid all the others. Therefore, the Ravager was solely focused on smashing his opponent. Sam gave him exactly what he wanted, and dropped his guard, shifting all his focus to breaking Deacon's grip on his collar. Rather than trying to peel Deacon's vise-like fingers free, Sam simply began to tear at his own shirt.

Deacon raised one high, mallet-like fist and smiled, seeing his opening to finish Sam off. Before he could bring down the blow, he seemed to notice something in Sam's look, and paused, half-glancing over his shoulder.

A moment later he was bowled over by the tumbling, rolling bull.

Sam ripped the chunk of shirt free and dove to the side, narrowly avoiding the impact himself. He was up and on his feet in a moment, trying to re-collect his bearings. Deacon had been swept away by the hapless animal, but he didn't know if the Ravager leader was alive or dead. In truth, he no longer cared. Revenge didn't matter, not when he could still save his friend.

He ran over to Vincente, still blessedly uncrushed by the miraculous falling herd of cattle, and began to free him from his bindings.

#

Abigail watched the front of the herd vanish over the high cliff, riding her bike among the rearmost of the cattle. One nice thing about being a Reaper was the extreme ease of driving an animal — or in this case a truly ridiculous number of animals — exactly where you wanted them to go. All you had to do was stand in the opposite direction and smell threatening.

This entire plan was the longest of long shots, and there were any number of things that could go wrong. Sam could be smashed by one of the falling herd, for example, or he could have already been killed. She'd scoped out his stand-off with Deacon before starting the stampede, but the action could have moved elsewhere in the brief time it had taken her to panic the beasts. All of these things and a thousand more could go wrong — really, her chance of success was charitably one in a thousand. *But on the other hand,* she thought, *what else is new?* She had to try. Sam was the only connection she had to the rest of this sorry world.

She had made her peace with the truth: she needed Sam, at least as much as he currently needed her.

Abigail twisted her motorcycle sideways and braked to a halt just before the ridge's edge. She let go of the handlebars and let the bike slide out in front of her, breaking into a run as soon as her feet touched the dirt. She gave her helmet's chinstrap one final tightening yank, gritting her teeth as she stared out into the open air in front of her.

*This next part is going to suck.*

She reached the end of the cliff at a full sprint and leaped out into the air, soaring above the Ravager camp far below. It felt, for the briefest of moments, like she had taken flight.

And then she fell.

From above, and at this height, the Ravager camp didn't look quite real. It resembled a slowly-moving color map of a camp, one someone would draw out with a stick in the dirt if they were hastily planning an assault or raid. Tiny white-and-red-speckled impact craters burst into being all over the map, as feral cattle plummeted into dirt, structure and Ravager alike. As Abigail fell, everything grew rapidly, taking on detail and depth; suddenly, it was all too real. Then the ground rushed up, smacking her out of the air with crushing force.

The impact felt like a bomb going off within every one of her bones at exactly the same time. She rolled forward to try and cushion her body as best she could, but still felt both of her legs, one forearm, and a handful of ribs break before she lurched and flopped to a halt, flat on her back.

She was still breathing, however, which wasn't too bad after taking an eighty-foot fall. Abigail winced, and with her remaining good hand pulled a canteen full of concentrated Plague-Head marrow out of her vest pocket. Ironically, it seemed the canteen itself was the source of her broken ribs. Tipping back the canteen, she began to gulp down the vile liquid. Almost instantaneously, she felt her bones begin to re-knit and her muscles re-form; by the time she had drained the canteen, she was back on her feet, extremely sore but once again functional. She tossed the empty container aside, drew out her pistol and unsheathed her machete.

It was time to go to work.

✝

Sam worked free the last of the bindings holding down Vincente. "Alright, couch potato," Sam said. "Quit just sitting around. I think it's about time we got out of here."

Vincente reached up and grabbed Sam's shoulders. Instead of standing up, he pulled Sam downward, out of the path of a fresh hail of zinging Ravager bullets. Crouching, Sam turned and saw that the Ravagers had apparently grown tired of hiding from the dwindling cattle-rain, and were back on the assault. Luckily for him, it seemed in the confusion that half of the Ravagers on the base's north side had taken the half on the south side for the enemy, aiming most of their fire in that direction. The southern Ravagers seemed to have the same idea of their compatriots to the north, returning fire with gusto.

Such chaos was marvelous to watch. But it wouldn't last.

Sam and Vincente ducked down behind the nearest dead bull, the carcass offering at least temporary cover.

"Right," Sam said. "Like I said, we gotta go."

"We can't leave here without that drive," Vincente said. "It's unlocked. Whoever has it has the power to kill thousands. Tens of thousands."

Bullet impacts thumped out a ragged drum roll on the carcass in front of them. "I'd love to know how you propose we do that," Sam said. He pulled out a small pistol he'd strapped to the inside of his arm before entering the camp and racked back the slide. "We've got one pistol and ten bullets between us, unless you've got some sort of extremely well-hid weapon still on you."

"The Ravagers weren't considerate enough to leave me armed," Vincente said. "I'm fresh out of guns. But she's not."

He looked over to the Ravager Roach, who was lying on her stomach nearby, trembling, her head cradled protectively under her arms. Whatever Deacon had injected her with, it seemed to have taken all the fight out of her. A silver revolver was strapped to one of her legs, a black semi-auto to the other.

Vincente pushed himself to his feet and, crouching close to the ground, he dashed over to the fallen Ravager. Sam braced his shoulders against the bull's stomach and fired a clip's-worth of shots toward the approaching Ravagers, giving Vincente some cover.

Sam heard a female scream, one of terror, and then a male scream, one of pain. He ducked his head back behind cover and looked toward Vincente and Roach. Vincente had gotten the black pistol free, but in doing so had apparently reawakened Roach's instincts for battle.

She had flipped over onto her back and kicked Vincente in the chin, dazing him and knocking him back onto the ground. Now free, she had scooted back several feet and was trying frantically to work the other pistol from its holster. Sam aimed at her chest and pulled the trigger. His pistol clicked empty.

*Not good.* He would never get the spare clip from his boot before she got her weapon free and shot both him and Vincente dead.

So he didn't try. He yelled out his best attempt at a battle cry and ran straight at her, lowering his shoulder at the last second and smashing into her at full speed.

Sam bowled Roach over backwards, but as she went down Sam's unchecked momentum carried him past her. He spun around and scrambled back to the Ravager, reaching her just in time for Roach to turn and land a right hook square on his nose, staggering him backward.

"Sam!" Vincente shouted, aiming Roach's black pistol seemingly straight at him. "Get down!"

"Time to die, Sam," a voice said from the opposite direction, behind him. *Deacon.* Sam turned in time to see the Ravager leader, bloody but very much still alive, level a second gun at him.

Roach grabbed his ankle and pulled. Sam fell backward.

Deacon fired. Vincente fired.

As Sam fell, he could almost feel the bullets pass by his head, buzzing and sizzling like molten steel hornets.

Sam hit the ground, flat on his back, the impact pushing the air from his lungs.

Deacon's bullet, meant for Sam, caught Vincente in the chest.

Vincente's bullet caught Deacon in the head.

Roach screamed. Sam screamed. Together, among the gunshots and explosions and dying animals and men and Infected, their voices melded into one terrible, bestial roar of anguish and horror.

As Sam took in empty, gasping breaths of air, Roach ran

past him toward her fallen leader. As soon as she was out of his sight, Sam forgot about her, just as he had Deacon, the other Ravagers, even the destruction raging all around him. He scrambled toward Vincente's fallen and unmoving form, hoping for the best, but this time more than ever fearing the worst.

✝

Abigail shot one Ravager, and then swinging her machete in one smooth motion, beheaded another. Before their companions could locate her, she was already hidden behind the next piece of scrap metal.

She moved, as quickly as she was able amid the scattered dozens of Deacon's Ravagers, toward the source of gunfire at the camp's front. Gunfire meant conflict, which meant someone fighting against the Ravagers. All she could hope was that Sam was among the fighters.

Still, there were just *so many* Ravagers ahead of her. There was no way she could fight her way through them all. She needed a way to even the odds. And she was fresh out of cows.

Her eyes settled on the cages to her right, and she smiled. It looked like the Ravagers had been courteous enough to provide a solution to her problems.

Bizarrely, the Ravagers had left two of their number behind to guard the imprisoned Howlers and Plague-Heads. *What,* Abigail wondered, *do they think a Reaper is going to fall from the sky and strike off the locks?*

The Ravagers were standing on their tip-toes, gazing toward the unfolding gunfight ahead of them. They should have been keeping an eye on their surroundings. Abigail cut through the pair silently, and considered the contents of the cages they had guarded.

She had a choice: one large cage, containing around a hundred Plague-Heads, or ten smaller cages, each containing a Howler. She couldn't risk the horde of Plague-Heads infecting Sam, so the choice was simple.

"You boys and girls are looking mighty hungry, aren't you?" Abigail asked the nearest Howler, smiling and peering into its yellow, animal eyes. She raised her machete and brought it down on the cage's padlock.

"Well," she said. "Time to hunt."

✝

The bullet had struck Vincente just under the collarbone. If he was lucky, the round should have passed through without hitting any major organs. *But when have either of us ever been lucky?* Sam wondered. Vincente wasn't moving, and time was short, so Sam did the only thing he could think of: he slapped Vincente in the face as hard as he could.

Vincente gasped and lurched awake. "The drive," he said.

"Good to see you too," Sam said. "Let's get it and go, before one of these Ravagers gets in another lucky shot."

He pulled Vincente to his feet and put the black semi-auto he had scavenged from Roach back in Vincente's hand. He reloaded his own pistol, and together the pair made their way, staggering from one cover to another, toward where Vincente had shot Deacon down. Several times Sam had to crouch and provide covering fire.

"Careful," Sam said. "I saw that Roach girl come this way. Keep ready."

"When did you start giving me advice?" Vincente asked, smiling. As soon as he spoke, the smile turned to a wince, and Vincente began to cough ragged, bloody coughs into his hand. Sam looked again at the gunshot wound and frowned. Vincente kept moving, however, grimacing through the pain; neither of them had time at the moment to stop and worry about it.

A shock of spiky red hair popped up, flame-like, from behind a jagged mass of rusted-out metal nearby. It was Roach. Turning, she began to run deeper into the camp.

"There she is!" Sam said. He saw the bright white object in her hand at the same moment Vincente spoke.

"With the drive," he said.

"We can still let it go," Sam said. "We can still turn and run."

"No we can't, Sam," Vincente said. "If we lose track of that drive, we may never find it again. It's our duty to go on."

Sam released the clip from his pistol and checked his remaining rounds. He still had half his bullets left. He supposed he could always find more.

"I know," Sam said. "Still, you have to admit, running tempted you a little bit, right?"

Vincente chuckled, then coughed. He tore a bandage from his shirt-sleeve, tying it over his wound as Sam reloaded his weapon. Together, they came out from cover firing, following Roach further into the depths of Deacon's Ravager base.

# 31

IT WAS AMAZING just how much damage a half-dozen Howlers and one Reaper could do to an army within a closed space. Abigail darted from cover to cover, watching as the newly-freed pack of Howlers set upon their Ravager jailers. The beasts tore out throats with their teeth, slashed chunks out of limbs and torsos with their razor-sharp claws; Abigail grinned, delighted to see Deacon's gang of killers and burners getting a dose of their own medicine.

Which didn't mean that the Howlers could win. There were still only six of them, to dozens of armed Ravagers, and it was only a matter of time before the creatures were put down from a safe distance by gunfire. For Abigail, this was fine. She didn't need the Howlers to wipe out her enemies. She'd just needed a potentially-lethal distraction.

A taller, bulky Ravager, covered in tattoos and scars, fired wildly at the rightmost Howler, screaming as he did so. This prevented him from seeing Abigail approach him from the left; by the time he noticed her she was already bringing her machete down on his neck. Another Ravager, this one a stout, dreadlocked woman, caught a Howler claw on the barrel of her sawed-off shotgun. This kept the bestial

Infected at bay long enough for her to drive a makeshift spear into the Howler's chest. In the process, however, she gave Abigail a clear target from only a few feet away. Abigail fired her pistol, and the Ravager went down.

That was when she saw Sam.

He and the older scout were running; Sam moving quickly, and the other with a noticeable limp. There was still a mass of Ravagers between them and her, but they were alive.

Sam was alive.

She felt a wave of happiness wash over her, and for a moment almost forgot she was in the middle of a war zone. Sam was alive. He seemed to be running the wrong way: *toward* her, and deeper into Deacon's base, rather than away from it like any sane person would be doing. She didn't understand it, but she also didn't care. Sam was alive. Something had finally turned out *right*, for once in her life. She redoubled her efforts, locating her next Ravager target and taking aim with her pistol.

Pain bit suddenly into her arm. At the same time, she heard the sizzle and snap of a bullet passing by. It wasn't until after she had thrown herself to the ground and rolled behind cover that she realized the grazing round had come from behind her, not in front. She jumped up and dove to the opposite side of the cover. Bullets rattled a moment later, peppering the spot she had just vacated; not the heavy, uneven blasts of Ravager shotguns and hunting rifles, but the metallic drum roll of automatic weapons.

She knew who was responsible before she ventured a look back. It was the mysterious group of Colonists that had set up shop in the back corner of Deacon's base. Each one of them was wearing fully-mechanized battle armor, and carrying heavy machine guns.

Bullets pinged off the metal, inches from her face, and Abigail pulled her head back. They had her location, and with those weapons, she wouldn't be able to move an inch into the open without being cut down. She was also a sitting duck for the first Ravager to turn around: her cover was now behind her from their perspective, and she couldn't even move to make their shot more difficult without opening herself up to the Colonist fire team behind her.

This was a severe problem. Ravagers ahead of her, Uninfected behind, and a pack of wild Howlers thrown in for good measure. She only had one option left, and she really didn't want to take it. She ejected the spent clip from her pistol and loaded in a new one.

"Everyone else has joined this party," she muttered to herself. "I guess it's time the Plague-Heads got in on the fun."

She took aim back at the giant cage holding the swarm. It was a difficult shot from this angle, but it was the only one she could take that didn't expose her to the Colonists' machine guns. Luckily, she had a full clip, and she only needed to hit the lock once to unleash a shuffling tide of Plague-Heads. Thankfully, there was only a small chance her shots would alert the Ravagers to her presence; less thankfully, this was because the air was already fraught with gunfire. But she should be able to escape in the coming confusion.

Yes, everything suddenly seemed to be coming up Abigail.

She took a final, steadying breath, and began to fire at the lock.

$\dagger$

Vincente stumbled again. Sam stepped over to him and

hooked an arm underneath his shoulders, helping him to remain on his feet. Far more of Vincente's weight immediately began pushing down on Sam than he had expected. Sam didn't want to think about what this meant for Vincente's injuries.

They continued to move forward, slower now, and Sam kept his eyes focused on the receding form of Roach. She had just reached the front lines of the Ravagers, and if he wasn't careful, he could easily lose track of her among the chaos.

And chaos it was. Something odd had begun to happen, even odder than cows raining down from above. Many of the Ravagers had turned away from Sam and Vincente, firing their weapons in seemingly random directions. It was almost as if, without Deacon's guiding will, they had fallen to fighting amongst themselves.

Sam saw what was really going on moments later. Somehow, the Howlers that the Ravagers had been holding captive were free of their cages. Now out in the open, among the throngs of people who had chained them up and starved them, they were reacting about like Sam would have expected. Dead Ravagers lay everywhere, rent by gaping claw-and-tooth marks.

Sam watched as Roach, still running at full speed, dropped and slid on her knees to avoid a bristle-haired, hulking Howler. The creature leaped, jaws first, at her head, distorted mouth trailing saliva; Roach managed to dodge clean under the thing. In its passing, it caught a shoulder on a metal pole and spun awkwardly into another Ravager, one who had just swung his shotgun toward Sam and Vincente. The Howler tore into its new target with primal, bloody enthusiasm, taking it to the ground before rocking back upward from a blast to the chest from the Ravager's shotgun. Vincente pointed his pistol at the fallen Ravager and finished him off, while Sam shot the Howler in the head, putting it out of its misery.

Ahead, Roach bent down to pick up a discarded hand-gun, and was immediately set upon by its former owner. As he made his way toward her, half-guiding and half-pulling Vincente along with him, Sam at first thought a Howler had engaged their quarry. However, the tasseled leathers and mohawk, along with the rows of tattoos and silver bands running up his arms, marked out the combatant as a Ravager. Roach kicked her assailant in the knee, and her kick was answered with a punch to the face, followed by a snarling headbutt.

The two blows knocked Roach back on the dirt. Vincente swung his pistol around in front of Sam's face and fired, taking out another Ravager that had appeared at their side. The shot blinded and deafened Sam for a few seconds, but he kept moving forward. His legs burned from the burden of Vincente's weight, his limbs sore from dozens of cuts and scrapes. His head hurt from dehydration and lack of sleep, not to mention far too many impacts over the last several days, but he kept on. When his senses cleared, he saw Roach had shot and killed her attacker. She was close enough that Sam could see the hot blood pumping from her kill's fresh bullet-wound.

Roach rose to her feet as the other, now-dead Ravager tottered and crumpled to the ground, her rise and his fall moving in concert, as if they were choreographed. She saw Sam and Vincente, and her eyes went wide. She fired at them as Vincente fired back, both bullets somehow miss-ing their targets. Sam kept pulling Vincente and himself forward, his legs begging him to rest and his brain plead-ing with him to give up, to drop Vincente and run. Sam ignored it all and pushed forward. He felt the impact of his leading shoulder against Roach's shoulder, and the three of them fell in a tangle of weapons and snarls and wild, animalistic punches and kicks.

All around, the increasingly senseless fighting and destruction raged on.

✝

The swarm of Plague-Heads, now free from their cage, began fanning out in all directions, attacking Ravager, Howler, and Colonist without discrimination. This new threat re-directed the hail of bullets that had been keeping Abigail pinned down, and she was again on the move. The armed and armored Colonist troops likely would fight off the mindless horde, but Abigail didn't need the Colonists to die. She merely needed time, and fewer bullets aimed in her direction.

It took her a moment to locate Sam again. He was rolling around on the ground, fighting hand to hand with a red-haired female Ravager. They were still a hundred yards or so ahead of her, but she could quickly close that distance.

And she would need to, quickly. Behind Sam, stomping toward him with a shotgun in each hand and murder writ large on his severely wounded face, was Deacon.

✝

Sam was thrown free of the scrum, while Vincente and Roach continued to tangle. Sam had lost his weapon in the fighting, and he scrambled around wildly trying to locate it. He saw, far ahead of him, that the Plague-Heads were free, their horde lurching in all directions, attacking anyone they could find.

But Sam had more immediate concerns. Roach had managed to get on top of Vincente, and was swinging down blows wildly with both hands. Vincente was fending her off with his forearms and elbows, but his movements were slowing considerably; Sam knew that by himself, Vincente had no chance against the uninjured Ravager. Abandoning his search for the gun, Sam threw himself at Roach.

Before he could reach her, a shotgun boomed, and she was thrown forward. Sam turned his head toward the shooter, just as he caught a flash of metal from the corner of his eye.

He saw Deacon's wounded, furious face for just a moment before the barrel of the shotgun cracked into his chin. Then he was face-down in the dirt, blood pounding in his ears, his jaw burning with pain.

Sam rolled onto his back. Deacon roared, his voice a tangle of rage and triumph.

"Give me the drive, Roach," Deacon bellowed.

Roach struggled to turn herself over. Sam could see the Kevlar beneath the tatters of her shirt. It had saved her from being torn apart by the shotgun blast, but she had still taken the full force of the shot from close range. Sam doubted he would have been able to move at all had that happened to him, but Roach seemed more angry than afraid.

"You lied to us. To all of us," Roach screamed back at Deacon. "I was too stupid to see it till you stuck me with that...that poison. But I see now, Deacon. I see you for what you really are. A liar, and a traitor."

"You don't know anything," Deacon snarled. Vincente was trying to crawl toward his discarded weapon; Deacon stepped past him and kicked the gun away, then pushed Vincente flat to the ground by planting his foot on his back. Sam tried to move to help his friend, but Deacon pointed a shotgun at Sam's face, freezing him.

"I open your eyes, give your walnut-sized brain a tiny bump-up, and the first thing you do is double-cross me. ME?" Deacon roared down at Roach. "I thought I was giving you a gift. Instead of opening your eyes, I should have slit your throat. And you call me a traitor?"

"What do you call it?" Roach demanded. "Holding back the great weapon from our king? Working with the sheep-men? Letting them experiment on our people? I watched you take KillDoz and Lemny into those tents, late at night, when you thought everyone was asleep. And I know they never came back out. That the secret mission you suppos-edly sent them on was bullshit. I knew, and it never sat right, but I couldn't fully think it through till just now. Till you changed me, made everything complicated."

A Howler bounded toward Deacon, who raised both shotguns and shot the beast in the face, killing it instantly. He lowered the weapons and leaned in closer to Roach, seemingly unconcerned with his base of operations being torn down all around them.

"Are you finished whining at me, girl?" Deacon said. "Cause I'm sure as hell done listening. You think you know what you're talking about, but you don't. And the 1.5 obvi-ously didn't make you any smarter, because your first move was to go against me. That's a dumb idea no matter who you are. So, all that's left now is for you to hand over that drive. Do it now, and I'll finish you clean. Make me look for it, and I'll take you with me through the tunnels. Then your end won't be nearly so quick, or easy."

This was the best opening Sam was going to get. He

pushed himself to his feet and dove at Deacon's knees. He managed to get the huge Ravager off-balance, just a bit, before Deacon corrected and tossed Sam aside like a sack of wheat.

Deacon pointed the shotgun down at Sam, smiling at the other end of the barrel. "We really have to stop meeting like this, Sammy."

But Sam was already looking past Deacon, goggle-eyed. "Abigail?" he said.

A look of confusion passed across Deacon's face, and he turned to follow Sam's stare.

"Well, shi-" Deacon began.

Abigail, having launched herself off the roof of the nearby warehouse, came down on Deacon like a falling cannon ball, leading with her machete. The tip of the blade skewered Deacon cleanly through the face, cutting through the back of his head and into the ground where he fell, half laid out over Sam.

"Let's see you survive that," Abigail said. She stood up and let go of the machete, the weapon standing straight up from Deacon's dead body and the ground.

"I was beginning to wonder if you'd really left," Sam said, sliding out from beneath Deacon's legs. "I'm sorry about what I said earlier. I think I just needed-"

"Sam," Vincente said, his voice a dry croak.

Abigail and Sam turned as one. Vincente was lying on his back, barely able to lift his head. He was pointing toward an open door in the earth, leading down into a dark staircase. Roach was nowhere to be found.

Sam rushed to his friend's side, Abigail following right behind.

"She took the drive," Vincente said, grabbing the collar of Sam's shirt. "You need to go after her. She can't reach the

Ravager king, or it will be over for everyone." He coughed twice, each ragged exhalation bringing with it dark, red blood. "The drive is all that matters," Vincente said. "You must get back the drive."

"Don't worry, we will," Sam said reassuringly. "Save your energy. We'll get you up and out of here, and then we'll figure out how to run down Roach."

Abigail began firing her weapon past them, putting down the first few approaching Plague-Heads. Dozens had taken notice of their small group, and were approaching at an eager (though still shuffling) gait.

"We've got to move, boys," Abigail said.

"Alright, V, you ready?" Sam said, moving into position to lift Vincente up off the ground.

"No," Vincente said. "Not me. You two go. I will only slow you down."

"Shut up," Sam said. "We're all going together."

"We can't all make it," Vincente said. He lifted his hand off of his wounded shoulder. His palm was covered with bright red blood, and his shirt was soaked through with it. "Look at me, Sam. My wounds will kill me even if I do make it out of here. You two can still make it, but you have to go now."

"I'm not leaving you here," Sam said, his voice cracking. "We're all getting out of here. Together."

Abigail kept firing until her pistol clicked empty. She tossed it away and pulled a new one from her waist, continuing to fire. "We are about 30 seconds from being overrun here," she said.

"Sam, it's okay," Vincente said. "I'm proud of you. You made it all this way, as far as anyone else could have. I'm proud to say that you are my friend. But, it's time to finish the job. Stop that Ravager, get the drive, and head for the Free Cities. Once you get there, you will know what to do."

Sam had begun to cry. "I can't leave you here to be torn apart," he said. "I won't."

"No, you won't," Vincente said. "You still have those explosives strapped to your chest. Give them to me and go. I'll buy you some time."

"You know he's right, Sam," Abigail said as she continued to fire. "We have to go."

"Vincente," Sam said, not knowing how to finish. He pulled the explosives from his chest and pressed them to Vincente's. He quickly rigged up his spare detonator, and put it in Vincente's hand.

"Goodbye, Sam," Vincente said. "I am truly glad I got to know you. Go and finish the fight."

Abigail grabbed Sam by the shoulder and pulled him toward the door and the stairway. The last thing Sam saw before descending into darkness was Vincente looking back at him, smiling.

✝

The tunnel was long. It was narrow, and it was very dark. Tiny orange lights every twenty yards provided the only illumination as Sam and Abigail ran forward, each over-whelmingly grateful to be reunited with the other. The tunnel exit had just come into view when they heard the explosion behind; they felt the ground shake, and Sam knew it was done.

Abigail and Sam came back up to the surface on the other side of the ridge. Ahead, shadowed against the distant hori-zon, they saw Roach, heading away from them at a break-neck pace.

Sam nodded to Abigail, and she nodded back.

Sam would see the job through. And he would do it alongside Abigail. Together, they would finish the work that Vincente had begun.

# EPILOGUE

SOLOMON LIMPED ALONG the outskirts of Deacon's destroyed outpost. With each step, his gait improved, but after the laborious process of recombing his body parts, which had been further crushed and ground into the dirt beneath hundreds of cattle, well...even his considerable recuperative abilities had been taxed nearly to the limit.

He had searched the remains of this primitive excuse for a base without luck for hours now, and while he had found numerous bodies to fuel his regeneration, he had yet to discover his prize. He was feeling almost...frustrated. It was an unfamiliar feeling to one such as him, who prided himself on, among other things, his near-infinite patience.

This was all Abigail's fault.

He had run out of patience with his one-time acolyte. He was beyond trying to bring her back into the fold, after her latest display of impudence. No, she had to be put down, along with her little Uninfected friend.

He would tend to it himself, after—

There, underneath that bit of scrap. He recognized the jacket, the haircut, and the scar. He had found what he had come here for.

Solomon pulled the corpse of the Ravager leader out of the ash and threw its considerable bulk over his shoulders, and he smiled.

He began his march toward the sunset, toward fate, and the bloody sky of the west.

Read this exciting excerpt from the next HORSEMAN book

## *About the Author*

Eric Wood has worked numerous jobs, all of which he liked far less than writing. He lives and works in Northern Michigan.

# THE HORSEMEN CHRONICLES
## BOOK TWO: THE FREE CITIES

THE TRAIL OF BLOOD led away from the dead men.

"You think this was her?" Sam asked, kneeling over one of the lifeless soldiers. He rifled through the dead man's pack, finding several full clips of ammunition.

"She was here," Abigail answered. "But this wasn't her. Or at least not just her. Ravager or not, she's not capable of all this."

Sam certainly hoped not. The forest clearing was scattered with bodies, at least a dozen by Sam's count. Around half were Howler's, their elongated jaws and thick, bristly body hair distinctive even from a distance. The other half were Uninfected soldiers of some variety, each wearing identical body armor and black metal face masks. Some sort of battle had obviously taken place here, and equally obvious was that this was the source of the gunfire they had heard the previous evening. But how did Roach work into all of this, Sam wondered? She had been traveling this direction for weeks now, staying just ahead of Abigail and his pursuit.

"Maybe all of this was unrelated," Sam said. "Just one big coincidence. Just a group of…let's call them mystery soldiers ran into a pack of Howlers. Roach could have snuck around them in the chaos."

From the corner of his eye, Sam could see Abigail standing with her hands on her hips, staring at him. He didn't have to look over to know she was rolling her eyes.

"A coincidence," she said. "Do you really believe that?"

Sam stood and slung the dead soldier's rifle over his shoulder. He walked over to Abigail. "Probably not, but you never know."

"I do know," Abigail said. She pointed at the tracks at her feet. "Look at these," she said. "One set of heavy footprints. They are too deep to be one person's weight. There were at least two survivors here. One of them carried the other up that ridge."

"It could have been one really fat guy," Sam said, moving up beside her and looking down at the foot prints. "Of course, it would be one with pretty small feet."

"Those prints are too small to belong to an adult male," Abigail said. "They belong to either a child or a woman. How many women or children do you know that are capable of carrying another person up that ridge?"

Sam followed the footprints as they headed up the hill. The wooded incline extended into the distance at least a couple of hundred yards, over rocky, uneven ground. It would be a difficult hike even without carrying a person-sized weight.

Along the foot path, a tiny dot of red, standing stark against the green of a sapling's leaf, caught Sam's eye. He walked over to investigate.

"Look at this," he said, taking the leaf gingerly between two fingers. "Blood."

Abigail followed him over and leaned in to investigate closer. She wiped the blood off of the leaf with the tip of her finger, and then touched her finger to her tongue. She rolled the blood around in her mouth, considering its taste.

"Ugh," Sam said, recoiling slightly. "Really?"

Abigail shrugged. "What? I thought we were past this, Sam."

"Well, yeah, but still. That's just random blood. It's a little gross. I mean, objectively."

She shrugged again. "Says you." She smiled. "Besides, this isn't just random blood. It's Ravager blood. This was definitely her. We are close."

"Well then, miss blood-taster," Sam said. "I guess we'd better follow."

With the same finger that had a moment earlier held Roach's blood, she poked him lightly between the eyes. "Yes, you big baby," she said. "I guess we'd better.

↓

"Do you smell that?" Sam asked.

Abigail's only reply was to point a single finger toward the sky above. Sam looked up, past the tops of the pines and the firs, and saw the puffs of black smoke in the sky.

"And do you think we should be concerned about that?" Sam asked. He tried to keep his voice even. After hiking uphill for much of the past hour, he was exhausted. He didn't want to let Abigail know just how out of breath he was. She, of course, was moving like a machine. Sam envied her inhuman endurance.

"Not in the way you think," Abigail said, continuing to scan the terrain ahead of them.

At the moment, Sam had any number of concerns. He was far past the western edge of even Vincente's furthest scouting trips, in the middle of undiscovered, wild country. He still didn't know what force those dead soldiers belonged to, and how many more of them might still be in the area. And then there were the Howlers: there had been five dead ones back at the battleground. Even with Abigail, he didn't like their odds if they ran into a pack that size.

On top of that, now he had to concern himself with a possible forest fire. Which direction did those things move again? He remembered reading somewhere that forest fires moved up hill. That made sense, he thought. Fire rises, after all.

The source of the smoke was somewhere ahead of them, and ahead of them was up hill. That would have been much better news if they weren't rapidly approaching the crest of the ridge. Just my luck.

Ahead of him, Abigail had reached the top of the ridge and came to a stop, staring out ahead of herself, seemingly stunned. When Sam caught up he saw what had captured her attention.

"Whoa," he said. It wasn't his most eloquent moment.

The ridge looked out over a wide stretch of empty valley, and beyond that was the largest settlement Sam had ever seen.

It looked like nearly an entire old world city had been restored. To the east there were old towers many stories high, their sheets of glass gleaming in the sun. To the west, former apartment buildings were connected to each other with makeshift bridges and studded with ad-hoc outcroppings, laundry lines and power cables draped over everything like black lace. In its open center, mazes of razor-wired fencing partitioned the square in two; on either side Sam could see the streets were crowded with foot and livestock traffic. At the far end of the enormous settlement he could see the source of the smoke in the sky: twin smokestacks, rising from a single factory many times bigger than even the largest back at the Colony. In fact, everything was bigger, down to the colossal walls encircling the entire town, spaced at regular intervals with guard towers that wouldn't have looked out of place on a medieval castle.

"I think we know where Roach has gone," Abigail said. "Welcome, Sam, to the Free Cities."

Excerpted from *The Horseman Chronicles: Book Two* Coming in XX, 2017.